DRAXX

AN ALIEN WARRIOR ROMANCE

FATED MATES OF THE SARKARNII

HATTIE JACKS

Editing: Polaris Editing

Cover: Reva Cover designs

❀ Created with Vellum

JOIN ME!

Why not join the Hattie Jacks Alien Appreciation Society? Subscribe to my newsletter for a free sci-fi romance novella: www.hattiejacks.com/subscribe

You can also join my Patreon
https://patreon.com/HattieJacksAuthor
Where I post chapter serials of my ongoing work in progress, the occasional poll and little snippets of character art.

Additionally, if you wish, you can stalk me on Instagram: www.instagram.com/hattie.jacks
or join my Facebook group:
www.facebook.com/hattieshotties

JEM

"Hello, pretty pretty," the alien warthog with four eyes croons disgustingly at me through the small hole in what I presume is a door, given I've never seen it open.

"Fuck off, ugly ugly," I reply and flick him a 'V' sign with my fingers, and I'm not indicating any sort of peace settlement.

I've had time to wonder if things could be any worse since I was abducted by aliens from *England*.

Brits don't get abducted. We leave that to other, far less uptight, countries.

Given I'd just crawled out of a divorce from my slimy politician husband, had been rejected by my biological father for the second time, as the first time he couldn't wait to hand me off to the adoptive parents who didn't give a shit about me, I genuinely thought all my bad luck had been used up.

But apparently not.

Alien warthog makes a sound which I'm presuming is laughter, with a dirty edge to it.

Fuck it. I hate him. I hate all of them, and most of all, I hate being at the mercy of whoever thinks it's okay to keep me in a dank, dark hole.

Despite myself, despite all my efforts to keep my shit together, my skin pricks with goosebumps over my spine. My life might have been crap, but I didn't deserve this, surely?

I sit down on the rough-hewn shelf which passes for a bed—here are no blankets or anything soft in this place, a bit like my personality—and glare at the alien through the flap.

Yep. There are aliens. Probably. I've given up hoping all this is a bad dream caused by late night cheese.

Aliens I can understand, which is why I initially thought they were a figment brought on by a particularly strong camembert. Because...aliens. Also, they don't have American accents, and the sci-fi I've watched makes a lack of such an accent improbable.

Turns out the movies lied to us...who knew?

There's a loud click, and the door to my cell springs open. I'm immediately on my feet, backing away. This is not normal, as far as normal goes. The door hasn't been opened since I got here, as far as I'm aware.

"Female." The creature which steps through the doorway is the one which haunts my sleep.

The thing which was there when I was pulled, terrified, from the pod, the one and only time I cried in all of this. Its pincers snipped at my skin. It was the one which shoved the needle in my neck and snarled at me to keep still.

Part lobster, part squid, part I don't know what, but all unpleasant. I'd take the filthy warthog aliens over this one any day of the week.

"No," I reply, my back against the wall. "Whatever it is you want, the answer is no. It will always be no."

It ignores my squeaking voice, so damn small compared to the creature advancing on it. I know I don't have anything to fight back with, but I'm going to fight. I've always fought back. It's why my adoptive parents hated me, ruing the day they brought me home.

I don't need these aliens to like me, but I'm absolutely not going to give in easily. The thing approaches me, claws snapping, tentacles shaking, and I kick out at it.

My leg is caught, and I'm hoisted into the air. Perhaps kicking out wasn't the best move ever. The creature makes a bubbling sound which could be absolutely anything, and then I see the bright spark of a needle.

"If you stick that thing in me, I will not be responsible for my actions," I snarl from my useless upside down position.

The thing burbles and bubbles again. It strikes me that it's laughing, and I don't believe it's a good laugh.

I'm half dragged, half carried out of my cell into a corridor which is dimly lit. I see other doors, a handful at least. The creature gives me a shake and, unable to help myself, I shriek at the sudden movement which makes my teeth rattle.

"Hello!" a small voice calls out.

A pair of bright green eyes peers through the opening in one door.

"Get back!" I shout. "If it's got me, it might leave you alone."

The eyes fill with tears, and then they're gone. I get another shake.

"Time to earn your keep, human," the creature splutters, and the needle is shoved into my upper thigh with a force which is entirely unnecessary.

"You complete bas..." My tongue fails me as my vision goes dark.

The last thing I hear is a human sob and find my addled brain thinking it's an entirely appropriate epitaph on my life and whatever is to come.

Sometimes you just can't catch a break, and this is one of those times.

DRAXX

"Let's see what you've got, *General*," the Mosom snarls at me. His beady eyes glint out from a mass of filthy fur.

He's only got one upper limb. His friends, all three of them surrounding me, also have missing body parts. I catch myself thinking they could probably make one good Mosom if they were put together.

Then I stop thinking. Thinking isn't good. It doesn't help. Violence helps, and I plough into these creatures of the pit with venom.

I could shift, but being in my full Sarkarnii form doesn't make it much of a fight, and I want this one to be as dirty as they come. Instead, I allow my tail for balance and my wings to aid in the fight but nothing more. The Mosom oblige me, biting, scratching, and one of them produces a blade and buries it in my back.

"Don't call me *General*," I rasp as I pull the knife from my scales and flick it back at the first Mosom, taking him out easily. "That title is no longer mine."

I don't deserve a command. My ancestors would be

horrified at what I have become. I am related to the High Bask, one of the first Sarkarnii to shift.

Now I am nothing.

All I deserve is this pit, this hole in a long forgotten moon which is now the galaxy's foremost prison. The Kirakos. The maze.

It is the place my brother and erstwhile leader, Draco, thinks will provide the key to unlocking our species, to finding any others of us scattered among the stars after our enemies destroyed our home. It's the reason he had us incarcerated here, collared and diminished to nothing but the scum of the Universe.

Despite the fact Draco has gained control of part of the Kirakos and had his mate remove our collars, my joy at being free was easily extinguished. Because we are not free. I am still a failure, and I still have to atone for what I did not do.

I didn't save them. I let myself believe the Sarkarnii were invincible.

And our enemies took every last one of my kin, save for my brothers and den warriors. I cannot be a general when I have no army to command.

And it's the reason I'm back down here, in the pit with the remainder of the creatures which were once something and are now unable to look into the light.

I don't want to look at the light.

I also don't want to wear pants again, but that's an entirely different thing.

Today the Mosom are not putting up much of a fight. None of them are getting back up, and I don't have enough injuries to make myself feel better. My tail extends, thrashes, and no matter what I do, it won't shift back.

Shifting into my Sarkarnii form is not fighting. Not

here. There are few left in the dregs of this underworld who pose a challenge to a fully shifted Sarkarnii. Today it looks like the pit is not going to serve up anything other than these half dead Mosom.

Some of which are now more dead than when we started. But then, they shouldn't have called me General.

I am no General.

"Draxx!" My brother Drega's voice echoes around the pit, and the limited light in this place is blotted out by a pair of powerful wings.

They whip up dirt and debris. The Mosom who can, scuttle away, dragging their fallen.

"By the bones!" Drega's lip curls as he shifts into his biped form. "Why do you come down here, Draxx? It nevving stinks."

He looks me over. I'm covered in both my own blood and that of the Mosom, along with the dirt from the pit. I still have a partial tail and my fangs. I release a stream of smoke, but doing so stopped providing any calm to my soul a long time ago.

"Don't come down here if you don't like it." My voice is low and filled with all the anger which flows through my veins.

Drega folds his arms and leans against a wall. "Someone has to come and get you, and Daeos was busy." He references my old second in command, a Sarkarnii warrior nearly as desperate as me for revenge and for the fight.

"I'm not finished down here, so whatever you want, it'll have to wait." I turn my back on him, stomping across the large fighting arena and over to the entrance to the tunnels where I might be able to scare up my next round of bloodshed.

It won't help. It never helps. I clutch at my head, willing

my shift away. Here in the pit, I am what I am—feral, dangerous, nothing.

I fight, I feed, I forget.

It might have been good to get the collars off, the ones which stopped us from shifting, but it was a temporary reprieve. My shifted form gives me little comfort. Returning to the pit makes the unbearable...well, it makes me think of something else.

Something slams into my already damaged shoulder. I turn with a snarl to see Drega holding up another rock. He huffs out an insolent smoke ring, which makes its way slowly up and up towards the light, a long way above us.

"I need your assistance, brother. I believe I may have found the other humans, but they're in the Warden controlled area, and it's going to be difficult, if not impossible, to get in." He weighs up the rock, tossing it from hand to clawed hand. "Given those odds, I thought of you."

"I don't want to find any humans," I spit. "I don't care about Draco's map. It doesn't matter what is out there. We lost them all, and that can never be undone."

I hear Drega's dry laugh from across the arena. "You might not care, but you love trouble, *General.*"

I round on him with a snarl, but he's already shifted, and his huge form is taking off, rising into the still, blood tainted air.

"If you want to come, I'll be leaving in half a tick. Draco has authorized weapons and explosives, and you know how much you love the explosives, brother."

Nev him. Nev Draco. Nev them all to the ancestors.

Drega knows how to both pique my interest with the offer of weaponry and nev me off enough I want to be able to give his head a good punch. Plus, I know Draco is behind this. My older brother, my den mate, is behind everything.

If he's allowing me the chance at destruction, he must want what Drega has found very much.

Rage rises within me. I wanted to stay down here in the pit, in the dark, doing what I need to do to keep the memories at bay. Instead my brothers call me out. They want my muscle, they want to taunt me with what I was and what I never will be again.

I am no general. I am no warrior. I will never be either of those things, not while my head is filled with screams I shouldn't be able to hear.

Not while I know I failed to save at least one Sarkarnii from our enemies who destroyed an entire species in a matter of seccari.

How can I be a leader when I have such blood on my claws? How can I even call myself a warrior?

"If anyone wants to fight, I am here!" I roar out, my voice ringing around the pit, echoing back at me.

I don't even know who I am anymore, but when the Rak sidles into the arena, holding up his mangled claw, his tentacles bristling, I don't need to think about it.

All I need to do is fight. And I guess I can do that anywhere.

JEM

J esus! Something is tapdancing in my head, and given I'm not on Earth, and definitely not in my cottage in the tiny West Country village I made my home after the divorce, I daren't hazard a guess at what it might be.

It would appear alien drugs are particularly potent, given the room I'm in isn't spinning, but it does have impressive rainbows everywhere. My stomach did want to revolt for all of half a second until it realized there was nothing in it. Now I feel queasy and strung out, and yet without the fun party beforehand. I haven't had fun for at least the last decade, and this is no different.

Alien abduction is for suckers.

Speaking of which, the lobster/squid sidles across the white room with its sparkling rainbows, weird legs clacking on the floor. I attempt to move, but, joy of joys, I'm strapped to a table or something. I can't see what.

"Is it crab season yet?" I hear myself say, knowing my mouth always runs away with me when I've had a drink or two. Only whatever I've been given is more like an entire bottle or a vat. "Nice legs," I add and cackle to myself.

"This one is broken." A voice comes from the other side, and I nearly jump out of my skin. "They're not this noisy."

I stare up at the purple slug-like creature with tiny arms and hands, its big blubbery face and watery eyes looking down on me.

"It's had paraxio." The harsh voice of the lobster/squid thing bites into my whirling brain.

"What's paraxio?" I ask, attempting and failing to sound sober.

"Paraxio should subdue something this small, not make it louder," the slug says.

"Paraxio." I roll the word around my mouth. It sounds weird. "Can I have some more?"

The slug throws up its little arms, and I giggle. "I can't work with this one, not in this state," it whines. "I need them quiet and compliant."

Those two words worm their way through the sludge of my consciousness.

"You what?" This time, my words have a hard edge because I want them to.

I might have let my ex-husband walk over me, but in my day job as a lawyer, I didn't take any shit. Not from anyone. My head clears a little more. There are other gurneys in this weird white room, all of them empty, save for two.

My head is strapped to the table, so I can't see much other than that they are wearing dirty white shifts like mine. One has red hair and the other white blonde tipped with pink. Neither are moving.

The slug, who I realize is wearing a white lab coat, makes a move towards the other tables.

"No! Wait!" I grab for him, my hand spinning uselessly

in the air. "I can be quiet and compliant. I can. I'll shut up right now, in fact."

The slug turns back, its pudgy face not showing any emotion, but its eyes, tiny and black, spark with interest.

"You will?"

I purse my lips and nod my head. Its segments shift as if it's relaxing.

"Good." It turns to the lobster/squid. "You can go, and take the other ones with you. Don't dose the *u-mans* with paraxio unless I specifically request it, or I will report you."

The lobster/squid bristles for a few seconds, then it spins on the spot and moves out of my eye line. There's the sound of clanking as gurneys are moved, but I daren't look away from the slug.

"Right," Slug says, rubbing his little three-fingered hands together. "We can get started."

A chill settles into my bones. At least whatever is going to be done will be done to me and not the other unfortunate humans, however many there are. I have to hope the number is limited to the ones I've seen and heard. I distract myself by thinking about how I can rescue them, how we can get away from wherever we are and if there are aliens out here in the galaxy who might be friendly to humans.

How we will get back to Earth.

How I will explain where I have been.

How things can ever be the same again.

"Ow!" I can't help but cry out as my upper arm is grasped in something which burns like hell.

"Quiet," the slug says, and the pain intensifies.

I grit my teeth, tears slipping from beneath my eyelids, unbidden and unwanted. I don't cry. I never cry. Crying makes me a baby, useless, worthless, something drummed into me from an age I don't even remember.

"No one's going to fight your battles, Jemma," my adoptive mother used to spit at me when I returned home from school, uniform ripped by the bullies who plagued me. *"Least of all me. You'll need to toughen up. It's a hard old world out there, and the sooner you realize it, the better."*

She was a hard bitch, and she did one thing right. She made me an even harder bitch in her image. No wonder I left the house which was never my home at sixteen.

No wonder I shacked up with the first man who showed interest. And it's absolutely no surprise at all he was the man I went through the messiest of messy divorces with ten years later. In between all of this, I managed to qualify as a solicitor. Something I should be proud of, given I worked for a charity providing legal advice to those who couldn't afford it, but even that was something he made me feel dirty about.

Love is for the birds. All life ever gives you for sure is pain.

Speaking of which, what's happening to my arm is getting hotter. It feels like this bastard wants to cut it off.

"What the hell are you doing?" I finally fire out, glaring up at the slug.

He opens his mouth to admonish me, but then everything goes to shit in slow motion. An explosion leaves my ears ringing and my face covered in dust. I blink through the grit, wriggling at my bonds which have suddenly become loose. I get a hand free—the other one feels useless given the slug's attentions—and I attempt to wipe my face free of all the mess.

Once I have my eyes clear, I pull at the rest of the straps holding me down and drop off the table. The room is still filled with dust, and debris covers the floor, and it's slowly settling. There's a jagged hole in one wall and outside there are sounds of...I don't know what...maybe alien weapons?

They zip and snap, light flashing as I attempt to recover my wits and work out how I'm going to get the fuck out of this place. Next to me is the body of the slug, weirdly deflated.

I don't look too closely at it. My arm hurts bad, although given I'm now covered in buff colored dust, I can't see what's been done to me, other than a ring of bright blood which wraps around my upper bicep.

The strange noises have stopped. I take my chance and scuttle across the floor, crouched as I aim for the unadulterated doorway.

That is until something unbelievably large and green fills my vision. Something with scales, claws, and...wings?

It reaches for me, jaw opening, a mouth full of sharp teeth.

So, this is how it ends.

Not a fucking chance.

DRAXX

As much as I hate to admit it, coming on the mission with Drega has been interesting. The use of explosives and weapons has been like a balm to my soul.

I'm not sure Drega agrees, given he's spent all his time so far telling me what not to do. Orders I ignored, of course, with some satisfaction. Drega was a healer, not a leader. He was never a general. I do what I think best, and if he doesn't want to follow me...

That's his problem.

It was relatively easy to blow open the nearest lab to our quadrant, the one where Drega said there were humans. I haven't quite been able to contain my shift as the sounds of the battle die away and I enter the room. It's similar to ones we all saw when we were first incarcerated, where they fitted the collars which used to control our ability to shift. Collars we are no longer bound by, and the Xicop guards know it.

I think that's what makes me want to shift even more.

My use of explosives has left the place fairly well

destroyed. To one side is a dead Belek technician, not quite Warden class, but disgusting nonetheless. I can't help but shift further when I see the filthy creature. They pretend to be a species above the rest, but I've met far more honorable creatures in the pit. Then something scuttles over my shifted feet. Something the same color as the rest of the place, of the dust which is gently settling. It squeaks as I reach for it, hoisting the thing up so I can take a good look at it.

A pair of incredible eyes glares back at me, a bright green, like the forests on my old world. The round pupils are pinpricks but the desire to kill me is clear.

I love them immediately.

Anything which wants a fight has to be mine. Despite all the muck covering this squirming life-form, it smells absolutely divine. I bring it closer to me to inhale deeper. It twists and sinks a set of blunt teeth into my side.

"What are you doing with that human, Draxx?" Drega bellows at me. "Put her down."

"This isn't a human female." I furrow my brow, finding it unusually hard to contain my shift. "I've met Draco's mate. Humans are not this...bitey." I twist the thing left and right, attempting to keep myself away from its snapping mouth. "They're soft and nice."

"It is a human and...what are you doing?" Drega folds his arms. My hips snap from side to side in a way I've never done before. "Are you *dancing* for your mate?"

"I am NOT his mate," the female says, swinging. "I am not his friend, not his anything, and if he doesn't put me down this instant, he will lose a limb. Maybe not today, but he'll be sleeping with one eye open for the rest of time if he doesn't *put me down!*"

I let go. The female drops to the floor and rolls over. Then she lies still.

Immediately, I go to scoop her up, take her into my arms.

And she bites me. Again.

"I warned you." She scoots back on her bottom to the other side of the room, leaving a trail in her wake.

A trail of blood.

She might bite, but she is injured, and it seems to override my brain. In fact, it overrides my sense of self-preservation because I'm striding across the room and then pulling her to her feet to inspect the nasty injury on her arm.

"Who did this to you?" I growl out, my mouth suddenly too full of fang. "Who hurt you?"

Those green eyes stare up starkly, defiantly, from out of the dirt and dust streaked face. They are eyes I'm immediately lost in, swimming in them like I've never seen a female before.

"The slug, over there." She points to the Belek's prone form.

I raise my pulsar and fire three shots into the thing. It jumps with each shot but doesn't move.

"It was already dead," she says, slamming her hands into my chest and pushing away from me.

I've learned my lesson, and I let her go. Unfortunately I forget how little she is, and she drops to the floor in a heap.

"Just get away from me, will you?" She attempts to get to her feet, sways, and clutches the wall for stability.

"I am a healer," Drega says, stepping between us and shoving me back. "Let me help you, little one."

Little one?

I release a snarl I've dredged up from the very depths of

the pit at my brother, although I'm heartened to see she holds him at arm's length too.

Although if he touches her, I will have to kill him, brother or no.

"Just go away," she says, shaking her head, her knees buckling. "I have to get to the others."

A high, shrill alarm sounds.

"That's not going to be possible." Drega gives me a worried glance. "Reinforcements."

"So?" I start to shift again, tail extending, wings rising, flanks extending.

The room is too small.

"Yeah, that." Drega lifts one of his pierced eyebrows, his blue scales glittering as his eyes dance with amusement. "It's the reason we were authorized to have weapons. These tunnels and labs are too small for our Sarkarnii forms."

"Nev it to the ancestors," I grind out, returning to my more usual state.

My female's eyes are closing, her small body giving up. Drega catches her as she falls, but this time, it's because she can't help herself.

"The others..." she whispers. "I have to get to the others."

"We need to go before we get stuck here and collared," Drega says as he unceremoniously deposits the female in my arms. "We'll fix her when we get back to the quadrant."

"What about the mission?" I ask.

"She is the mission." Drega races out into the corridor and lays down covering fire for us. "I wanted another human and now I have one."

I look down at the unconscious female in my arms. I have no idea what Drega thinks she is, but I know one thing.

This female is mine.

JEM

This is more like it. A mariachi band thumping away inside my head after a night I don't remember. I groan, reaching to grab at the offending body part, and then I recall....

The big scaled aliens! The green one who dangled me in the air by one leg, sniffed me, and wouldn't let me go. Who shot an *already dead* slug alien because I said he injured me.

And the other blue one who said we were mates, when I've definitely never met any green scaled alien, especially one with muscles which go on forever, eyes like fire, and a tail like a fucking dragon.

I'd remember a date like that, I'm sure. And, although I don't have many friends, I'm sure none of them are hiding lizard qualities under their shirts.

"Agh!" I'm sitting up, ready to fight, ready to do anything to get away from these fucking aliens, one of whom thought it was all right to pass me around like I'm an upside down parcel.

But what happened after the explosions and the dangling? It's all a bit of a blur. Someone asked me for my name, someone wrapped a cooling bandage around my arm. And now...

I'm in a small concrete room without windows, and it's made even smaller due to the same alien from earlier sat immediately opposite the bed I'm lying on, his eyes open, unblinking, his scales shining, glittering with some sort of supernatural light. *A lizard man.*

No, he's far too big, far too muscular, to be a lizard. Maybe crocodile or a dinosaur...or a *dragon?*

"You are awake," he says.

"Well done, Captain Obvious." I sit up, swing my legs over the side of the bed, and ignore both the spin and pain in my head and arm.

I'm still covered in dust and filth, although there is a bandage in a weird material wrapped around my bicep. Blood has already soaked through.

"I am not a captain," my alien growls. "My name is Draxx, little female."

He actually growls, a proper, honest to goodness growl. No one growls. This is insane. I must have finally gone mad.

"It's an expression." I decide to roll with whatever my psyche is doing. "It means you just said something which is self-evident."

Eyes with slit pupils follow my every movement. He doesn't say anything else. All I can hear is his rasping breath, which is weird enough...until he snorts out a stream of smoke as if he's taken a drag on a cigarette.

The scent of him hits me like a sledgehammer. Spicy, musky, smoky like a bonfire in autumn. I get to my feet. Just because this alien doesn't smell like a mound of rotting rubbish like the others I've met doesn't mean he's good or he has my best interests at heart.

"My name is Jem, and I'm going now," I say.

He unfolds himself from his seat, and he just keeps getting taller. And taller. He has to be well over seven feet in height, maybe more. I wasn't wrong about the bulk and the muscles. With all the green, he is a hulk in so many ways. Only this alien's face doesn't look like someone punched it repeatedly.

Chiseled doesn't even cover how angular his face is, how handsome, how the scales flow over his features, appearing and disappearing seemingly at will. He's an alien who would absolutely give any model a run for their money.

As for the rest of him, he has abs which would make any Mr. Universe weep.

He's also not wearing any clothing.

At all.

But instead of an eyeful of alien junk (because at my five ten, while his crotch isn't at eye level, it's certainly close), there's only a bulge of scales. Admittedly it's a big bulge, but still...I'm not sure whether to be relieved or surprised.

For a second, I hesitate, expecting him to stop me, but instead he says and does nothing as I take several wobbly steps to the door, which snaps open suddenly at my approach.

Outside is a similar colored passageway to the room. I dart left, waiting to see what my green companion will do.

"It's the other way," he rumbles behind me. "If you want to get out into the main square."

I have literally no idea what he's talking about, but the word "out" catches my attention, and I will my limbs to move as fast as they can down the passage towards what seems to be a brighter light.

And no, the irony is not lost on me.

I hear him behind me, because something as big as he is can't be quiet, as I burst out into the open, chest heaving and all my senses on high alert.

The huge square is walls many stories high of blank concrete-like slab and is *filled with dragons.*

Actual dragons with wings, flames, and all the other things I've seen in CGI and never expected to see in real life. So many colors whirl around me, so many huge bodies, huge carnivores with teeth and claws and all the things I'd quite like to avoid.

I stumble backwards and hit a wall of heat. Above me, a rumble and a huff of smoke.

"What the...what are they?" I gasp, my heart thundering in my chest, unable to keep my eyes off the writhing mass of scales.

"Sarkarnii. My brother warriors," my alien rasps, his voice velvet dark, filled with smoke.

"But you're...you don't look like them." I'm stumbling over my words, my head, my eyes, my nostrils full of all new things. All strange, all terrible.

He uses a clawed hand to steady me, then takes a step back. As I watch, his form changes, growing huge, scales expanding, wings sprouting, tail lashing.

He is a dragon. He is an alien. He is both.

An enormous head dips towards me, huge snout with smoke curling from the nostrils. It turns, and a massive eye, with a gaze so intense I feel it could consume me, hovers in front of me.

"I am Sarkarnii." A voice, his voice, comes from the

beast. "I am *the* Sarkarnii, and you, little female—you are my treasure."

The head withdraws, lifts, and as the flanks of the creature inflate, a huge sheet of flame fires from his mouth.

For the first time in my life, my consciousness deserts me. The last thing I see is the dragon resolving into a man, clawed hands reaching for me once again.

DRAXX

I want the treasure. I want her. I need her.

Her scent is unmissable, all clean air, freedom, and the promise of a rut. I could breathe her in for the rest of time and never be satisfied.

I can't have her.

Drega comes out of her quarters and frowns at me.

"Nev it, Draxx, why did you have to shift? Draco's mate says humans call us dragons. We're some sort of story made up to scare their young. You've frightened her."

He shakes his head in despair.

"She needed to know what we are, what I am," I state.

"If that's how you feel, you need to stay the nev away from her if you know what's good for you. Humans are the key to finding the map, and if you nev it up, Draco will come for you, whether you're in the filthy pit or not." Drega is spitting fire and steaming towards me.

He means to take the female from me. I curl my body over hers, glaring at him.

"Map." I spit out a flame at the floor. "It's meaningless.

We lost everyone to the Liderc. You know it and I know it. Even if it exists, even if the human is the key, why should I care?" I snarl.

"I know you lost your promised mate, but the way you reacted to this human says she was not the one for you." Drega looks unbearably smug. "Looks like you have your fate after all, here in the Kirakos."

I hate him. I hate the human. I want to go back to my pit, brood, and fight. It's all I'm nevving good for. So, when he reaches for my human, with a great reluctance, I place her on the floor to one side of us, sliding my tail out in order to block her from his view.

"It means nothing. I reacted to her as I might a shiny piece of metal. You know that." I huff at Drega. "She is not my *szikra*. She was not chosen for me, and fate has nothing for me, not anymore."

"Idiot." Drega shakes his head, scratching at his hide on the back of his neck with his long claws. "I'm taking her to the control room once she has recovered. If you have no interest, I don't expect you to stand in my way."

The growl I release is one I keep for the pit.

"Then take her." I can't believe the words leave my chest.

The very last thing I want is for her to be anywhere near any other Sarkarnii who might attempt a claim on her.

A swift movement catches my attention. She was there, watching us, listening, and now she has gone back in the room, just as Drega sidesteps and blocks my way.

"If you want to mourn the loss of something you never had, be my guest, but don't upset her," he snarls, folding his arms as I attempt to look around him, back to where the female is. "The humans are the key to what we need."

"She has a name," I growl. "Jem."

Jem.

I roll it over in my mind, imagining whispering it to her as her back arches and my cock slides inside her.

"By the bones!" Drega interrupts my thoughts with his sharp tongue. He's shaking his head.

"What?"

"Nothing." He stalks towards me and gives me a shove, staring pointedly at my crotch. "Go back to the pit and forget about this female, if she is *not yours to claim*."

His voice has an edge to it. Drega is, as usual, deliberately goading me. But I've spent too nevving long fighting to forget I can't work out what it is. I should do as he says. The pit is my home. Only the scent of her lingers everywhere, on my skin, in the air. When I look down, I see my cock is pushing at the slit of my pouch.

This will not do.

I let Drega force me back to the main square. He shifts immediately and is in the air, dancing in what passes for the sky in the Kirakos, not even looking back at me. I guess he's going to report to Draco.

Draco thought if I wasn't collared, I'd be better able to cope with the Kirakos. He failed to consider the incarceration we are all still facing. He is basing such an assumption I managed, just, to keep things together while we were aboard the *Golden Orion*, his ship and our only home. But, while we might control this quadrant, we are still in the prison to end all prisons, and so far, my brother has shown not an inkling he wants to be free. My bones can't take it. I need to see the stars again.

Instead he insists on searching for this nevving star map. The one which is supposed to locate any other Sarkarnii left in the universe. The one we came to the Kirakos, the prison maze, for.

The one I never believed in.

I snort out some smoke and flame, resist the urge to shift, resist the urge to turn back straight away and take the female in my arms. Instead, I make my way through the maze, Jiakas running in my wake, back to the open maw of the pit.

Stench rises up. All those who are lost live down there, and there are many lost souls in the Kirakos. I lost mine the day our species was decimated, my den warriors, other than those with me on the *Golden Orion*, Draco's ship, gone. Our sires, gone. The mate, the Sarkarnii female I was to dance for and join with for the good of our den, Almeria.

Regardless of whether I wanted a mate or not, I can't even remember her face. It is all gone. The rage and the fire took me instead. When I found myself in the pit and gave into the fight.

When all is blocked out, all is forgotten.

The darkness embraces me, and only tendrils of the females scent remain with me, like invisible strings. I do my best to shake them off.

"Let's see what you've got, *Sarkarnii*." A rasp in the dark, hardly even a string of words, more of a mood.

I don't need any goading. I need to break my links to the maze above me. I need to forget about her.

As the first claw slams into my side and pain explodes throughout my body, I lean into it. I spin, I thrash, I slice.

I maim.

I'll do anything other than go back to the surface. To help my brothers, to see my female. This fight, this endless night, this unshifted form, it's all I am.

I thought removing the collar would quiet my soul. It didn't.

But meeting this female, saving her, being close to her. It has set me on fire.

One I know I can't put out.

Arrogant. Bastard. Arsehole.

I fling myself down on the bed in the weird little room. Not only did the alien cause me to faint, and I've never fainted in my fucking life, but he then decides that I'm not worth his time or energy.

I'm both his and not his. And I never asked to be *anything* to him.

Well fuck *Draxx*.

"Don't judge my brother too harshly," the big blue scaled alien says. "I'm Drega." He places his hand on his chest and gives me a little bow. "We are the Sarkarnii."

"Great," I say. And I turn over to face the wall.

"We have a few things to discuss, but I'll come back when you feel better," Drega says.

"You do that." I talk at the wall.

If I thought it wouldn't hurt my hand, I'd have punched Drega in the face. He's also startlingly good looking, although not nearly as handsome as Draxx, my green behemoth.

Why am I even thinking these things? Draxx turned

into a fucking *dragon*. Then after growling "mine" all over me like some sort of cave...alien, he tells his brother he's not interested.

Fuck that. Neither am I.

Rejection is my middle name. I'm used to it. Adoptive parents who hated me, an ex-husband, I am the epitome of everything everyone didn't want. I shouldn't be surprised some alien decided, on balance, I wasn't worth his time. Especially one as bloody annoyingly good looking as Draxx.

I'm not exactly Earth's greatest catch, after all. Dark hair and green eyes, yes, but my bum is big, my boobs are too, and I don't exactly balance them out in the middle. Plus, at five ten, I'm a big girl.

My ex used to ask me to tread lighter and not wear heels because I'd be taller than him. So, now I'm a thirty-five-year-old bundle of insecurity.

Who has also been rejected by a fucking alien.

And the fact I fucking fainted in front of him—I'm not going to forget it in a hurry. He made me show weakness. In a place where all I am is weak, I hate him for making me look weaker.

I lie on the bed in the strange room, which still has hints of musky smoke in the air. I will my body to get back under control, to recover enough I can make good my escape and get back to find the other human women.

A chill steals through me. I'm surrounded by alien dragons. What if they want to eat me?

I wave that question away. They've already had ample opportunity, and I'm still here, mostly intact. But what if they want me for something else?

"What the hell could massive dragon aliens want from you?" I fire out at myself.

The ice returns.

They want me as a pet. That's why the big green one went all growly.

I'm the equivalent of an alien hamster.

Oh, fuck. I've got this all wrong. I thought he was *interested* interested.

How wrong was I?

This hamster isn't going to stay in her cage. I get off my bed and spot a pile of what looks like clothing on a square block. I tentatively pick at it, finding there is a pair of pants, a silky top, and something which looks like a corset. I'm still wearing the now pretty stained and filthy shift I've been in since I woke up at the mercy of aliens.

I'm not going to think about any of this. I pull on the pants, wriggle into the corset because the girls need to be contained if I'm going to do anything, and shrug on the silky top. It clings to me in all the right places which is strange, as I never thought of myself as having 'right' places.

Could be worse I suppose. I could be naked, but then that might scare the aliens...

I half expect the door to the room to be locked, but it isn't. It rolls to one side as easily as the first time I left. Only now I know what to expect. If the main square is full of dragons, this time I'm going right, not left. Maybe going right will take me back to where I started.

I wish I had a weapon of some sort as I stalk my way through the dimly lit passageway. I can do unpleasant things with a pointy stick. I've practiced.

But the scratchy walls and the dirt floor remain stubbornly stickless. Looks like I'm going to have to use my charm and wit to survive.

Which means I'm screwed.

The passageway gets darker, and it's sloping downwards. I think where I came from was deep inside somewhere, or at least it smelt that way. Maybe I'm going in the right direction.

I carry on for a little while longer, the light getting worse and the skin on the back of my neck prickling like crazy. Eventually I come to the conclusion this passage doesn't go anywhere and I'm being an idiot.

I'd be better off taking my chances with the dragons. I turn around, and a shadow moves. Not in a good way.

In an oily, dangerous way.

I guess my brain is still not quite right because I forgot the one rule I've always lived by. If it's new, it's not to be trusted.

This is new.

I shouldn't have trusted it.

The shadow moves, but the light stays the same. I don't have a pointy stick. I don't have anything.

"Er...hi?" I venture. "I'm just passing through."

The darkness doesn't move. But it does grow teeth.

Oh, shit.

This was a mistake. A really, really big mistake. How could I have been so fucking stupid to think I could take on an alien...planet or space ship or whatever this is. I've already found slugs, assassin crustaceans, and dragons, so shadows with teeth has to be par for the course.

Only I'm not going to survive this encounter and that pisses me off.

I back away from the teeth. I'm desperately trying to think what the protocol is when dealing with a large predator, except the largest predator we have in the UK is a fox, and shouting 'the bins are round the back' is usually sufficient.

I don't remember what you're supposed to do about

bears or big cats. My mind is a blank of white fear because those teeth are getting bigger.

"Perhaps we can talk about this?" I suggest, because I'm hoping the thing is sentient.

"Perhaps the yeykok can die," a voice rumbles behind me. "For threatening my female."

I hit the hard wall of muscle before I even see Draxx. Then I'm slammed into the wall as he thunders past me, claws outstretched before they sink into the dark. For a second, he disappears entirely, then with a burst of snarls, growls, and roars, he and the shadow are spinning, limbs, tail, scales, darkness, I can't tell where one begins and the other ends. The noise is tremendous in the confined space, and I clap my hands over my ears, wanting to get away but not wanting to risk finding something even more terrible.

There is a snap. It echoes unpleasantly in the sudden silence. And then a wave of scales rises up in front of me, resolving into the powerhouse which is Draxx. I'm pinned to the wall, a large clawed hand around my neck as he bends down to my face.

His other hand is by his side, dripping with dark...something. The shadows which were moving are no longer doing so.

"What," he rasps, "are you doing down here?"

"What"—I bristle under his touch, hating him with all my being—"do you care?"

He huffs out smoke, and it curls from his mouth like he's taken a drag on a cigarette. I feel my insides squirm as his eyes flash in the gloom, bright gold lights zipping between his scales.

"I shouldn't care." The words are torn from him. "But you are mine."

"You keep fucking saying that," I retort, rage rising

within me. "But I don't belong to you, or anyone. I am not your pet. Just let me go, Draxx."

He leans in, his face millimeters from mine, and he smells so damn good, my knees go weak. The hand tightens around my neck, not constricting my airway but enough for all the heat in him to pour into my skin. He smells like a bonfire, and it's all I can do not to inhale him.

"You belong to me," he snarls, his lips brushing over mine, sending shockwaves through me. "No one touches you, or I will end them."

DRAXX

That didn't go as well as I hoped.

For a start, the yeykok nearly killed my female, and now she's glaring at me like she wants to set me on fire. Our mouths so close I can almost taste her.

All of her body vibrates under my touch. She wants to kill me. I want to kiss her.

It could be because I simply can't help myself. As soon as she's close, I want to claim her, make her mine. Dance for her. Sheath myself in her.

Nev it to the bones of my ancestors! I can't take a mate. I've already lost too much. We're stuck in a prison, one which is not entirely under our control and with no sign of us leaving. For me, taking a mate would be more than foolish. Taking *this* female would be foolish.

Everything I touch turns to dust. Everything I care for dies. I'm not willing to put myself or any other creature, especially the one beneath my claws who smells like the old country, all sweetness and promise of what could be, at risk.

She doesn't move. She stares and stares, as if her eyes

could do what she wants. I might have saved her from the yeykok, but she doesn't care.

Jem wants me dead.

"Are we going to stay like this forever? Because I'm hungry," she says, eyes still burning.

My female is hungry! I have failed to provide for her!

Something thumps in my chest, and it's not my heart. I release her and rub over the surface of my skin, attempting to work out what the issue is. I cannot.

"Then we will eat." I go to pick her up.

"No," she snarls.

"No?"

"No. Don't touch me. Don't ever touch me again." She takes three paces back and nearly steps in the puddle of yeykok.

"It's this way." I gesture ahead of me. "To my quarters. I can arrange for a meal to be brought. I don't need to touch you."

I haven't been in my quarters in half a revolution. I'm not even sure they're still there, but it's an option, and it's my only option until I can get far enough from her scent my head works again. And also regret my suggestion I don't need to touch her.

Because I do. Very much.

Jem huffs at me, but there's no smoke. I rather like it. She makes my chest feel strange again as she stalks past, and with a quick glance over her shoulder to make sure I'm following, she marches through the passageways. I want to touch her so many times, if nothing else to see what she will do, but I refrain. Just.

We reach the dead end which is the entrance to my quarters, and I get another baleful glare.

"What are we doing here?"

"The maze is not what it seems. It never has been."

"What do you mean 'maze'? Isn't this a planet or a space ship?" she queries, some of her fire draining from her.

"This is the Kirakos. The galaxy's most impregnable prison. It is also a maze designed to torture its inhabitants."

Her chest heaves, and I do everything in my power not to look at it. I fail.

"I'm in a *prison*?" Her voice rises.

"We're all bad here," I growl, moving past her, dragging my eyes away from her body because whatever I am now, I am not that sort of warrior. "All criminals." I press the hidden catch, and the door swings inwards.

"Figures." She storms past me, her scent streaming behind her.

I harden my resolve. If she thinks I'm a criminal, maybe I should be one. If it means she doesn't want to have anything to do with me, all the better.

My quarters smell musty, and it's already too late when I realize the last thing I did in them was rip most things to shreds in my ante room. The collar had been particularly restricting, refusing to stop shocking me when my tail wouldn't shift back. It was shortly after that I went into the pit and did not resurface for a long time.

"What the hell is this place?" Jem has her hands on her hips.

"My quarters," I reply, attempting to keep my cool. I flip over some of the furniture, and it is remarkably intact. Presumably, I wasn't in as foul a mood as I thought.

"This is where you live?" She stares at me, and then her eyes drift over the destruction.

"Sometimes."

"Fuck me," she says. The phrase doesn't translate, but I get the meaning.

Then her stomach growls.

"Wait here," I say, leaping to the door and attempting not to wince at the state of the floor.

Out of the door, I spot Drasus. The purple scaled warrior is ambling past, stretching out a shifted wing for a brief preen, obviously on his way to the feasting hall.

"Food for my female. Now," I growl.

That did not come out how I meant it to come out. Drasus is a good warrior. But I can't seem to get my brain and body to obey each other.

He grins at me, genially. "You have a female? Will wonders ever cease?"

"I'm not asking again."

"Can I see her?" He cranes his neck. "Nev it, Draxx, you didn't put her in your quarters, did you?"

I can feel my shift. It burns at me.

"Just do it." I want to pull rank. I am one of the ruling families of the Sarkarnii, or I was. Draco, our leader, our captain, is my brother. I should not need to fight this warrior for a platter of food to take to my female.

A female I cannot leave unprotected.

Drasus snorts out some smoke and narrows his eyes. "One time, Draxx, but you'll get me one of the new pulsar weapons as my payment."

"Done."

I don't have access to the weapons, but Drasus doesn't need to know. Draco won't let me near anything which might make a noise...or a hole in something. Not anymore and not without supervision.

He knows what I might do. I might mount my own escape attempt and spoil his party.

Drasus ambles away as I hop from foot to foot, my tail attempting to trip me up as I guard my treasure and try to work out what the nev is going on in my chest. It feels like something is dancing in there.

A dance which makes it to my hips. Drega's words echo in my ears: *Are you dancing for your mate?*

But Jem cannot be my mate, and I shove the thought away. I don't rut. I don't mate. I fight, I survive. That's all.

Only, I can't leave her. My cock aches in its pouch. My head is filled with need. I have to get back to her.

"Little female?" I call out as I enter my quarters.

Only silence echoes my words back to me.

My rooms are empty of anything soft and delicious.

And it's then I hear it, loud and clear. The thump of my mating gland, firing the mix into my system like molten metal.

That she has gone shouldn't be a problem, if I don't rut or mate.

It is a problem. A big one. One which will only be solved with a significant amount of destruction.

JEM

I'm not sure what I was expecting when Draxx said he would take me back to his quarters, but I've never seen anything like it.

Of course, I'm also in an alien prison, and I've never seen anything like one of those. I've not even seen the inside of an Earth prison, so perhaps I shouldn't have any pre-conceived ideas about what to expect.

Only this place looks like a hurricane hit it. Furniture is overturned, split into pieces. There are stains on the walls which were probably once decorated but now are ruined. The entire place looks unloved and unlived in. I don't understand why Draxx brought me here.

I shift from foot to foot, watching the door he left through. On the one hand, I don't want to have anything to do with him. On the other, my lips are still tingling from where he brushed his for one second over mine.

Fuck! I run my hand through my hair, hating all the emotions swirling inside me. I've been abducted, I've been tortured, and I'm in a prison. I do not need to catch feelings for anything or anyone, certainly not an alien who blows hot and cold as if he's psychotic, and...

My hair feels disgusting.

It sticks to my hand alarmingly. When I pull at the long strands, it looks like it's covered in porridge.

As this room is now devoid of huge hulking dragon alien, I fancy I can hear the sound of running water. Do I risk finding somewhere to clean up?

I look down at my clothing. It's not in a bad state, even after my tangle with the shadow monster, but my skin underneath itches with the dirt and dust I got covered in after my so-called rescue.

I still don't quite know why I'm with these aliens, and they didn't leave me strapped to a table at the mercy of the slug. Although I don't suppose they have to keep me tied up, not given what I've encountered so far.

Fuck off massive dragons are going to keep anyone in line without much need for a leash.

I don't know whether to trust my long learned instincts here, in this alien place. Something tells me the Sarkarnii are not bad, not completely anyway. Something tells me they don't want to hurt me.

I incline my head to listen for the water again, and I find myself walking down a passageway to one side of the ruined room. It's well lit by skylights up above and in much better order than the room I just left.

I'd even venture it's clean, to a degree anything left unused for a while remains clean. There is dust. I leave tracks in it. To my left, a door snaps open, and I peer into a huge room, dominated by an even bigger, circular bed. This place too is not in any state of disarray. It's as if all the destruction was kept for the first room and then left.

The noise of the water is louder in the 'bed' room. I spot another door, and as I approach, it opens too, into a room filled with moist warmth and something which resembles a swimming pool rather than a bath.

Does the door behind me lock? I turn and see a small set of lit squares next to it. I press the green one, and it slides shut. I press the red one, which I presume means I've locked the door.

With a sigh of relief, I shed my clothes as I head towards the swimming pool, leaving a trail of garments behind me like a teenager until I'm naked and slipping into the clean water. As it stings against my skin, I groan with happiness, and I don't think anything has felt better.

Other than the closeness of Draxx to me in the passageway.

I growl at the stupid thought, the noise echoing around the room, and then I dive under the water, running my hands through my hair over and over again and concentrating on holding my breath, not thinking about big green scaled dragon aliens with muscles which go on forever and who smell like smoke and sin.

I very nearly choke myself to death with that last thought, rising to the surface to cough and splutter. I'm wiping water out of my eyes and snot from my face when I see them. A pair of thick, muscular, and, of course, green calves. I follow the shining scales up and up until I'm looking directly into Draxx's face.

In one hand, he holds a platter of food. In the other, he holds my clothes.

Immediately, I fold my arms over my chest, not knowing how much of a good look he got, given most of me is underwater.

"What are you doing in here?" We fire out at the same time.

"I'm having a bath! Get out!" I rage back.

"This is my bath, my personal aquium," Draxx growls.

"I didn't see anyone's name on the door."

He flings my clothing to one side and slams the food down as he drops to his knees. A pair of wings unfurl from his back, and he leans closer to the water, to me, something rumbling from deep inside as smoke rolls from him.

"I don't have to tell anyone this place is mine." His voice is dangerous, low, and sends a weird feeling through my body.

"I needed a bath," I snap. "Someone got me covered in dirt. I haven't had the opportunity to get clean since I was abducted and brought here against my will." I glare at him, willing him to turn into a dragon so I can inform him he is deliberately making things worse.

"I saved you. From the Belek," he rasps and then tumbles headfirst into the water.

His huge bulk displaces so much I'm washed to one side as his scales glitter under the surface. Freed of the air, he swirls in the water sinuously until he bursts out, water splashing everywhere and a wave engulfing me. It goes straight up my nose and sends me into a coughing fit.

"You call this saving?"

In a rush of liquid and scales, I'm caged against the side by Draxx. Even in the water, he smells strongly of oak wood fires and tobacco. The hugeness of him, every muscle defined by scales, water beading on his skin and glittering like jewels—he is...vast.

And he is sexy.

"I call it claiming what's mine," he says. "And now I

have you in my quarters and in my bath, I'd say you are ripe for claiming fully, wouldn't you?"

Fuck. Fuck. Fuck. I am so naked.

And so screwed.

DRAXX

Nev it to the bones of my ancestors! When I have Jem in my aquium, all pink and scaleless, every part of her glistening with water, I cannot help myself.

Being next to her, having her so nevving close to me, at least quells the drumming in my chest which I thought would never stop after I found her missing when I returned to my quarters

The sound of the water drew me away from smashing any remaining things to the trail of her clothing through my bed chamber.

To find her in the one place out of all the maze, other than the pit, I missed. My aquium. The place I shed my skin every half a revolution, where I soaked my body when all it wanted to do was shift and ached for the change.

When I thought my mind was gone because we have lost everything.

And, no longer collared, I can shift, I have a female in my grasp, and everything is how it should be. Jem is to be claimed. By me.

Which is where I make my first mistake. I relax.

Jem takes the opportunity to scramble out of the water, grabbing at her clothes, and all I see is the delicious round globes of her ass before she's out of the aquium and into my bedroom.

It takes me all of a seccari to heave myself out of the bath, grab the food, and follow her. Unfortunately, it seems she has taken that seccari to pull on her clothing, meaning she is able to focus her not inconsiderable ire on me.

"Do you ever wear clothes?" She folds her arms as her gaze rakes down my body.

"No," I growl.

"Do you do anything other than growl and attempt to intimidate people?"

I think about her question for a beat.

"No?"

She snorts out a distinctly smokeless breath and sits down on my bed.

I really wish I was wearing pants for a change. My stiffening cock is yet again pushing at my pouch. This female should not be enticing me, making me want her, making me do anything for her. That is how Sarkarnii females behave, and their venomous bite can incapacitate a male, even one my size. I'd happily fight her, but I don't know how to subdue a human.

All I know is she bites, except, her eyes are not on me. Her eyes are on the platter of food, and they are *hungry*.

By the bones! I wish I had pants.

I offer her the food. She snatches for the plate, and I pull it out of her reach, an idea penetrating the fog filling my head and something I'm not entirely sure I should have in Jem's presence.

"Hey! You said you were getting food for me, so what are you doing?" she complains.

"It's my food, and I want to make sure you get all the sustenance you require." I grin at her as the plan slowly unfurls in my distinctly crowded mind.

"So?" Jem cocks her head to one side, and I do everything, everything in my power to stop my cock from emerging.

It is painful in the extreme. She is so delicious, so beautiful with her wet hair pulled to one side. I shouldn't even be looking at her in this way. I don't know what it is that continually draws me to her, making me want her, making me want to claim her entirely.

I was to take a mate. A sweet female Sarkarnii promised to me. We met once. She seemed receptive, or at least she didn't try to envenomate me. I was sure once she went into her heat, we would mate, and things would be better. It was my duty, after all.

And then the Liderc destroyed all my species, my parents, my mate, everything.

There was nothing I could do to stop them.

My vision darkens. What am I doing with this gorgeous creature in front of me? Everything I care about turns to dust. It's the reason I'm in the pit, fighting, all the time. It's the reason Draco keeps me from the weapons and explosives. I can't bring myself to die, but I want to be as close to death as possible.

I hate the churn in my guts, the fog in my head, the fact some part of me desires this little human and the rest of me won't allow us to be...anything.

The more I prolong our contact, the worse all of this will be when I lose her, like I lost everyone—my warriors, my legions, everyone save for my nevving bothersome brothers who are only interested in themselves.

As if to prove a point, I hear Drega calling out in my ante-room.

"Nev it," I mutter under my breath. Drasus must have told him about me being here.

I put the food down next to my mate. "Stay here. I'll deal with this."

She looks at me like I've grown an extra head and then reaches for the biggest chunk of roast tralu meat on the platter. Taking a big bite, cheeks bulging, she looks at me as if she's scored the biggest victory yet.

I was a general, who once had forces unimaginable at my every command.

If she thinks she's won, she has not.

JEM

I do not understand Draxx. At all. He's infuriating and goddammit...he's stupidly, strangely, wrongly compelling.

If I hadn't got out of the bath when I had my chance, I don't know what would have happened. And his apparent refusal to make himself slightly presentable in terms of clothing means I know he has something between his legs. Something which grew larger as he stood in front of me, teasing with the food, a smile which lights up my stupid heart.

He switches from puppy to brooding in a blink of an eye when he hears someone calling his name. It does mean I get the food, and the meat I chose is particularly delicious. I chew the massive mouthful in triumph.

However, I do not want to play with Draxx. I don't know what he wants from me, but whatever it is will need to wait until I've got to the other humans and freed them too. They have to be my priority. In fact, all he's done so far is get in my way. I mean other than saving me from the Belek slug things, and the shadow monster, and from starving to death...

So Mr. Scaly and Handsome saved me twice from certain death, and he makes my guts twist uncomfortably when I have him up close and personal.

Especially when he's up close and personal.

This is not happening.

Nope. Not at all. I shove as much of the meat in my mouth as I can, swallow, and hastily consume more. I don't know when I'll get to eat again so, as long as it doesn't taste like garbage, it's going down.

Not that any of the food tastes bad. In fact, for a selection of dishes I can absolutely say I have never tried and it's unlikely anyone on Earth has ever done so either, the food is flavorsome and I cram as much in my mouth as I can.

But I'm still not going to let Draxx tell me what to do or keep me away from anything. I'm definitely not going to be "claimed" by him, whatever that means.

I don't belong to him, even if it's what happens here in this prison.

I mean, I might need him. He's big, dominant, and, by his own admission, growly as hell. Draxx could be useful. But it doesn't mean I'm indulging him. Whatever it is he wants from me, he's going to have to work for it.

I'm done with rejection. If I'm not on Earth, the rules, whatever they were, don't apply. I can be whatever I want to be.

The liberation which fills me is incredible, I almost feel like I'm being lifted off the bed I'm sat on and into the air. Freedom from what is expected shouldn't be this good, but it is.

I shove little sweet berries in my mouth, square my shoulders, rake my fingers through my, thankfully clean, hair, then I flounce out of the room into the corridor and follow the sound of voices.

"Draco wants to see her, brother. I need her. You can't keep her here." I recognize the voice, Drega's, and I stop before I get to the main, ruined room. "Plus this place is hardly fit for a female." I hear the sneer in his voice, and something about it makes me bristle.

"Then I will take her to Draco," Draxx replies. "Not you. And I haven't been in my quarters for half a revolution, you know that."

There is a long sigh, and smoke curls around the corner, puffing into my face. "Why do you always have to be so nevving difficult?"

"I lost every nevving thing which mattered to me to the Liderc and got stuck with you and Draco," Draxx says, but rather than sounding triumphant, he sounds defeated.

My heart does a slow flip in my chest, and I find my legs carrying me forward, out into the room of destruction. Draxx stands, hands at his sides. He is taller than Drega, although not by much. But the power imbalance between them is obvious. Drega has his arms folded. He is in control.

"Jem." The blue one does a bow as Draxx turns, his face initially grim, brightening for an instant when he sees me, and then settling back into brooding mode.

"That's my name. It would be nice if you buggers could possibly explain to me exactly who you are and what is going on, rather than attempting to drown me or terrify me," I fire out.

May as well use my newfound resolve to have zero filter.

"Drega, high healer of the Sarkarnii Bask, leader of the Scaled Battalion and lord of the sky sea." Drega bows at me.

"And incarcerated in the Kirakos like the rest of us," Draxx grumbles.

I manage to hide my snort of laughter. Drega looks askance at both Draxx and me.

"Well, *General*," he says. "Looks like I can ask Jem in person."

"I want some answers." I fire at him. "Can Draco give them to me? Or can you? Because I'm getting a little tired of cryptic crap."

Drega smiles with glittering eyes, and a tail curls around his feet. "Both Draco and his mate are dying to meet you, little female, and you can ask all the questions you like, but..."

"There's no but," Draxx snarls. "Jem goes to Draco with me. She does not need to give you anything."

Somehow, I'm pleased he's standing up to his brother, pleased he wants to take me to this mysterious Draco, and intrigued Drega called him 'general'. It seems there's more to this alien hulk of muscle, scales, brooding, and lack of clothing than meets the eye.

Goddammit, I love a mystery to unravel. It was my favorite part of being a lawyer. And when that mystery is wrapped up in a package which is as easy on the eye as Draxx? I feel like my decision to make my own freedom was the best one I ever made. This way, I get to choose what I want to do.

And today, I am choosing Draxx, whether he chooses me or not.

I step up to my big green powerhouse. "So, what are we waiting for?" I put my hand on his arm. "Draco's waiting."

Draxx clearly has no idea which emotion to feel, and it's wonderful watching various thoughts flash across his expressive face. Expressive, that is, when he's not brooding or snarling.

I find my wrist caught up in a massive clawed hand, my body pulled close to his as he dips his head and inhales deeply.

"Provided Draco also has food, I will bring my female," he says to Drega. "She requires more feeding."

And just like that, I hate his guts again.

DRAXX

This is better. I haven't been able to taste my little morsel of a female, but I got the opportunity to drink down her scent meaning some of the pain and thumping in my chest has lessened.

I do not want to take her to Draco. For a start, my brother, our erstwhile leader, always has an ante-room filled with other warriors. Although, admittedly, he also has a mate, food, and a growl which could empty a planet.

He is my brother after all.

Jem is not impressed I have hold of her wrist, and she attempts to pull it from me, but I struggle to let go. When she finally wrenches it from my grasp, she does not look happy.

But she does look edible.

Drega goes to usher her out, but I extend a wing and slam him into a wall.

"This way, my little Jem." I give her one of my best smiles, plenty of fang.

She looks at me as if I've shifted, her lips tight. But she exits my quarters and ascends the stairs into the small square outside. It leads to the main square where Draco's quarters lie. Drega is, as he has always been, a secretive Sarkarnii nevver, and his quarters are situated far away from ours.

Ancestors forgive him if he had to share anything with the rest of us. Drega is all about control, where as I am all about the lack of it.

He doesn't know most of the undercroft tunnels lead into all our quarters, and I've visited his many times in the past. He has to suspect something, given my removal of his treasure occasionally to mess with his head, but if he does, he hasn't said anything.

I like shiny things. All Sarkarnii do, but I can't help myself. If I see something I like, it somehow ends up in my mouth or pocket...if I'm wearing pants.

I really should start wearing pants. Again.

Jem has gone quiet as she walks alongside me, Drega sensibly bringing up the rear and rubbing at his shoulder, the big Sarkarnling.

I notice her look up into the sky, and I move closer to her, shielding her with my body.

"I'm fine," she snaps.

"Good. You can be fine with me here next to you too."

Jem makes an odd growling sound, her fists bunching up delightfully. I wonder what she'll be like underneath me while I slide into her. Will she dig in those little pink nails? Will she let me hook her?

A hand clamps on my shoulder, and I turn with a snarl, Jem getting away from me as she heads across the square.

"If you want to get anywhere with that female, you're going to need pants, Draxx," Drega says, eyes dancing. "Long before you dance for her."

"What I do and don't do is none of your business." I

spin back to protecting my mate as I guide her around the edge of the main square and towards Draco's quarters.

The smell of smoke is strong as we near. He must be entertaining the other members of our crew, the warriors who were with us on the *Golden Orion* when we were captured. Or rather allowed ourselves to be captured.

My skin tightens, as if it needs to shed. The thumping in my chest rises. I want to get close to Jem again, but she's already descending the steps which will take her to my brother's ante-room. I give Drega a snarl for distracting me and follow her.

As soon as I reach the bottom of the steps, the sounds of multiple warriors has me grabbing for Jem.

"Stay back." I stride forward, every ounce of my being on high alert.

Sure enough, Draco's ante-room is filled with all my den warriors. Drasus gives me a smug smile. Daeos, the red-scaled nevver, is attempting to start a fight in one corner with three other warriors. He's the only warrior who ever ventured to the pit, even fighting alongside me on occasions. I might be feral, but I've seen him fight. Daeos has something broken inside him, I've seen it in his eyes.

It's the reason I told him to stop coming to the pit. There was no need for both of us to lose ourselves there. I must have been persuasive, as the only time he came back was to find me before Draco took on the Wardens during the last run for freedom.

And we're still not free.

"Draxx, finally." Draco is sat on his throne, ignoring the chaos going on around him. "Did you bring the female?" He peers behind me as I tuck Jem farther back.

Drega steps in front of me and Jem.

"The female is with him, but there is a problem."

I bare my teeth as a warrior gets too close to us, the growl I release coming from somewhere deep and dangerous.

Draco leans forwards and glares at me. I glare right back. I also feel Jem moving out from behind me, and when I risk a glance, she too is giving Draco a stare to end all stares.

I should be going wild, but the way she looks at him, with death daggers, makes something warm in my chest, my breath coming in short pants of delight as I look at her.

"Get out," Draco snarls at my den mates. "All except Drega and Draxx."

There's some grumbling, but then Draco stands, and the room clears very quickly, leaving only a haze of smoke.

"Sit your female down, get her fed," Draco says, taking his seat once again.

"Where is your mate?" I don't mean to growl at my brother. Draco may be many things, but I've always respected him.

And he's always made sure I've stayed on this side of our ancestors, no matter what. Until we ended up in the Kirakos, we had adventures galore. He kept me from the door of despair for a long time.

"My Amber is resting," Draco says, his eyes softening at the mention of his female. "This conversation is not for her."

Draco's tail, the one part of his shift he's never been able to control, even when we were younglings, thrashes with interest.

"Jem?" he queries. "Would you be so kind as to sit and take some of my hospitality?"

The room is filled with growling. It takes me a seccari to realize the noise is coming from me.

Somehow, I don't think this meeting is going to end well.

"As you ask so nicely." Jem pushes past my hand as it attempts to hold her back, her pretty head held high. "Yes, I will."

She seats herself on a couch next to Draco's chair. He gives me a baleful look, his eyes flicking to the food on offer. I am frozen with bubbling rage, not entirely sure which brother to kill first.

"What exactly is this place, and what do you want from me?" Jem says.

"You mean you haven't told her?" Draco narrows his eyes at me.

"No," Jem says, a smile hitching the corner of her mouth. "Draxx hasn't. So, now I expect to hear it from you."

And just like that, I don't want to kill my brothers anymore. Instead, I want to see just how my mate will destroy them instead.

JEM

The big gold scaled alien sat in a chair like a throne looks at me as if he's trying to see right through me. With my newfound resolve not to take any more shit, I return his look. There's a plate of food next to the upholstered bench I'm sat on, and I pick up some of the meat Draxx had earlier.

Only the second I put it in my mouth, I realize it's not the same. It has spices which nearly blow my head off. Instead of appearing cool, calm, and collected, I start to choke and cough. My eyes stream. I become aware of a massive green body beside me, and a cool container is put in my hand. I take a sip and find that, although it's not water, it's clean and refreshing.

Draxx lifts my chin up with one huge clawed finger. I blink rapidly at him, still struggling to get my breath as he slowly swipes an equally huge thumb over my cheek, wiping the tears away. He lifts the other hand and does the same with a touch so light it could almost be a feather.

How can a beast like him do something so gentle?

Draxx appears to be all muscle, and yet here he is, almost as if I can't feel his touch at all. Instead, I get the heat from his body and the curl of smoke from one nostril as those incredible whirling eyes, filled with fire, gaze down at me.

Embarrassment should be heating my cheeks for being such an idiot, but instead Draxx makes me feel like a princess, even if I am covered in snot.

"What were you saying?" I stumble out at Draco, not wanting to take my eyes off Draxx who has taken hold of my chin.

"We're looking for a map. It's being stored somewhere in this prison. Humans are the key to unlocking it."

"Uh-huh." I'm still looking at Draxx. He licks over his lips with a dark tongue, and my insides turn to liquid.

This huge alien fills my senses. My lungs are still on fire from the spice, my eyes sore, but Draxx's scales glitter in my vision, the scent of him, all smoke and tobacco, fills my nostrils, and his heat infuses into my skin.

"By the bones! Can you put her down and concentrate!" Drega fires out.

Draxx rounds on him with a snarl, and the spell, or whatever it is, is broken. I wipe my nose on the back of my hand and edge to one side.

"Is he in rut?" Draco asks Drega, who rolls his eyes.

"That's the problem."

"I am not in rut for this female," Draxx rasps.

"Fuck's sake! I'm here, you know, and I am not 'female', I'm Jem." I grit my teeth and look around at the three of them. "Any chance you can start from the fucking beginning and explain why I'm here, what you want from me before we get onto maps and humans..." I suddenly find myself swallowing hard, the tears pricking at my eyes not related to spice. "I've been taken away from everything I know, and my planet hardly has space flight to our nearest moon, let alone anywhere else. Most humans don't even believe in alien life."

I cough again but shift away from Draxx so he can't put a dragony spell on me again, and he twitches violently.

I clear my throat.

"So?"

Draco looks around at the other two, gold lights twinkling beneath his black and gold scales.

"So, you're right, little female, you should know what you're getting yourself in to."

I listen with growing horror and anger as Draco explains he, Draxx, and Drega are a species called the Sarkarnii, a species which can change their form at will and that they are on the brink of extinction, most of them being killed in a genocide I can't even comprehend by another alien species called the Liderc. After this bombshell, things take a slightly muddier turn into exactly what this trio, and the other Sarkarnii, were doing up until the point they, allegedly, got themselves captured and put into the Kirakos, apparently a prison to end all prisons.

Not that Draco is doing badly out of being incarcerated. His quarters are opulently furnished, there's plenty of food, albeit some items I'm never going to try again, and it's displayed on plates which look like gold. The entire place is so very different from Draxx's quarters, and my heart does a funny squeezy thing in my chest when I think about it.

I feel bad for him. I feel bad he has suffered, far more than I ever have. After all, as much as my birth father and adoptive parents' rejection and my divorce hurt me, I didn't lose nearly everyone I knew in some horrible one-sided war.

"And that's the reason we need humans," Draco concludes.

Both he and Drega look at me with anticipation. I risk a glance at Draxx. He glowers at his brothers.

I have absolutely no idea what Draco is talking about because I've not actually been listening. I've been thinking about Draxx.

"I see," I say, hoping he might possibly expand.

"To unlock the map," Drega adds hopefully.

"My female is not going on some nevving quest to unlocking a map we don't even know exists," Draxx growls.

I'm inclined to agree with him, but also I have other fish to fry.

"There are other humans. I saw them in the place you took me from. I want to go back and free them," I announce.

Draxx rumbles beside me, a deep, low sound which reaches parts of my body it should not.

"Other humans?" Drega queries.

"At least three. There was one in a cell near mine and two in the room you found me in."

Draco's head swings between his two brothers. "Did you see other humans?"

"No, only this one," Drega is quick to say. "There might have been others, but not only could we not stay long, *someone* made sure the Belek scientist had gone to meet his ancestors and the guards had called in reinforcements."

"Nev it, Draxx!" Draco fires sparks out of his nose. "What have I told you about interrogation?"

"They have to be alive to be interrogated." My huge green monster sighs the words as if he's said them many times before, his shoulders dropping. "But the Belek was hurting this human, and she was unarmed. It had no honor."

For the first time since I woke up in this horrible place, I actually feel like there is someone on my side. And it's absolutely not the creature I would have ever expected.

A big bad green warrior with a destructive streak and a way of growling *mine* I can't ignore, sends strange signals to parts of me not used in a long while.

Which means I'm in way, way over my head.

DRAXX

Draco's lip hitches, displaying an amused fang. We left our planet long before the Liderc did what they did to our species. Draco, in a usual display of temper, quit the place because he thought the leading Council wasn't going to listen to him.

He was right. They did not, and our bloodline counted for little in the grand scheme of things. It meant we left behind our old lives, our old ways, our old titles, our friends and family. The mates chosen for us. Instead, we did what we wanted when we wanted.

I don't deny it was an adventure, one which piqued my interest after a strict warrior upbringing, but I wish we had been there for the greatest battle of them all.

One where we might have saved everyone. I don't blame Draco, far from it. I blame myself.

"Spoken like a true Sarkarnii warrior, my general," Draco says without a shred of irony.

I growl under my breath.

"Fact remains, regardless of whether the Belek scientist was dead before or after I shot him, we don't know what he was doing with the humans other than hurting them, and I agree with Jem. We should mount a rescue mission."

"Why the nev should I expend resources and warriors to rescue more humans when we have the one we need?"

Jem makes a choking noise, and every muscle in my body tightens. If she is unwell again, like she was after eating the meat flavored with izes, I need to be prepared to help her. The spice is a favorite among most Sarkarnii, but not something I like much. It would appear it doesn't agree with humans either.

"What if I'm not the *one you need*?" She does a passable impression of Draco, and I have to hide my smile from my brother. "But anyway, I don't care. I'm going to get them, and you can't stop me...unless I'm a prisoner of you as well as this place."

I think I hear Draco grinding his teeth, even from this distance, as he surveys my mate.

He opens his mouth, but all of our attention is drawn to the corridor leading through to his rear quarters.

Amber stands there, staring at Jem with her mouth open.

"Draco! Why didn't you wake me?" she exclaims.

My big bad brother is off his chair and by her side in a swish of his tail. He molds himself to her. "You were resting, my heartsfire," he croons. "I did not want to wake you with this triviality."

"Finding another human is not trivial," Amber says, but she traces her hand down his cheek in a soft motion I wish Jem would use with me. "You should have woken me."

"Next time, I will," Draco says and releases her to walk over to Jem.

"I'm Amber Jenkins." She holds out a hand to my mate who rises, her eyes huge.

"Jem...Jemma Sharp," Jem says. "You're British?"

"Sheffield, born and bred." Amber smiles broadly, and I see my Jem relax.

"Bristol," she says. "Same side, farther down," she adds with a laugh.

All of which is incomprehensible to me, but as it seems to make my female happy, I find my muscles unwinding too. Jem is happy. Jem is safe. I'm not keen on her being here with Drega and Draco, but it's made easier with another female present.

"We think Jem is the key to the map," Drega ventures.

"Do you?" Amber fixes him with a look. "Well, she's not going anywhere or doing anything until she's had a chance to properly acclimatize. Then we can discuss what needs to be discussed," Amber says fiercely, looking between Draco and Drega.

Jem is surprisingly meek as Amber puts an arm around her shoulder and ushers her away, into the rear quarters.

I stand to follow, but I get a heavy, gold, scaled hand on my chest. Draco is exposing rather a lot of teeth.

"My quarters, my female," he growls.

"My female," I respond with a snarl.

"Nev you both and your ruts!" Drega snaps.

"I am not in rut," both Draco and I fire out at the same time.

"You're always in rut." Drega sniffs at Draco. "And you're in rut for the first time, which is going to be painful and unpleasant," he says to me.

"I am not in rut." But as the words come out of my mouth and my chest pounds, the look in Drega's eyes says it all.

I am in rut.

For Jem.

And as it's my first rut, it will be agony until I can hook my intended mate. A female who is so far away she might as well be back on our home planet.

"Good luck, brother." Draco punches me in the arm. "That female is going to be one tough mate to dance for."

"Nev you." It's hardly the best retort as I crane my neck to see where she has gone.

"I'll call you once my mate is finished with yours, although from what Drega tells me, you need to clean up your quarters if you are going to entertain her properly." He looks me up and down. "And pants. Females like pants, mostly, although they are prepared for us to forgo them when the time is right."

"I like to shift," I grumble.

"You don't shift in the nevving pit. Just put the nevving pants on," Drega growls back.

"Like either of you know anything."

"Nev me!" Draco extends his wings and claps them together in frustration. "This is like the nevving space worms all over again."

"I wore pants then," I retort.

"Barely and you know where that got us." Drega sighs. "Let's just hope Amber can persuade Jem to assist us. I'm sure she's a key, just like Amber was."

He's referring to Draco's mate's ability to open up all the hidden passages in the Kirakos. Drega is convinced any humans held here will have specific abilities which can aid us.

"Jem belongs to me, Drega." I grab hold of his neck and slam him up against the wall, causing a crack. "Don't forget it."

For once, my brother doesn't respond or shift. Instead he gazes at me with a rather smug expression.

"By the bones, I thought you were bad when you spent all your time in the pit, but now you're in rut, I wish you'd stayed there."

I drop him with a grunt, and he lands on his blue ass, glaring at me.

"I'll wear pants when I want to and not before." I stomp my way out of Draco's quarters, knowing all I'm going to do for however long it takes for Jem to emerge is spend my time soaring above the central square.

And looking for a pair of pants.

JEM

For some reason, the minute I'm out of Draxx's presence, I want to be back with him. He's annoying, large, and very tactile, all things I want to hate.

But I don't. I can still smell him on me, rich and musky. I can still feel his breath on my cheek. And I can't forget how he stood up for me against his brothers when I said I wanted to go find the other humans.

"Come through," Amber says as she ushers me down a quiet corridor and into a well lit room. There is a set of doors opening onto a garden.

I gape. The courtyard is small, but there are plants growing there. Nothing like I've ever seen before, the colors are hard to place, and the fragrance is...interesting.

"Have a seat. Let me get you something to eat," Amber says.

"No, wait." I grab her arm. "How long have you been here? Are you really...with...Draco? Is this place really a prison?"

Amber laughs. She's pretty. Her tawny hair stretches down her back in loose curls. She's curvy, about two inches shorter than me, and wearing a pair of loose pants and a long tunic top which looks very much like it was tie-dyed in greens and blues. I feel rather dowdy in comparison, especially as I'm wearing things which appear to have come from some sort of alien jumble sale.

But at least I know how I ended up with a pair of human sized boots.

"God! I know, it's so much to take in. But please, let me get you something to eat and drink as I bet no one has so far."

"Draxx," I mutter, suddenly feeling very tired. I plonk myself down on a squashy couch.

"Draxx?" Amber bustles out of the room, leaving his name hanging in the air.

She's back quickly with a tray laden with food, which she sets in front of me. I eye it warily.

"None of that spicy stuff on here is there? I got caught out earlier."

Amber screws up her face. "The Sarkarnii and their spices. They breath fire, you know, and it appears they have an iron constitution. I can't stand the spiced meat, not now I'm..." She pauses and then pours me out a glass of the clear liquid. "Anyway, you need answers, and I also have questions, so dig in, and I'll do what I can to explain."

I pick my way through the food, listening to Amber explaining she spent some time in another part of the maze before being dropped, literally, at Draco's feet. How she became his partner, something the Sarkarnii refer to as a 'mate'. How I have little robots inside me which means I can understand other languages.

My skin crawls.

"It turns out I'm what they call a key. It means I can open doors in the maze. I'm not entirely sure how it works.

Drega thinks it's linked to human DNA, but why, he can't say," Amber concludes.

"He seems to think I'm something special too," I say, mouth full of food. "Although I don't think Draxx agrees."

I am so hungry, I hadn't realized. The few bites I grabbed of the food Draxx got for me didn't do much to fill the void which is my stomach. I want to be more ladylike, but I guess that's not happening.

"Oh, that Sarkarnii thinks you're something special." Amber chortles. "Very *special*."

I cough again. "What do you mean?"

"Has there been growling? Snarling? The word 'min'" bandied around as if it's going out of fashion?" she asks.

I stare at her, my eyes feeling like they are out on stalks. "How did you know?"

"It's what they do. Sarkarnii males are not like anything you've ever encountered."

"You're telling me!"

"I don't just mean the changing into dragons, the size, the scales. I mean in terms of how they are with their women, their females. It's nothing like a human man. Once you're chosen, you stay chosen. Forever."

Her words make my stomach contract.

"So, what does it mean if one of them does all of those things?" Food turns to ash in my mouth.

"It means you've just got yourself a big, green stalker." Amber grins.

I do not find it funny in the slightest.

"Look, I don't mean to be rude, but I'm not here to get laid. I'm not here on purpose, but what I want to do is find the other women I saw and any other humans before the slug things hurt them like they hurt me." I lift up my sleeve and pull at the bandage on my arm.

Amber draws in a breath. "Shit."

"They're not playing nice with us, Amber."

She closes her eyes and rubs her stomach. "No, I know they're not. I guess I just hoped..." She flaps a hand at me, eyes filling with tears. "I hoped any other humans were being treated better than I was," she sobs.

Now I feel like a complete arse. The last thing I wanted to do was upset Amber. I reach out a tentative hand and take hers.

"I'm sorry."

"Fuck it!" She fans her free hand in front of her face. "I don't think I ever swore as much until I met Draco." Amber laughs soggily. "Ignore the waterworks too. Hormones."

"Ugh!" I tip my head back. "Time of the month?" I make a groaning sound. "I'm a banshee when I'm on my period, so I can relate."

Amber gives me a wan smile. "Something like that," she says quietly.

"Are there only males in this prison? What do we do about...you know?" I point at my crotch. "Pads and stuff?" I whisper. Amber goes a little pink.

"Er...there are females!" she exclaims after a pause. "Not Sarkarnii, another species called Jiaka. Don't be too alarmed. They have more than two arms and eyes, but other than apparently being inveterate thieves, which is why they're in the Kirakos, they are harmless. Which means we have plenty of female things if we need them."

"Okay." I rub my hand over my face and shake my head. "This is going to take more getting used to."

"I've been here a while, and I don't think I've got used to it yet," Amber says kindly. "Having Draco helps, even if I can't go anywhere without him becoming impossible." She laughs, and her entire face lights up with love.

Amber is in love with an alien. A massive gold scaled one who, if he's anything like the others, can turn into a dragon. I'm not entirely sure what to think about that. Looking back on my life, I've never been in love, with anything, not in the way it makes you smile a secret smile like Amber has just done.

Perhaps it's something in the water? Heat rises from the pit of my stomach, flooding my veins, making my skin prickle. Amber's room is dark and quiet. It reminds me of the cell. It reminds me of what the other aliens were doing.

The cloying feeling of uselessness grips at my heart, and breathing becomes difficult.

"I could do with some air. Do you mind?" I get to my feet, my vision starting to dim as I stagger to the door and out into the fragrant courtyard.

"Hello, my treasure."

The voice is unmistakable. Leaning against the wall is Draxx. He has his arms folded over his broad chest. He is wearing a pair of dark leather-like pants.

Dammit! He looks like a green Greek god, all chiseled muscles and a face I'd throw my knickers at any day of the week. In his outfit, he is all day a bad, bad biker alien. Why does he have to do this?

As my chat with Amber has confirmed, I do not need any more complications in my life. I definitely do not need a big, scaled complication who is intent on turning my insides into mush.

"What are you doing here?" I fire at him.

I hear that rumble in his chest, again. The one he made when we were discussing how Drega and Draco wanted to use me. Draxx hitches up a top lip to expose a sharp fang.

"I wasn't busy."

He wasn't busy.

He wasn't busy.

I do not know how to process the new heat which flows through me. Or what to do when Draxx lifts his head, scents the air, and then in a fluid movement where I see a hint of wings and tail, stalks towards me.

"What do you want, Draxx?"

"You, wrapped around me, screaming my name until you see stars."

My jaw hits the floor. No small talk, no easing into anything. Just what he wants. I should hate it, but instead I find my stomach liquifying and an inability to respond.

I walk backwards a couple of steps until I hit a hard object, the rough concrete cool on my back. Maybe Amber will come to my aid?

Draxx plants two huge hands on the wall, one on either side of my head. Smoke curls from his nostrils, which is gone in a second as he sucks the air back in and closes his eyes.

"I don't know what you think this is," I breathe.

"I think I'm close to the female I desire." His body crowds in on me. Heat rolls from him. It penetrates my bones.

If I thought I was lightheaded before I stepped out into this courtyard, I'm pretty sure my head could leave my body and fly away right at this moment in this proximity to Draxx. He's so damn huge and he smells so fucking good I could spread him on toast.

This is wrong, so wrong.

And somehow he's got closer to me, his face millimeters from mine.

"I am not going to kiss you, little treasure. Do not fear me," Draxx rumbles.

"I'm not going to kiss you either," I pant. "I'd rather die."

"I don't want you to die, unless it's from the pleasure I'm giving you."

Draxx's tongue flickers out from between his lips, stroking over mine. I gasp at the touch.

He dominates me. Sweeping, incredible, I'm lost. I'm completely lost. I have a hand on his chest, and he cups the back of my head until there's no space between us at all.

And then it hits me. I pull away for a second, staring and staring at him as my brain finally catches up with my body.

"Draxx! You have two tongues."

"And you, my treasure, are about to experience them both."

DRAXX

Now I've tasted her, my mating gland pumps the mix into my veins with all its might.

I am in rut.

I rut for Jem.

The mix sets me on fire, and any semblance of what could be considered propriety within my mind is gone. Unless I have her, unless I claim her, nothing will do. I will go up in flames. I will rip out my wings until the moment we are joined and I am hooked in her, my barbs buried in her and my seed swelling her belly.

But two hands are planted on my chest, and I'm being pushed away from my Jem.

"I don't...I can't do this," she gasps. Her face has two high pink spots, her eyes are glazed, and I'm sure I can smell her arousal.

Then she ducks under my arm and runs back into Draco's quarters. I'm several steps into following her when there is a rush of wind behind me.

"I wouldn't if I were you, brother."

Draco is behind me. I look around to see him, arms

folded, wings shifting away and a smug look on his face. What the nev is it with my brothers and smugness?

"I don't need mating advice from you, *brother*. I had a mate waiting for me on Kaeh-Leks, you know I did."

"Ah, but you didn't mate her, did you?" Draco maintains his air of annoying righteousness.

He forgets sometimes I know all his secrets. I know what happened with the space worms.

"What does it matter? And since when did you get so nevving good with mating?"

Draco huffs out some smoke at me, and I snort a flame back at him. I want to follow Jem, but it's more than just my unused accelerant burning at me, it's exactly what Draco wants from her. From me.

"Okay, I'll bite." I extend my fangs to shifted length. "What is your advice?"

He loses some of his composure for an instant. "Just give your mate space when she needs it," he says.

"Because you do that?" I laugh. He's virtually joined with his mate, hardly ever leaving her side.

Draco rubs at the back of his neck, his scales fluttering. "We need to get the key to the map."

"I know, but Jem wants to get the other humans. And as much as we're all so nevving reliant on Drega, what if she's right? What if she is not the key and one of the other ones she saw is?"

"It would have helped, Draxx, if you'd kept the Belek alive long enough to find out," Draco grumbles.

I shrug. "I doubt it would have helped. Belek are wardens here for a reason. They only fear the loss of their station. Look at Warden Noro."

I reference one of the senior wardens of the Kirakos who wanted to use the Sarkarnii to find the star map for himself on our recent run for supposed freedom which was, in fact, entertainment and a source of income for the Belek.

"Gondnok hasn't been in touch, has he?" I ask.

One of the other senior wardens, Gondnok, had, apparently, asked for my brother's help in exposing Noro, who was taking profits and not sharing them out, meaning a drop in rank for our fair-weather friend. What Draco got in return is debatable, but it does mean we no longer wear the collars which contained our shift, and we control our quadrant of the maze.

But we are still prisoners, and until my brother gets the star map he believes will lead us to any Sarkarnii not killed by our enemies the Liderc, we will remain here.

And once he has it...once he finds them, I don't know what his plans are. I go along with him because I don't want to think about what I lost. It's easier that way. Like fighting in the pit. Fighting, maiming, killing because it's all I was ever good at.

"He has not." Draco releases a contemplative smoke ring which floats up above us. "And I don't like it."

"We keep our enemies close, Draco. Gondnok is a Belek. He lives for politics, and he has an agenda, but then so do we. And I believe we have to start with rescuing the other humans."

"Then do it," Draco says with a sparkle in his eye I do not like much. "Weapons are authorized." I grin, but he holds up a hand. "However, you will need to take Jem with you."

"What? No!" I growl.

"If you're rescuing humans, you need a human." Draco's grin is even wider, sparks leaping from his nostrils as he is clearly enjoying my discomfort. "My mate is having my Sarkarnling, so she cannot go, and I cannot go. Jem is the only human we have available. Plus"—he holds up a claw to make his point, and I want to bite his hand off—"if she is a key to the map, she may be able to help further."

I can't fault his logic, but I can growl as if I want to rip into his torso. I might have lost myself to the pit, but I was the general. The term is not a goad, it is a taunt from fear. Just because I'm in the Kirakos, it doesn't make what I was on Kaeh-Leks or on the *Golden Orion*, any less.

"I don't like it, Draco. Not at all. Is this an order?"

His grinning face becomes solemn.

"I would not order anything involving you or the humans I wouldn't do myself. Jem is safer with you than anyone," he says. "But in answer to your question, yes, this is an order." Nev him, the grin is back again. "And I'll let you tell me later if you could have gone without her."

I pull myself up to my full height, shift out my wings, and fill my accelerant sacs. This is the last thing I want to do, and yet if it gives me time with Jem, I'll do it.

Except if she ends up in harm's way because of me? Everything wars within me, and I need to shift, to fly and to fight.

"Tomorrow," I growl through my deepening shift.

"Good." Draco slams a hand on my chest. "So, tonight we feast." He laughs. "It's not every day my brother finds his mate, after all."

JEM

I shouldn't have listened in to Draco and Draxx's conversation, but before Amber led me through to another part of Draco's extensive quarters, I definitely heard the bit about Draxx 'having another mate'.

Why I'm letting those words tear through me with the force of a thousand suns, I don't understand, but I feel eviscerated.

Only it's not as if I wanted Draxx or any of this. After all, I've been abducted by bloody aliens! Not so long ago, I was in a cell and being tortured by a different species. I can't catch feelings for Draxx in such a short time, it's insane.

Even if he kisses like he will never let me go.

He has a mate, and I don't think he means a friend. Something curls up in my stomach. I don't know for sure, but I had an inkling my ex-husband was cheating on me before the divorce. Not that I cared so much—we hated the sight of each other by the end—but the feeling of being lied to, of someone not telling the truth, causes bile to sour my mouth.

A mouth Draxx plundered with his damn forked tongue. The one he threatened to *pleasure* me with. Of course, I ran away because my insides went gooey and my heart filled with something I've never experienced before.

A want.

A need.

Turns out my head was in control, and it was damn right to tell me anything too good to be true probably doesn't exist, like a massive, green alien dragon warrior following me around like a lost puppy.

Amber says Sarkarnii take their mates forever. So, where the hell is Draxx's mate?

"Everything okay?" Amber says as she sorts through clothes from a pile she threw down on the bed. She holds up her hands. "I know, stupid question."

"I'm struggling, if I'm honest." I breathe out. "I should be British about all this and keep a stiff upper lip, but there's just so much to take in."

"At the risk of continuing to sound like I'm stating the bloody obvious, you have all the time in the universe to get used to this. After all, we're not going back to Earth."

The sentence hits me like a sledgehammer, and I sit down suddenly, blood rushing to my head and making me feel faint.

"Not again." I groan.

"Shit!" Amber sits next to me and puts her arm around my shoulders. "Put your head between your legs. There's no such thing as a bag in the Kirakos or I'd get you one to breathe into."

I've already dropped my head forwards, but I turn to look at her. She's serious. I snort.

For a second, her face remains filled with concern, until

it dawns on her what she said. Then a smile flickers across it, which she attempts to control. Badly.

We burst out laughing at the same time, mine rather manic, hers tinged with relief. Tears spring to my eyes, with mirth, with grief, with a flood of emotions I can't put my finger on. I wipe them away as our laughter dissipates. Amber hugs me tightly, and I pull an element of calm from her.

"I guess we do just have to keep calm and carry on," I say.

Whatever Amber is about to reply is lost with the door opening and Draco striding inside. If he's in any way bothered I'm on his bed and covered in snot, he doesn't bat an eyelid. Instead, he takes hold of Amber and winds himself around her. Her chin in his hand, tipped up to his face, he plants a kiss which I can almost feel, given I've been on the receiving end of a Sarkarnii tongue not so long ago.

"It has been decided. We feast tonight, and Draxx leaves in the morning," Draco says when he lets Amber come up for air.

"Draxx leaves?" I hear myself say, even though it seems like my throat has constricted to the point of nothingness.

"He has a mission. My general needs work to keep him out of the pit, and now I have work for him," Draco says.

I make a sound which could be an ''oh, but is more a whisper than anything. Amber gives me a narrow-eyed look.

"Then we both need to get ready for tonight." She pats Draco on his huge golden scaled chest.

"But I..." His words are stopped by a pink finger slamming against his lips. "Okay, I'm going," he grumbles. "But you will make up for this later, my heartsfire." He growls, and once again, she is engulfed in him.

When she is released, Amber is bright pink, and Draco

flashes me a grin before disappearing through the door again.

Amber pushes back her hair and releases a shuddering breath. She looks as if she might have been drugged until she gives herself a little shake and turns to me with a smile.

"Sarkarnii mate forever?" I query.

"They mate hard. Once you are hooked and claimed, that is the pinnacle for them," Amber says walking back to the bed and the pile of clothes. "Nothing else matters. You only ever belong to your Sarkarnii warrior. And you'll only ever want to."

While I think she's trying to be reassuring, actually it isn't helping at all. My insides feel hollow. I'm not some lovesick teenager though. I'm a grown woman, so I need to suck it up and behave like one. If Draxx is fucking off somewhere, then he can fuck off. See if I care.

I'm certainly not going begging for anything to him. He might be able to kiss like he's the centre of the universe, but it means nothing if he's already spoken for. It just makes him a cheater.

"This should fit you." Amber holds up an emerald scrap of silky material. "You'll look gorgeous in it with your coloring." She nods appreciatively.

"I don't think I need to look gorgeous or anything," I say, my voice dull. "And I definitely don't feel like going to a party."

JEM

A mber is a sneaky one. Somehow she persuaded me, wrapped into a huge towel, into her bathroom, which was at least the same size as Draxx's, but this one had shampoo.

When I came out, my clothes, along with Amber, were gone, and all there was on the bed was the damn green dress.

I will kill her when I see her...If I make it past her huge Sarkarnii that is. I put on the dress rather than remaining naked. No underwear which is a little disconcerting, but the dress sort of moulds to my shape and at least gives me a bit of uplift in the boob department.

The dress itself sweeps the floor, fluttering and flowing like the scales on a Sarkarnii. The shimmering green puts me in mind of Draxx's scales, and a lump hardens in my throat.

I ball my hands into fists. It doesn't matter. I don't need Draxx. I can ask one of the other Sarkarnii for a weapon and directions back to where the other humans were. It sounds impossible, but then so was alien abduction and look where I am.

Plus I'm not some helpless female. I kept myself fit on Earth with boxercise (let's face it, I used it for my pent-up aggression). I took a self-defense class once. Providing all aliens keep their junk in the same place, I'm golden.

Only then I remember Draxx and his lack of pants.

What if they don't keep it in the same place?

The thought has the same hysterical laughter from earlier rising, and I clap my hand over my mouth to tamp it down. Dealing with all of this would have been bad enough if it wasn't for the fact somehow Draxx has crept into my psyche and...

I drop my arm away and huff out my irritation. It looks like Amber is not coming back for me, and I'm on my own, so that's her definitively struck off the Christmas card list. I exit the bedroom and follow the sounds of male voices and the smell of smoke back to the main room where I first met Draco.

It is full of Sarkarnii again, although here and there I spy something smaller, scurrying through the huge warriors who are clearly enjoying themselves. Booze, or the alien equivalent, is being drunk, food consumed.

I duck back down the corridor, my heart hammering in my chest. Not because I caught sight of Draxx, leaning against a wall on the far side. Not at all. Not because his lips hitched in a slight smile at something another Sarkarnii said and he looked so damn handsome I could cry.

He has a mate. Sarkarnii spend the rest of their lives with their mates. You didn't. You're not mate material.

I feel my hands curl up into balls and my stomach contract. I'm not here to be bothered by gorgeous alien warriors. I shouldn't be here at all, and the other women I saw and heard should be free. Even if freedom is a room filled with seven- and eight -foot males with claws, fangs, scales and occasionally, a tail. Terrifying and weirdly intriguing.

"Jem?" Amber's voice cuts through my thoughts. She's stood in the entrance to the corridor wearing a similar dress to mine only hers is scarlet.

It hugs her figure, and she's plumper than I expected somehow.

"Coming," I say, throwing my head back and lifting myself up.

If I pretend I'm confident, I am, right?

"Come over by Draco and me." She smiles, leading me through a throng which parts ahead of her. Warriors don't even glance, they just move aside.

Draco acknowledges me with a fanged smile, and Drega, his scales glittering, hitches a pierced eyebrow. Amber hands me a metal goblet which is like something out of a Thirties movie about kings and queens.

"Ale-wine," she says and then gives me a conspiratorial wink. "I watered it down for you. The Sarkarnii like their alcohol strong."

I manage to hold back from saying they'd need to, given their size, and take a sip instead. It's still strong but has an interesting slightly sweet flavor which isn't bad. I give her a smile.

"Thanks." I look around the room, feeling uncomfortable and searching for small talk.

"You look really pretty," Amber says.

"I feel strange." I lean into her. "You didn't give me any underwear."

Her eyes widen. "I thought you already had some," she whispers back.

I shake my head, and at that moment the absurdity of my situation hits again, a giggle rises, and I slam my hand over my mouth. The ale-wine must be stronger than I thought.

My squeak attracts the attention of Drega who gazes at me like I'm a puzzle he's trying to crack.

"My treasure," a voice rumbles in my ear. A hot body is at my back.

It's Draxx, and I ignore him, taking another sip of my drink as the room seems to both swim and contract to a pinprick. I can smell his smoke, his musk, the sweet sour of tobacco—it swirls around me, far more intoxicating than what I'm swallowing.

Instead I stare at Amber, but at the point when I think Draxx might leave, Draco takes her arm and draws her away.

The room might be full, the air thick with talk, smoke, and everything else, but I have nothing else to think about, nothing else to concentrate on. And I can't help myself. I turn and look up the green-scaled chest, the defined and chiseled abs, up to a thick bullish neck topped with a blunt jaw and that handsome face. Only now it's serious.

As if he's never smiled before.

"You look"—he sucks in a breath, his eyes closing briefly—"beautiful."

"Yeah, well..." I don't even look down at my dress. Instead, I look past him at the rest of the room.

Until something takes hold of my jaw and my chin is firmly pulled up so I can't see anyone but Draxx.

"Tell me you did not dress for them." The words rasp through my body. It heats, it cools, and I'm not sure I can even speak. "I will kill each and every one for laying their gaze on you, regardless of whether they are my brothers or den warriors."

"Let me guess, is that because I belong to you, Draxx? Because I don't," I spit out. "You're fucking leaving, and you have a mate, why the hell should you care?"

"I have a mate, and she is coming with me tomorrow," he rumbles.

"Good for her. Maybe you can get her to wear a stupid dress like this one." I hate the fact tears are pricking at my eyes. I hate my heart is pounding at his touch, at the flicker of his dark tongue against his soft lips.

I hate him. I hate Draxx for making me feel alive again.

"She already is," he growls, and his lips are on mine before I can reply. "And she looks good enough to eat."

JEM

My body is on fire as Draxx's forked tongue laps me, my brain unable to function. My instinct taking over, leaning into him, my lips parting to allow him entry and then absolute nothingness as I sink into the bliss which is his kiss. My limbs are loose as his arms enclose me.

I shouldn't want this, but I do. My entire existence has narrowed to a pinpoint where there is only me and Draxx. His incredible tongue sweeps my mouth, and I'm lost. This close, he smells amazing. His skin is hot and smooth. Where his hands grip me, there is roughness, but it is combined with something gentle, even if I can feel the pricks of his claws in my flesh.

And the sharpness of his fangs as yet again, my treacherous body betrays me, and I become reciprocal with the kiss. If I thought the simple peck we had earlier was hot, this is setting me on fire completely.

I don't want it to stop, ever.

But it does, and I blink up at the handsome green warrior, noticing for the first time the slit pupils he has are blown wide, but I can still see the sea-colored sparkle of his irises. That tongue, forked and dark, slides out and wipes over his lips. He hums with pleasure.

"I can't wait to taste the rest of you," he rasps, eyes fixed on me like a predator.

Something in me breaks. I still can't quite breathe from the kiss, but it doesn't matter. I twist out of his hold with a sudden wriggle and back away.

It doesn't stop Draxx advancing on me again. I can't look away from him. I'm still panting, hand spanned over my breast, unable to keep my eyes off him.

"If you run," he growls, "this time I will chase you."

Those pupils are even bigger, even blacker, and he is hyper fixated on me. I want to run, and I want to stay, the emotions warring within me.

Draxx has a mate, I heard him say so. This is a situation I should run from. Snogging an alien is not how I envisioned my escape from my cell to be. Only I didn't snog an alien. I was the subject of a kiss from Draxx, the huge gold-green Sarkarnii warrior who honestly does look like he wants to eat me.

A shudder runs down my spine at his veiled sexy threat.

"Brother!" Drega appears as if made from smoke and slaps a clawed hand on Draxx's shoulder. It's enough of a distraction for me to be able to slip behind another huge purple-scaled warrior and make a dash for the door to the outside of Draco's quarters.

I don't know why I'm running, except the prickle of excitement rising over my skin, making my hairs stand on end as I mount the steps and find I'm outside and it is, sort of, night. The air has a metallic tang and, as I look up, there are no stars, but a faint glow like a sunset...or a sunrise.

And there are noises. Noises which are like nothing I've

ever heard. Somehow, dragons, or aliens which turn into dragons, seem less frightening than being out here in the dark.

But if I'm going to go after the other humans, I'm going to have to steel myself to this new world, or prison, or whatever.

And, as a sigh wracks my body, I know I'm going to need help.

"You ran." A dark, cigarette filled voice says in my ear.

I squeak and jump in alarm as I'm spun on the spot by a pair of huge green hands to look into Draxx's face. Those eyes are still huge, his body strung taught, muscles standing out all over the place.

"I had to fight to get to you," he growls as his eyes close slightly and he sucks in the air.

"What did you do?" I whisper.

"What I needed to, in order to find my treasure," he says. "And if you run again, I will take you, I will mate you, and you will be mine."

I have no idea what his words mean, but there's a quake inside me as he stalks closer I can't hold down. I back up, but there's a rough wall behind me. I look to either side, but it extends forever into the darkness.

There's nowhere to go. There's just Draxx.

And me.

And a tiny scrap of silk separating us.

DRAXX

The rut is overwhelming me. My mating gland, because that's what's been thumping in my chest beside my heart, is filling my veins with the mix. I am both on fire and chilled to the bone. All I want is the female caged against the wall. The scent of her, the sight of her, my desire for her sent me into a frenzy the second I spotted she was missing.

Drega very nearly lost a limb, but the nevver was laughing so hard he slipped from my grasp, and the other warriors who came to his aid, were sent flying. All I heard was Draco snarling as my half-shifted form followed Jem's scent out of his quarters and into the main square.

If he didn't want me to spoil his celebration, he should not have kept me from my female all afternoon. Sending me all over the nevving Kirakos on errands he insisted were important and I took because if I couldn't be with her, I would end up back in the pit.

And I wanted her.

Jem glares up at me and then bites her bottom lip, the one I tasted only a few minz ago and which tipped me over the edge. I long to plunder her mouth again, except I want more, so much more, and she has such incredible possibilities. The dress she's in shows me as much.

If Draco had wanted order, he should have kept her out of sight, but to let my Jem loose, dressed in my colors, her scent filling the entire room as a ripe and ready to be mated female, he should have known better.

My mate, loose in a room of warriors was never going to end well.

"Draxx," Jem says, her voice breathy.

I want to hear my name on her lips as she bellows it to the ancestors while I'm buried deep in her. Except when she says it, I have no option but to capture her lips and swallow her words. Her little hands slam against my chest, and then, as I press against her, they slide around my waist band, and I can feel my cock pushing from its pouch, the pre-cum wetting the inside of my pants.

Turns out pants were a good idea after all.

"Draxx," she says again as I let her up for air, my hands sliding down her body, taking in the slippery fabric which only just covers her.

She smells divine. I know she will taste even better. Encircling her tiny waist with my hands, I lift her higher until she has no option but to wrap her legs around my waist, and now I have access to her. My hand slides up, pushing back the material until I feel her shudder and jerk against my touch, her soft heat weeping onto my fingers as I tease between her folds.

She drops her head back, and then it snaps up as I explore a little farther, dipping inside. By the bones, she is tight. One digit is barely able to get inside her. She will need to taste me and be prepared before I can take her and claim her.

"Draxx!" This time, her voice is more insistent, more able to slice through the fog of the rut.

She is staring over my shoulder. I'm aware I've partially shifted, and my wings are open. I can feel Jem's heart stuttering against her chest as I press her against the wall, my fangs scraping over the skin of her neck.

She presses her cunt against the bulge of my cock, and the intake of breath from her is loud in my ear.

"Jesus! What have you got in there, Draxx?" she exclaims.

"Something which will have you hoarse with pleasure, my *szikra*." I'm rewarded by another heave from her chest and a flood of her scent. "Something I will impale you on in due course. But not just yet."

I drop to my knees, pinning her to the wall at just the right height. I hitch her leg over my shoulder, and she gasps beautifully, her thighs falling apart for me.

The scent which hits me is so intoxicating, for a seccari, I cannot breathe. Her slickness glistens for me in the dim light.

"Draxx," she moans as I press into her with my nose, coating myself in her scent. She squirms at my touch, and I withdraw.

She pants out loud.

"If you want me to feast on this pretty cunt, little mate, you will stay still and let me devour you whole," I growl into her thigh.

Her entire body hitches. Her hand is tangled in my hair, gripping at me, but she stops moving.

"Good mate." I lap through her folds, teasing at a little nub at her apex.

Jem whines, I feel her muscles straining, but she doesn't move, allowing me to tease up her thighs as I enjoy her delicious flavor. She whimpers again as I slide my tongue into her pussy. A flood of her nectar hits me as she shakes, hard, her hand pressing on my head, leg shaking.

"Are you close, *szikra*?"

"Yes." Her voice is a breathy moan.

"Are you going to call my name? Are you going to tell the entire of the Kirakos who is plundering this exquisite pussy?" Her hands tighten, her body stiffens. "You will shout my name, Jem. You will tell this maze who you belong to."

I clamp my lips over her nub and folds, my tongue plundering her as I suck in her deliciousness. Jem stills for an instant, and then her entire body convulses against me, rewarding me with her juices and a scream from her lips which is unmistakably my name.

Unable to stand it any longer, I want to take her to my quarters, lay her down, lick over her entire body, and then sheath my cock in her tight cunt. The one which has milked my tongue for every last drop it can consume. Behind us, there is a scuffle, and I spin around with her in my arms, still clutching at me, to find a tralu staring at us with a large eye.

"What the hell is it?" Jem hisses in my ear, her arms tightening around my neck.

My stomach contracts, and a bark escapes my lips. It's a laugh, and as it rises, I throw my head back, reveling in the feeling of mirth which I haven't felt for a very long time.

"It is nothing to be afraid of, little mate. I will protect you."

"Will you protect me when we go to look for the other humans?" she says, her eyes clearing as her body tightens against me in a different way from her pleasure.

"If you think I'm taking you into the Kirakos, you are wrong." I laugh because now I've found it, and her, I don't want to let her go. "It is not the place for a sweet female like you."

"Bet you'd take your mate," Jem spits, filled with a fire I adore immediately, even if I'm confused by her words.

I furrow my brow. "I just said I would not take you. You are too precious, *too delicious* to be put in any danger."

"Your *other* mate."

"I have no other mate. Every female I knew died on Kaeh-Leks. Including the one chosen for me by my family."

Jem glares at me. "She died?"

"Yes. We were never mated, only promised to each other by our families. There was one meeting between us."

With a huff, she pushes against me, wriggling until I let her go to the ground. My cock pulses at my pouch. I needed her, and now I've lost her.

"I'll see you tomorrow. When *we* go to get the other humans." She prods me in the chest with her finger and winces.

Then, almost as quickly as she left Draco's quarters, she marches back into them.

JEM

Draxx doesn't follow me. I don't know if it's a good or a bad thing. My head is aching, and it's not the weird ale-wine I've been drinking.

He had a mate and she died.

I don't know how to process the information. If she's dead, maybe he wishes she wasn't, maybe that's why he told Draco he had a mate. And then he's spent all evening calling me his mate, culminating with him strumming my body like a musical instrument.

And how he touched me!

No man has ever eaten me to completion, ordered me around and plucked an orgasm so intense, I saw stars. If it hadn't been for our stupid exchange about his mate, I'm absolutely sure I would have found out what Draxx is keeping in his pants, and whatever it is, it's fucking huge.

Yet another thing making my head pound. I've seen him naked, there was nothing where I expected it to be, but the iron baseball bat of what had to be a cock I felt pressed against me says otherwise.

I'm confused, aching, and hungry, so when I set foot

into Draco and Amber's quarters, I'm pleased to see the party has dissipated and there are a couple of warriors sat chatting quietly in one corner with Draco and Amber on the central chair. Drega stands with his back to them, clutching at a goblet.

"Hi!" Amber waves me over. "Pass me some roast tralu," she says to Draco, who passes her a hunk of meat.

I take it. "I think I just met one of these." I eye the meat carefully, and my stomach reminds me I had no such qualms about beef on Earth, so I take a bite before wolfing down the remainder.

"It's not the only thing being eaten around here." Drega snorts.

My cheeks flame. Did he see us?

No, Jem, he fucking heard you. You screamed loud enough to wake the dead.

"Er, I don't like to ask, but do you have anywhere I can sleep? I'm bushed." I tell Amber.

Because a huge green Sarkarnii made me come so hard I think I saw last week.

Crinkles appear at the corners of her eyes. She opens her mouth to say something but is cut off.

"You mean Draxx has not claimed you?" Draco rumbles, obliviously shoving a hunk of meat into his mouth.

He has one leg hooked over the arm of his chair, leaning back in it insolently. Amber is sat on his lap, his huge hand covering her midriff.

"No," I growl, and both Draco and Drega huff out smokey laughs of disbelief. "But he is taking me to find the other humans tomorrow."

Drega opens his mouth to speak, but Draco throws up a hand to silence him. "Good," he says. "You may stay in the quarters adjoining mine." He sits up straighter and gives me a good-natured smile, or at least as good-natured as a smile can be when it's accompanied by fangs and smoke.

Drega gets to his feet, but Amber's already up.

"I'll take her," she says, before leaning back into Draco and kissing him softly.

The huge golden scaled creature closes his eyes in pleasure.

"Probably best," Drega grumbles. "If Draxx finds out either of us have been near you, I'm going to need more than just a medi-kit." He grumbles.

Draco barks, and it's similar to the sound Draxx made earlier. I realize it's laughter.

"You should have known better than to get between a Sarkarnii male and his female, especially when he's in rut. And to think I thought you a healer, Drega."

"Nev you, Draco." Drega's eyes burn at his brother, and he turns away again, staring into his goblet.

Amber turns to me, and for the first time, I see she has a little rounded stomach. As much as she looks pregnant, I'm not going to say anything.

I've made that mistake before and hell, it was embarrassing.

Even my new 'fuck it' attitude doesn't extend to pissing off the only other human I know. Amber gives me a big smile and beckons me as she heads for the door. She shows me into a small, comfortable suite a little way down the dark corridor once we come out of her quarters.

"Get some rest," she says kindly. "Are you really going to go and find the other humans with Draxx?"

I sigh deeply. "It looks like it. I just can't sleep knowing they're somewhere in this place, and if you'd seen them how I saw them..." I run my hand over my face.

"The Wardens had me chased around a mini-maze by

monsters for several weeks before I ended up here. So, I can believe it," Amber says, her jaw hardening. "We've been trying to find the other humans—the ones the control room said were here—for a long time, but the Belek kept moving you."

My brain is wired, but my body, the fucking treacherous thing, once zinging for Draxx's touch, now only wants to crash.

"Control room?" I say as I sit down on the oversized bed.

"Yeah, it's the place Drega initially thought would hold the star map the Sarkarnii are looking for. It might still, but it seems human DNA is the key to unlocking its secrets, much to Drega's annoyance." Amber smiles at me. "He's not into mating," she clarifies. "He's a big old grump who loves his science. Females are a distraction." She uses bunny ears around the word.

I'm not sure I've ever met three brothers who are so different.

"And what is this map?" I stifle a yawn, hoping I manage to get out of the dress before I fall asleep.

"Draco believes it's a way of locating any Sarkarnii left in this galaxy or beyond after most of them were killed by their enemy, the Liderc, while they were all escaping the planet they inhabited in huge ships called arks."

"So, there are Sarkarnii females?"

Amber shrugs and mirrors my yawn, her hand absently rubbing over her stomach. "Maybe. Basically they don't know."

"And what happens when they find the map?"

"Draco plans to break out of here, get to his ship, and find the others, reunite with them. He's hoping at least one of the arks survived. It could mean there are thousands and thousands of Sarkarnii left."

"Even ones presumed dead?" My voice trembles as I say the words.

"Possibly. Draco and his den warriors had no way of knowing who was killed and who wasn't," Amber says. "Anyway, once we find the other humans, once they have their map, we'll know, won't we?"

"You're staying with Draco? Even once they escape?" I feel like I have to ask the question, even though it seems they're both very much into each other.

"I am." The hand runs over her stomach again. "We're having a child together, and I love him."

"Congratulations." I don't know what else to say. I give her what I hope is a supportive smile.

My growing up diet of sci-fi movies means all I can think about when it comes to alien young is x-rated chest bursting, but obviously that isn't the case because Amber looks quite normal.

"Thanks," Amber says. "I didn't want to scare you earlier, which is why I didn't mention it. But I wanted you to know I had a reason to not go looking for the other humans."

"I understand completely." I nod earnestly, still unable to get the thought of Draxx finding his chosen mate among the stars out of my head.

"Okay," Amber says carefully. "Night then. I'll see you tomorrow before you leave, I'm sure."

"Night," I repeat, as if we're parting after a visit to a pub.

Once she's gone, I lie back on the bed, everything whirling around me.

What if Draxx's mate isn't dead? What if all he wants is to find her again and he's using me to get what he wants?

I blow out my cheeks as I stare up at the rough concrete-like ceiling above me. It wouldn't be the first time a man has said what he thought I wanted to hear in order to get what he wanted. My ex for instance. He thought marrying me would mean he was entitled to a nice payout from my rich, absent father.

How wrong he was.

But it didn't make me any less of a fool.

DRAXX

I can still feel where she touched me on the chest. I can still scent her on my skin. I can still feel the shudder of her against me. When I lap at my fingers, I can taste her sweetness, her promise. The promise of a mate and of mating.

It's the only thing stopping me from going back to the pit, back to get drunk on mayhem and destruction. The thought of not being close to Jem means I have to stay in the upper parts of the Kirakos tonight. My only respite is to shift and stay in my Sarkarnii form. My chest buzzes each time my heart thumps, and the ache of not being near her makes me want to choose violence.

I rest on the top of the maze, looking down at Draco's quarters. The last thing I want is to nev him off by hanging around outside. It's unlikely he will change his mind about allowing me to accompany Jem into the warden-controlled areas, but he might want to send other warriors with us, and I want her all to myself.

I want to be able to show her what I was once. Why they called me 'General'.

Why my warriors would follow me into battle.

Why I always led from the very front.

Why my enemies always feared me.

Because, no matter how efficently I could rend flesh from bone, or how terrifying I was in battle, my strategies meant we always won.

Always.

Only I couldn't save my family, the mate chosen for me, all the other Sarkarnii on Kaeh-Leks. Which makes me nothing. Not even a general.

A sudden flash of blue and darkness has Drega landing on the ledge next to me and shifting into his other form. As much as I want to ignore him, I can't. He's going to run his smart mouth no matter what I do.

"Draxx," he says as he stands beside me. "She's not coming out."

"I know that. And I'm not going in."

"Sensible."

My shift is the only thing keeping the heat from my rut from overwhelming me, but it's always easier to talk in my smaller form. I grudgingly shift, not looking at Drega. We need to discuss the mission tomorrow, and I can't exactly avoid him.

"I don't want her to come with us."

"Why, don't you think you can protect her?" Drega says insolently.

He jumps as my tail sweeps under his feet with an aim of unbalancing him. He manages to avoid a sneaky wing snap too. But it was a lazy move.

"You forget, *brother*. I am older than you, and you over-step your mark," I snarl.

"And you forget you're in rut, Draco has a mate with a

Sarkarnling in her belly, and all I want to do is stop the pair of you emptying accelerant sacs everywhere." Drega folds his arms. "Neither of you have ever had the best of tempers."

I growl under my breath, most probably underlining what he is saying. Having an even temper is not needed for a Sarkarnii general. Being the best warrior I could be was my reason for existing, even when we lost everything.

"I have no desire to fight with Draco. That nevver fights dirty."

"Which is saying something coming from you." Drega laughs.

"I fight because I have to." I sigh.

My brother settles next to me, wary of my tail and wings, as he should be. We used to spar together all the time, on our planet, on our ship.

When he wasn't deep in his work, or getting into trouble chasing something he wanted.

"Don't I know it." Drega grumbles at me, staring out over the Kirakos, where here and there are lights denoting the other creatures who scrape a living here.

"Our ancestors willed it, Drega. You might think you're a healer, but I know what you are."

"Don't get all ancient ancestors on me, brother. I know exactly what you do in the pit." Drega snaps.

"And I know you too."

He huffs out a long stream of smoke, attempting to center himself. He's always hated it when I tell him what I see. A secretive, guarded male, clever to a fault. A Sarkarnii who would kill before asking questions, even if he will insist he's planned it all in advance.

"If we can just concentrate on getting the humans and

the key to the star map, perhaps? Then we can get the nev out of this prison, and things can go back to what they were." Drega says, quietly.

"Things can never be how they were, Drega." I stare down into the main square, watching a couple of warriors wrestle in the dim light. "We are all filled with fire, and we have all lost everything. Map or no, it will not change facts. We are broken."

"I don't want to be broken, Draxx. And neither do you. We are Sarkarnii. Our line is descended from the very first ancestors, the High Bask. I am not going to let the nevving Liderc beat me or my family. Are you?"

He shifts immediately and takes off with strong down-strokes, flame biting into the night air. I could follow him, teach him some manners, only, as I drop my head and stare down to where my female is, as out of reach as if she were with our ancestors, I know in my heart he is right.

I let the pit take me because I believed we were beaten. Only I never stopped to check if we were. And now I have something to fight for.

Jem.

My fated mate.

The beautiful creature draped in green, who tasted like nectar and who came undone on the very tip of my tongue.

Imagine how she will be when I have her hooked?

My cock pushes at my pouch, the tip leaking pre-cum in a steady stream. I want nothing more than to take myself in hand, but all of my spill is for her body alone. I cannot waste it in a fruitless bout of thrusting.

Although, as I shift back to my Sarkarnii form and my cock hardens further, I feel my self-control slipping.

But then, self-control was never my strong point.

If I am to have my mate, I need to dance for her, and

something tells me dancing for this female is not going to be easy. I need to reconsider my approach so far, not be the feral Sarkarnii everyone thinks I am. I need to strategize like the general I know I was.

I need to claim my female as soon as I can.

JEM

Yeah, sleep. Seems I could never get enough when I was locked in an alien cell, but the time I could do with it, before I go out like an intrepid explorer to find the other incarcerated humans? Nope. I lay awake, my head churning with everything and my body simultaneously pulsing with the filthy thoughts I kept having about Draxx's forked tongue between my legs.

Like the touch of his fingers, huge and yet soft, one sliding inside me. I imagine him curling it up and...

It was a rough night, which left me sweaty, uncomfortable, and unfulfilled, until finally, finally, I heard noises in the corridor outside and opened the door to find a sheepish looking Sarkarnii holding a pile of clothing.

"For you, my lady," he says, shoving the pile at me and taking a hasty step back, his scales glittering in red, one eye on the stone steps down into the entrance to Draco and Amber's quarters. "Draco's mate says to join her for the morning meal when you are ready."

I turn away, yawning. The door slides shut, and I'm sure I hear sounds of scuffling outside as if there's some sort of fight, but I'm too tired to check. Instead I locate the bathroom at the rear of the suite, use the facilities, and then dress.

Amber has sent me something far more practical than the shimmery floaty dress from yesterday which I did end up wearing all night and not because it smelled like Draxx.

Absolutely not.

Suitably suited and booted, I make my way down the corridor and into the outer room of Draco and Amber's quarters.

It's empty.

There's food arranged out on the same table as last night, and my stomach growls loudly. Thing is, do I risk any of it?

"Eat," a deep voice rumbles behind me, and I can immediately feel the warmth of a big, big body.

Huge green arms appear, and in one hand is a large platter.

"You will need your strength and wits today," Draxx murmurs in my ear as the plate is shoved into my hand, and I'm not quick enough to do anything other than take it.

And because his scent, his warmth, and his bulk are somehow intoxicating me. When I recover my wits, he's moved away and has taken a heaped platter for himself.

I pick at my offering, not quite as enormous but still far more than I could ever eat. Having tried a few things, I'm pleased they're all palatable, and I look around for Draxx. He's sat quietly eating his food on a comfortable bench. I feel like a bit of a bitch leaving him on his own, especially as all he's done is make sure I'm okay and not any growling, snarling, fighting, or using the word 'mine' today.

Although, there's still time, obviously.

The room is beginning to fill with Sarkarnii, but the

noise remains at a low buzz. I see each of the warriors who enter give Draxx a little nod. Out of respect? I'm not sure. I edge over to him and sit down.

"Thanks." I say without looking at him.

"Eat."

"I am." I finger some of the food. "What is this?"

Draxx swipes at the pink frilly thing which looks like a cross between lettuce and seafood. He spears it on a claw and then holds it up to my mouth.

"Disno. Good meat. Some of my favorite."

I'm pleased to hear it's meat, although given I've seen tripe before, I'm taking my life (or rather my tastebuds) in his claw if I'm going to try it. However, everything else he's chosen for me was pleasant and tasty, so I open up and let him put the food on my tongue.

The flavor bursts in my mouth, meaty, part bacon, part beef, and all goodness for this early in the morning. If only I had some ketchup. I moan with delight, closing my eyes to savor the first really good thing I've had to eat.

Beside me, Draxx growls. His eyes are dark, slit pupils blown as he stabs another piece of disno and holds it to my lips. I hesitate for a second, and he pushes the food at me. Instead of resisting him, I open up and allow him to put the food in, but I accidentally close my lips over his claw.

Draxx's eyes flare, and I pull back sharply. His chest rumbles, scales flow over his skin, and, before my eyes, a tail extends, tip flicking like a cat. There are spikes all the way along the length, large and bony albeit a darker green than the iridescent scales. They remind me of something, but I'm not sure what, only that my core heats with anticipation.

"Are you ready?" Drega appears beside us.

Draxx snarls up a storm, and he takes a step back.

Finally, with some effort, the big green behemoth next to me recovers some of his composure as Drega eyes him.

"I have weapons and supplies. Who is accompanying us?"

"Drasus and Daeos."

Draxx nods sharply. "Eat," he says to me again as he rises. "I will be outside once we are ready."

Without another word, he rises and stalks out of the room, Drega shaking his head as he departs.

"What's going on?" I say in a hoarse whisper.

"If I know Draxx, it will involve explosives," Drega grumbles. "You best do as he asks. We're going to be using the undercroft tunnels to reach the warden-controlled area, and it's a long walk."

I've always enjoyed the outdoors, so I know the value of a good hearty breakfast before a long hike. I put some of the drier meat in my pockets for snacks later and finish as much as I can before Drega raises his hand at me, and I follow him and two other warriors out of Draco's quarters and into the cool air outside.

As I troop out, something whistles in the sky above us and a huge green dragon lands with a thump, raising clouds of dust which resolve into a not quite as huge Draxx. He is covered in what look like weapons. And here's me thinking in space, it would be all ray guns.

While some of what he's carrying might actually include ray guns, Draxx bristles with two double-headed axes strapped to his back and a set of four daggers at his waist along with several thin metal tubes. In his hand, he carries a long stick which might be a rifle. Tucked behind him is a bag bulging with I have no idea what.

"Ready?" Drega says, throwing a couple of the long

sticks to the other warriors. They both look to Draxx and not Drega.

Draxx nods slowly, and they turn, heading across the central square. Drega looks at Draxx again, snorts out a smoke ring with a hitch of his lip, and follows.

"Expecting a fight?" I raise an eyebrow at Draxx.

"Where I go, the fight goes," he rasps back before turning to me. "And where you go, I go."

My knees go weak as he looms over me, one hand capturing my chin, tilting my face up to his.

"Should anything harm a hair on your head, they will die. That is my promise to you."

My heart flips in my chest as his lips hit mine. This is not how I wanted today to start, but it looks like I have no choice. I'm about to go into the heart of the maze with an agent of chaos.

His name is Draxx.

DRAXX

I know I shouldn't be kissing her. I know I should ignore the throb of my cock in my pouch. I know I should be thinking about freeing the other humans. Because once it's done, I can dance for my mate.

But instead, I am kissing her, and she tastes like promise and perfection. I curl my hand into the soft strands of her hair and enjoy how her body arches to mine, stretched taut, ready to be plucked.

I am so, so ready to be mated to her.

"We...we have to go, Draxx," she breathes.

My name on her lips! I would die a thousand deaths on the battlefield to hear it from her again as I plunder her body and make every part of her sing.

"We have to go." I give her a final kiss, and she pants as I release her.

Then her eyes harden. "I hope you're not going to do this the whole time. I want to find the other humans."

"I give you my word as a Sarkarnii general, I will not kiss you the *whole* time," I say, surprising myself at using my title.

Jem narrows her eyes, huffs out a little breath with no smoke, and then turns away from me, marching in the direction Drega and the others took. It is my honor to protect her, and so I enjoy the view of her delicious ass as it swings from side to side. I imagine how it will look as I take her from behind.

By the bones! I am not going to get anywhere with a cock pushing at my pouch and a mind filled with delicious dreams of my little female. And I'm certainly going to struggle to protect her if all I have is a fog of rut.

In fact, she's managed to get all the way across the main square and is disappearing down into the undercroft entrance with Drega and the others while I've been contemplating my cock. I curse under my breath as I hurry to catch up with her.

Drega gives me the dirtiest smile as he plants himself between me and Jem, with Daeos and Dresus ahead of her. I want to kill him. I want to kill them. My mating gland pulses hard in my chest, and the level of self-control I have to exercise is unbelievable. It's only because I worry my Jem might get caught up in the killing I hold myself back.

To add insult to injury, Drega shifts his tail, so I have to walk even farther behind. At least until I manage to tread on it hard, and even though he does his best to hide the squeak of annoyance, I can still hear it. So, when he looks over his shoulder, I give him my best grin, fangs and all.

Thing is, when he looks, so does Jem, and the alarm on her face sobers me immediately. I'm supposed to be preparing to dance for my mate, to make her see I'm a worthy warrior of her affections, to hope she doesn't decide to disable me with her venom.

Wait. Do humans have venom? Do they envenomate their mates like I was always told Sarkarnii females do?

I feel like I should have asked Draco some more questions. I also probably shouldn't have laughed at him quite so much when he was preparing to dance for his mate.

The time when I was supposed to be preparing to dance for mine back on Kaeh-Leks seems a thousand evs ago. A mate chosen for me, one I had met once, in a crowded gathering and spoke but two or three words to, before Drega dragged me away. Hand-picked by my family because as the younger brother to Draco, I didn't get a choice.

Not like Draco.

Seeing him settled with a mate is funny. And that's why I laughed at him. Of course, I'm the one in rut now. Suddenly it isn't quite so amusing.

Having finally had enough of Drega, I shove him against the wall and storm past so I can walk behind Jem. She looks back at me again and then shakes her head, concentrating on moving forward, following the glittering red bioluminescence of Daeos. She has a small glowing light stick in her hand and seems confident here as she has light and me to protect her.

"How far is it?" she asks, still staring forward.

"It will take most of the tick to get there. It's easier coming back because the Wardens know we've been in their area, so we can just shift and fly back, but there's no point in announcing our presence before we get to where we need to be," I reply.

"I wouldn't have thought much would bother a Sarkarnii," Jem says, and this time I'm sure the glance she throws me is something akin to interest.

"Yeah, well, none of us want to be caught and collared again," Daeos calls back. "Least of all Draxx. He nearly drove us insane with his behavior when collared."

I snarl so loudly it fills the passageway. Daeos goes rigid for an instant but carries on walking.

I see Jem looking back at me, and I don't like what I see in her eyes. The last thing I want is pity.

"I'll explain later, when we're finished here," I tell her.

Her shoulders drop, and for some reason, I feel like she's unhappy with me. I glare at Daeos. The red-scaled nevver can't be trusted. He has absolutely no filter, but unlike me, he didn't develop an unhealthy obsession with the pit while we were collared and unable to shift. He used it to work out whatever it was he needed to work out and then disappeared.

For the first time since we got to the Kirakos, I'm starting to think my behavior could have been tempered, and although it pains me greatly to admit it, maybe Drega was right.

Maybe I could have been a better Sarkarnii and a better general for Draco.

And for myself.

JEM

lthough the red-scaled warrior called Daeos made the comment about a collar as almost a throw away thing, the look which passed over Draxx's face made me wonder if, whatever the collar is, is not something any of them bore lightly.

Especially him.

It certainly doesn't sound good, whatever it is, and it makes my chest constrict in a weird way. The thought of Draxx being hurt, or to experience the sadness he tried to hide, it makes me...care about him?

Oh god, I want to care about another so very much. I stopped caring about myself and had no one else who cared about me, or to care about, for a long, long time. All I did was my job. I saw clients, I went to court, I argued their cases. I was on autopilot.

Sure, I cared. But I didn't feel. It didn't set me alight.

Maybe that was why I ended up traversing Dartmoor in the middle of the night, having booked the Airbnb on a whim to get away. After all, what was the worst that could happen?

Okay, so I didn't expect alien abduction, but here we are.

I also didn't expect to start caring for a seven-foot-plus scaled alien blockhead of a warrior, who just snarled so damn loud I thought my eardrums would burst in this confined space.

But that look. The dulling of his eyes, the dimming of his lights as it hit him and the squaring of his shoulders as he pushed the emotion away. It grips at me. It intrigues me.

Maybe I do want the explanation...later.

For now, we're still walking and walking down this dark, winding passageway. I have a light, so I'm not stumbling over the debris under my feet, plus the lights under their scales which these Sarkarnii give off—it might as well be Christmas in here.

Until there is a noise up ahead and, as I freeze, all four of them wink out of existence, as if the lights had never been there at all. If it wasn't for my glow stick, the entire place would be in complete darkness. Ahead, I hear some slithering followed by a squeak.

"Melabuk." A voice comes back to me. I think it's the purple warrior called Dresus. "A big one too."

For some reason, a shiver goes down my spine.

"What's a melabuk?" I ask Draxx.

"Good eating," he replies. "Make sure you keep some for later," he calls ahead.

There's some grumbling, grunting, and some noises which have to be a knife slicing through flesh. Daeos leans back against the wall and does his level best not to look at me. Draxx is so close I can feel the heat from him. Finally, we move on. I look for a carcass or any sign of whatever the melabuk was, but there's nothing.

After even more bloody walking in the dark, the

passageway suddenly opens up, wide enough we can all walk side by side. Draxx stays close to me, while the others walk slightly ahead.

"We can rest here," Draxx says. His voice takes on an interesting quality in the larger area. It was already strong, but here, it rings with confidence.

Daeos and Drasus drop to the floor and start to fiddle around with a couple of bags they're carrying. Drega looks at Draxx and then heads up the widened passageway on his own. Draxx hunkers down next to the other warriors for a short while, before rising and walking over to me.

"Sit. Rest," he says.

"I'm fine standing. I used to hike all the time back on Earth," I tell him.

He rumbles, and his eyes flare, then he plonks himself down, although his height means he's not that much lower.

"Sit," he growls, patting his lap.

I feel my eyes widen, but somehow my body obeys, and I sink down onto his hard thighs. I can't believe Draxx has ordered me to sit like a dog and yet, I am complying.

And I like it.

Except...

I wriggle on his lap and grumble. "You're uncomfortable. I should just sit on the floor."

A hand clamps over my midriff. "You will stay," he rasps in my ear. "Daeos! Food!" he calls across to the two warriors.

Daeos rises, and although he has a little smirk on his face, he soon drops it before picking up some sizzling meat and bringing it over.

Wings shift out as he takes a bow, presenting the steaming food to Draxx.

"Nev off, warrior," Draxx says as he swipes the meat,

but I spot the brief flash of fang, and Daeos gives him a huge grin before returning to his comrade.

Draxx peels off a strip of meat and blows on it gently. He offers it up to my lips. "Melabuck is best served fresh," he says.

"I'm not hungry," I reply, somewhat dubious about what I might be eating, given it was found in a dank passageway.

"You will eat," Draxx says, the smoothness and depth in his voice hitting a place in my crotch it really shouldn't. "Open."

The warm meat is at my lips, and for a second, I think of defying him, just to see what will happen, but instead I part my lips and let him put the food between them. My teeth bite down, and I capture the tip of his claw as he removes it.

Draxx shudders a tiny bit, a muscle ticking in his jaw.

I chew as I stare at him. He pulls off another strip, and before I've even swallowed, there's more food ready for me.

"You need some too," I manage to say in between mouthfuls.

"I can survive for weeks on very little. My Sarkarnii form allows me to do so," Draxx says.

"I insist." I make a grab for the meat, but it's speared on his huge claws, and he pulls it away from me.

"You do not get to insist on anything, unless I say so," Draxx rumbles.

I open my mouth to protest and have some more meat placed in it while his eyes and scales glitter. My body heats at his treatment, but not because I hate it.

Because I like it.

Back in the dark, there is an almighty roar and flare of flame. In an instant, Draxx is up, I'm placed on my feet, and the other two warriors are bristling with weapons.

A whipping of blue scales, wings, and teeth has Drega

resolving into his more humanoid form, his nostrils smoking considerably.

"We can't go that way," he says, evenly. "It's blocked by...something new."

"What?" Draxx fires out. "The only other way will take a further ev to reach the warden-controlled area."

"It has a vesso," Drega says with some finality.

"What's a vesso?" I ask.

"Mostly teeth," Draxx replies.

DRAXX

I do not like the fact there is a vesso in these passages. The creatures, vicious, organic eating machines, were used by the wardens in the same way they use the yeylock and the melabuk as ways of slowing down any prisoner attempting one of the runs where the prize was supposedly freedom.

It wasn't. It did get rid of many inhabitants of the Kirakos though, which was part of the reason they took place.

The other reason was entertainment and money for the wardens, each run being watched by those rich enough to buy in.

But the runs will be this prison's downfall. In the last one, we managed to gain control of our quadrant. All we need is the map, and then Draco intends on taking the control center and getting us the nev out of here. I'm hoping we get the chance to blow the place to atoms before we go.

And then I'm going to find the nevvers who watched and enjoyed the bloodbath of each run and give them a taste of what it's like.

Jem is close by my side as a low keening cry echoes through the passageway. Drega grumbles out a curse.

"We could do with a key right now. I gave the vesso a good blast of flame, but it won't stay back there for long, not with the scent of food."

"Food?" I see Jem looking at the cooked meat Daeos is pocketing.

"Not that sort of food," Drega says. "I mean us."

Jem blinks at him in horror, and all I want to do is punch him through a wall.

"But you're dragons?" She looks up at me, her beautiful eyes wide. "Nothing can harm you?"

"We can't all shift in here, and it's not big enough to fight properly. We can deal with a vesso out in the open, but in a confined space, even with the weapons we have, there's a risk you might get hurt," I say gently, but she huffs and turns away.

I capture her jaw in my hand. She glares up at me.

"I can fight," she spits out.

I smile. "I'm sure you can, but you don't want to fight a vesso. However, maybe you can help in another way?" Jem furrows her sweet brow at me. "Draco's mate is able to find hidden doors in the maze. Maybe you can too?"

"Find hidden doors? How?"

"It seems human DNA has ended up being encoded within the Kirakos, either by accident or design," Drega explains, looking over his shoulder at the darkness behind us. "The whole maze is riddled with passageways, exits, and entrances. Amber was able to find them for us."

Jem looks around at the expectant warriors. "You're kidding me? This is a joke, right?"

"Try over there," I say to her, nodding at the closest wall to us.

From my experience in the pit and the surrounding areas, it looks like a part of the maze which might hold a hidden door. Without a key, the only way you found out if there was a hidden door was if you accidentally tripped the mechanism.

Jem gives us all a narrow-eyed stare and then steps up to the wall. Placing her hands flat on the surface she takes in a deep breath. Nothing happens.

She turns to look over her shoulder at me. "This is stupid. I'm not a *key*, and there's nothing..."

True to form, the moment she speaks, a trap opens beneath her, and she drops away from me. I make a leap for her, but I miss her hand by a scale's width, and instead I follow her head first, bellowing for my fellow warriors to come down behind me.

The chute we're in is narrow but slippery. Up ahead, I catch a glimpse of Jem's head and the light stick she still has hold of, but I'm not gaining on her, despite my bulk. I also cannot tell if the others are behind us.

The positive in this situation? The vesso most definitely will not fit down here, so unless there's another one waiting when we finally get out, our situation will be marginally improved.

Save for having to find another way to the warden-controlled area where the humans are. And the possibility we might end up in a worse position, somehow.

The chute is getting increasingly narrow and my speed slowing. Not being close to Jem is making my skin itch as if I need to shed, so I attempt to streamline my body and slick down my scales. It works, and I slip faster until I hear something up ahead. It's a fork in the nevving chute, and I have no way of knowing which one Jem took. I inhale as deeply as I can, hoping her scent is stronger down one of the passages, but it is no help.

The last thing I want to do is stop now as, if the others are above me, the resulting Sarkarnii pile up will not be pleasant. I pick the left one and hope to the ancestors I am following my mate.

Because if I lose her, I will have to take the Kirakos apart to find her.

JEM

That was...not fun.

My stomach rolls from the twisting and turning. My ankle throbs at me because I landed awkwardly when I dropped out of the slide from hell.

Whose clever idea was it to find hidden doorways in this weird place?

Draxx.

The big green muscle machine who is nowhere to be seen.

Only...

I manage to scramble to one side of the cave I've fallen into as something large shoots out of the hole I exited and tumbles over a few times.

And immediately transforms into a dragon, filling the space until I'm squashed up against one of the rough walls, my vision is blocked with green scales.

"Draxx...get...off," I squeeze out with burning lungs.

There's a rumbling in the flank beneath me, or at least I think it's his flank, given I can't see anything and can hardly breathe for the enormous creature filling the space. I attempt to move, to gain more air, and the pain in my ankle spikes. I'm not one for making a fuss, but the sudden sharpness causes me to cry out, especially when I stupidly recoil from the pain and it only gets worse.

"Jem." My name, spoken as a growl, as something unworldly, fills the rest of the cavern and rattles through my body.

There's no way Draxx saying my name like that, while he's a fucking dragon, should have any effect on me other than terror.

But instead it makes my core clench and heat pool exactly where heat should not be. Instantly, the thought of his two tongues and what he can do with them fills my mind.

We're in the heart of an alien prison, I'm being squashed to death by an alien dragon, something horrible is coming to eat me, and all I can think about is Draxx and his forked tongue.

I suppose there might be worse ways to die.

"Can't...shift." Again, the words are rumbled through me rather than spoken.

Pain fires through me. I thought I'd sprained my ankle, but now I'm not so sure I haven't broken it.

"Please, Draxx," I whisper, the last of my breath leaving my body.

I'm suddenly missing the heat and the press of his dragon form as Draxx resolves himself into a more humanoid shape. His fangs are still long and he struggles to close his gorgeous lips over them. That tongue, the one which I can't get out of my head and obviously want elsewhere sweeps out, licking and licking until the fangs are gone.

And I feel a little sad.

"Are you injured?" He stalks toward me, picking up various weapons as he goes, slinging them back across his chest.

He is sans pants once again, but I guess that happens when you change into a dragon.

"I hurt my ankle when I fell out," I explain as I shuffle more upright against the wall behind me. I don't want to even look at my foot.

"Let me see."

"No!"

I draw back from him, but the pain in doing so has me hissing.

"Don't argue with me," he intones. "You will do as I ask. Let me see."

Something floods through me, and it's nothing I can put my finger on, other than I feel the way I did earlier when he wanted me on his lap.

The massive green-scaled behemoth drops to his knees on the sandy ground. He lifts my leg with a gentleness the huge claws on his fingers bely and unlaces my boot.

"Tell me if any of this hurts," he says, his words hushed as he concentrates on his task.

With the boot loosened, he carefully holds my calf and slips it free. I bite back a groan of pain. My foot, sockless because underwear is not a thing in this prison, is puffing up red against his green. Horrible mottled blue bruising blooms down the side of my foot.

"I'm not sure, but I think it might just be a sprain." I look at where there is a darkened area under the skin. Without an x-ray, obviously I can't be sure, and I'm racking my brain to remember my old first-aid training.

"We cannot stay here, my mate," Draxx says as he looks

around us. "We are trapped if anyone finds us, and I do not like it."

His scales ripple as he surveys the area.

"What about the others?"

"They can take care of themselves. You require rest and healing," Draxx says, and his tone brooks no argument.

And I have none. Not to this massive male who touched me as tenderly as a newborn. I guess he's not quite what I thought after all.

As if to hammer home his point, Draxx hands me my boot and scoops me up in an easy motion which makes me feel like I'm feather light. I open my mouth to grumble generally about being carried, but the stern look on his face has me snapping my jaw shut.

I like stern Draxx.

My ankle throbs, and perhaps him being dominant with me is not a bad thing, otherwise I would have insisted on walking. We reach the entrance to the cavern, and Draxx takes a careful look around. Outside, it looks different from the maze. We're high up, not quite on a cliff face, but enough to see the valley bottom spread out below. Draxx sucks in a breath.

"What is it?"

"It's the Igered," he says, eyes narrowing, pupils little slithers of darkness, his hands tightening where he holds me. "And it shouldn't exist."

DRAXX

"Tiger-red?" Jem queries, studying my face.

I'm doing my best to keep my expression neutral, but what with the mating mix flowing through my veins, throbbing anger at the fact my mate got injured *on my watch*, and the shock of finding a place which we were always told by the longtime inmates of the Kirakos was a myth, I feel the muscle ticking in my jaw.

I am failing again. A growl rises from my belly. I don't like the color of Jem's ankle or the fact her face is equally pale. She requires healing, and my nevving brother is nowhere to be seen as usual.

"This place. It's supposed to be the center of the maze," I say. "But I never believed it. I expected the center to be where the Wardens congregated, not a calm in the middle of the storm."

"I'm going to hazard a guess this is not where you thought we'd end up when you made me poke that wall," Jem says, and her voice has an edge to it which I recognize as pain.

"No," I reply as I start into the lower parts of this new area.

I'm lucky the weapons I brought with me were scattered around the cavern. Although no longer attached given my shift occurred the second I exited the chute, I have most of what I need to defend my mate in this new and strange place.

Although with night coming, we're going to need shelter as much as she is going to need treatment. Myth or not, I don't take any chances in the Kirakos.

It's never safe here. Not for a seccari.

A familiar scent greets me as we make our way down the side of the cliff by way of a narrow series of ledges. I'm impressed that Jem does her best to keep her weight distributed on me as I jump from rock to rock, the height and drop not bothering her in the slightest.

I think about shifting, but I don't want to attract the wrong attention. So, instead, we work our way steadily down the slab side until we reach the vegetation.

It's been a long time since I was anywhere with greenery. The pungent smell of dirt and freshness hits me like a wall, and I inhale deeply.

"I wonder why this is here, if we're still inside the maze. I didn't see anything like this where you and the other Sarkarnii live."

"There is some plant life in the rest of the Kirakos. The tralu feast on it, and some of it is made into dishes by the Jiaka." I curl my lip up.

"Yeah, I've noticed how you big boys like your meat." Jem pats my chest with a half smile.

"I am Sarkarnii. I do not do garnish," I growl, and she laughs.

The sound is incredible. It makes every scale on my body ripple. I stare and stare at her, feeling frozen to the spot. I understand the mechanics of the rut, the desire my body has to fill her in so many ways, but this is something different.

This is something glorious. I want to consume her laughter so I never forget it.

"I guess with fangs like yours, you're built for meat eating." She traces a finger over my scales, and heat follows her touch.

"I can do far more with my mouth than just feed," I rasp. "I can eat too."

The perfume of her arousal rises up to me, and my head spins. "I might just let you have another taste," she says, then she winces.

Nev it to the ancestors! I let my desires get the better of me. Her ankle is puffed up weirdly and not the same color as the rest of her. I lift my head and scent my surroundings. It's mostly fauna, but I'm sure I detect a hint of smoke.

And it's not me, despite having full accelerant sacs. There are life forms in this place, which means there has to be shelter.

The entire place glitters with green, a multitude of colors I can appreciate, some of which look like the dress Jem was wearing the night I enjoyed her. I can hear water running, and it makes me think of the natural aquium which Draco favors for his shed. If there is water here, then it has to be the life force for this place.

We reach a small trickle of the water running down the cliff, not the roar I can hear in the distance, but a clear stream which makes its way through a long, carved channel. I gently place Jem down beside it and drop in my hand. It's cool, and as I take a sip, it has no taint.

"It's good," I offer her what's left, and to my delight, she pulls my hand closer and buries her face in it, her lips touching my skin and sending my cock pushing at my pouch.

Fortunately, she withdraws, splashing a little on her face and rubbing it over her hands.

"I'm going to leave you here while I check out farther below for shelter."

Jem nods. "Any chance of something to defend myself while you're gone?"

My mating rut returns with a roar. I take her face in my clawed hand, making sure she is looking up into my eyes.

"You have me, and that is all you'll ever need," I growl.

"You're right," Jem says with a quick smile. I hear the chime of an activated plasma pulsar between us. "But just in case. I'll also take this."

I look down slowly. Jem has hold of a pulsar from one of the holsters on my chest, the slim tube looking huge in her tiny hand. Her eyes blaze with triumph.

"I will allow you to keep the weapon if it brings you comfort, little mate." I grin at her. "But you will pay for your misbehavior later."

"I'm counting on it," she replies.

JEM

Fuck it! When he gives me that look, the one I know will haunt my dreams, the one where his nostrils flare and his jaw tenses—he one which makes me want to disobey him and also turn into a puddle at his feet.

Instead, I allow myself to ogle his delicious green behind which shimmers with green scales as he pushes through the undergrowth and disappears.

Draxx is not what I thought he was at all. He doesn't have another pretty Sarkarnii female waiting for him somewhere, he isn't an agent of chaos (well, not always). He is considerate, clever, and kind. He can be in control when he wants to be.

Except when he isn't, and oh, boy! I love tipping him over that edge. It makes me want to see that part of him so much more. The Draxx not in control, the Draxx who wants to *dominate* me.

I never thought I'd feel like this in my entire life because it's always been about control. About not letting others get under my skin, like my adopted mother telling me I was worthless, or my ex-husband telling me I was not good enough for him. Only somehow, at some point and despite every effort, I've let Draxx in.

Because he always turns out to be exactly what he appears to be. Strong, handsome, completely bonkers, and one hundred percent true. It's been my own judgement coloring everything else about him.

That and the fact I don't believe in love at first sight. Something tells me I might have been wrong about that.

The bushes in front of me rustle, and I point the silver tube I have no idea how to work at the shivering vegetation. It parts and Draxx appears, holding up his hands in a universal gesture while grinning at me.

He advances slowly and then plucks the tube from my hand.

"Hey! You could have got yourself hurt," I exclaim.

"I think you'll find it's the other way around, my treasure," he says, putting the tube back in my hand. "You were pointing it the wrong way." He taps at a black spot on the end facing away from me. "So you know for next time."

He leans in as a curl of smoke rises, looking every inch the delicious bad boy. "I will show you how to handle a weapon properly. Later."

Dear god!

"In the meantime, I have found us some shelter, and I believe I have something to help your injury."

I'm scooped back up in a pair of strong arms, and Draxx carries me through the vegetation along an overgrown path downwards. Eventually we come out at what has to be the bottom of the valley and there is a broad stream. Its bright blue waters are a direct contrast to the dark green of the surroundings. Draxx turns right and follows another, more well-trodden path until we pass through some tall waving grasses and find ourselves in the midst of a settlement.

There is a large open area where a fire burns without much smoke in a pit, and under the trees, I see tall creatures moving around.

"Draxx."

He turns as his name is called, and I only just manage not to do a big intake of breath. Stood before us is a human-sized praying mantis. I grip at Draxx's arm, not entirely sure what to do other than stare.

"Litur." Draxx does a little bow. "This is my mate." He smiles

"Ah, a little human," Litur says, "I had heard the Sarkarnii were compatible with other species, but I hadn't expected it to be one from the old galaxy." It shakes its head. "But you live and learn. Come." It beckons at us.

"What the hell is this?" I hiss at Draxx.

"The Ragad are an ancient species," Draxx says quietly. "Some of them lived for a while on my planet, and I learned much from them."

"What are they doing here?"

"That is a question they will answer in due course. In the meantime, they have somewhere you can rest, and I can treat your injury." He walks after Litur towards something which looks like a teardrop made out of reeds.

As we get closer, I see it is suspended from one of the huge trees growing at the side of the river. There's a mechanism to lift it up into the air, which must be to keep it out of the way of either any water or predators.

"Everything you need is within," Litur says with a little bow. "Tend to your mate, Draxx. We will talk later." The praying mantis stalks away on its spindly legs, and I repress a shudder.

Draxx ducks down as we enter the teardrop. He kicks

out behind us, and I hear a whirr of mechanics before the thing rises swiftly into the canopy.

"I want you all to myself, my mate." Draxx looks down at me, his eyes soft. "I hope you don't mind."

"I guess I don't have much choice." I put my finger to my bottom lip and look around.

Inside the hanging room is about as far away from a reed hut we could possibly be. It's clean and smooth, like plastic. A huge bed dominates the main area. It looks like it's molded out of the same slightly translucent, pale cream material as the rest of the place.

Draxx sets me down on the edge of the bed which is surprisingly comfortable.

"No." He gives me a grin filled with fang. "You don't. You'll need me to look after you."

With some reluctance, he turns away from me and walks to the other side of the round room. Outside I can see an incredible view down the valley. The light is dim now as night approaches.

"If we're in the center of a prison, how is there light and dark?"

Draxx walks back to me, carrying a basin. He drops to his knees, and I'm immediately reminded of our previous night's encounter, which causes parts of me to clench.

"There is an artificial sun. The entire moon is, we believe, enclosed in an outer skin. It's the reason there is rivers and some other natural resources."

"Seems very elaborate for a prison."

"It is. The Kirakos was not always a prison and not always a maze."

Draxx gently elevates my ankle onto his thigh and dips a cloth into some tea-colored liquid. He wipes it over my swollen flesh, and it initially tingles, then, when the tingling is verging on painful, a feeling of warmth slides through me, and the pain disappears. I watch with eyes on stalks as Draxx continues to bathe my ankle and the swelling visibly reduces.

"That stuff is incredible!" I gently rotate my ankle. There's no feeling of anything grating which is a good thing, although a hairline fracture could still be possible. "If we had it on Earth, it would be…"

I stop talking because Draxx is staring at me, his eyes searching my face.

"You miss your home?"

In an instant, I see him.

I see Draxx.

Not chaos, not warrior, not even general.

I see the male who has nothing.

Who lost everything.

My heart leaps into my throat. I'm not sure I can speak because all I want to do is hold him, cradle him until there is nothing but us.

"No," I say truthfully. "My life on Earth wasn't anything special. In fact it was pretty crap. I had an ex-husband who took my eyes out in the divorce, an adoptive family who couldn't care less about me unless they wanted money, and a birth father who wanted nothing to do with me."

Draxx continues to study my face. "I don't know what any of that means."

"It means I don't want to go back to Earth." I put my hand on the side of his face, marveling at the way his scales ebb and flow over his skin.

I surprise myself with the sentiment. But when I search inside, I know it's true. Even if it were possible, what have I got to go back for? Nothing. So, when I chose to be free, it seems I also chose outer space.

"You don't want to go back to your planet? Your people?"

Draxx is frowning, so I place my other hand on his cheek, stroking my thumb over his sharp, angular bones, my heart flip-flopping in my chest.

"I'm sorry, Draxx. I'm so sorry. I didn't mean it to sound like I don't care about my planet or my species. I do, in that I wouldn't want them destroyed, but it doesn't mean I want to go back. I know you cared about yours so very much."

He turns his head away but not so my hand breaks contact with his skin.

"I cared that I couldn't save them. That's what I cared about. Going back to Kaeh-Leks is not my aim."

"What do you want?" I ask.

"I want you." Draxx turns back to me, eyes blazing, smoke huffing from his nostrils. "Under me, filled by me, mated by me, and claimed by me."

Oh, shit.

DRAXX

That my mate does not want to return to her planet has sent my heart spiraling and my mating gland thumping like never before. If I thought the rut was bad up until now—the heat, the overwhelming desire to burn something, to shift, the friction of my ever-hard cock against my pouch—this is something else entirely.

I don't know what this is, but I am burning for Jem.

She gazes at me, one hand on her chest and one hand on mine. Heat rolls from her, and I feel like my skin is on fire at her touch. I capture her hand in mine, but she twists, and she has hold of me. Lifting my fingers to her mouth, she kisses my claw.

And then parts her lips, letting me slide it into her.

I groan at the wet heat, knowing this is what her pussy feels like when I am sheathed in her.

"How is your ankle?" I growl.

She releases me with a 'pop'.

"Better."

"Good, because I am going to prepare you for mating."

"Prepare me?" Jem queries. "What do you mean...? Oh!"

I stand as she speaks, my cock fully emerged from my pouch. It hangs in the air between us, pre-cum running in a stream. Her eyes are wide as she takes me in.

"Draxx." Her voice is a hiss. "You are *huge.*"

I take myself in hand and slide it up my cock, pumping some more cum out. "Which is why you need to be prepared."

"How?"

"You will see, little mate."

I lean into her, gently fisting her hair in my hand as I offer up my cock to her mouth.

"Open," I demand as I tap the tip on her lips, enjoying the sight of her pout smeared with my cum.

When Jem does as I ask, I very nearly orgasm on the spot. It takes a huge effort just to push my cock between those beautiful lips, and as she licks, I can't help but groan at the sensation of utter bliss coursing through me.

Breaking the rut will be the most exquisite thing I've ever done in my life because I have Jem.

"Fuck! What is that stuff?" Jem's eyes are half-lidded with pleasure as she reaches for my cock, stroking up and down the shaft, the thing looking obscenely large in her tiny hand which can't even encircle my girth.

"Sarkarnii seed has special properties for a female. It assists her body in accommodating him, stops her from wanting to envenomate him."

Jem laughs, and once again, the sound envelopes me like the heat from a flame. I want more of her, so much more, and yet, making her laugh is perfection itself.

"I don't want to envenomate you, Draxx."

"I would hope not. I would be useless to you for some time if you did."

Jem laughs and dips her head back to the tip of my cock, sucking at my slowly developing hook and sending me spiraling. My shift threatens, but I cannot take her in shifted form for the first time. Her body has to accept me first, and given how tiny she is, the more cum I can get into her the better.

She is also far too clothed for my liking. I pull my cock from her mouth, despite my desire to keep it there.

"Lie back," I growl. "I want to see you bare for me before I enjoy your beautiful cunt."

Jem's eyebrows bunch. She hitches herself back obligingly. I carefully remove her other boot and then slip her out of her pants. She shudders as the cool air hits her, but the aroma of her arousal is as intoxicating as ever.

I want to see more. Every instinct in my body is telling me to tear away what's left of her clothing, but instead, I peel at it, removing layer after layer until her gorgeous breasts appear, skin smooth and tipped with bright red nipples. I tease at one with my tongue, and she groans, her back arching, pushing herself into my mouth.

This female will be the death of me yet.

JEM

"My Jem. My treasure," Draxx growls over my nipple, his forked tongue teasing at the taut peak and sending shockwaves down into my pussy. "You are made for me."

My mind is a mess of all these new sensations. Not only does Draxx have a cock, but it emerges from a slit, and it is, quite simply, a baseball bat of a meat truncheon. I know he is huge and green, but his cock is something else entirely. I can't get my hand around it, every inch of the thing is covered in hard, ridged scales, and the tip is both broad and shaped like a hook with yet more armor plating.

Whatever he might think about his seed, that thing is *not* going to fit.

But hell, I am going to try. The way he plucks my desires from me, makes my body sing, and my heart beat, it's something else.

I *want* Draxx, more than I've ever wanted anyone or anything. I want to ride this monster to completion.

I clutch at him, but he's not giving way, even if that huge cock is pressing between my thighs, the slick of his pre-cum smearing my skin and tingling even more than the stuff he put on my ankle.

I'm hopelessly wet, not sure if I've ever been wetter in my entire life as he slides a hand down my body and dips between my folds.

"Hmmm," he rumbles over a nipple, captured between his teeth as he sucks and sends stars rolling through my vision. "This juicy cunt wants Sarkarnii cock, doesn't it?"

"Y-yes." I'm shoving myself into him because the scent of his smoke, his musk, the feel of his soft, slippery scales against my skin, his bulk pressed over me, is overwhelming. "Let me have it," I moan into his ear, nibbling at the soft shell and feeling him buck.

The only sign of his self-control slipping. Oh god, I want it to slip. I want him inside me.

"I've already warned you, mate," he rasps. "I need at least two orgasms before I impale you on my cock. If you do not do as you are told, there will be consequences."

My pussy rushes with moisture at his words. I've never wanted *consequences* more in my life.

But then I also want to see if I can take the beast he has between his legs. I squirm under him and earn myself a growl and a stare, followed by the most incredible dominating kiss which leaves me panting as he drops down my body, tongue tasting every inch of me until he reaches my mound.

"Such a delightful wet cunt, ready to come on my tongue," Draxx rumbles, one hand spread out on my stomach, covering the entire thing and holding me down.

My body wants to react, but I cannot help obey his command. He stares at me for what seems like a long while, then he licks up his finger and bites away his claw before liberally and slowly coating the clawless digit with the pre-cum which is still running from him like a tap. With the wickedest of smiles, he teases between my folds, and the tingling I felt on my tongue when I licked him is replicated in my pussy.

"So delicious and tight for me, beautiful jewel," Draxx rumbles, and he slides his finger farther in.

I gasp at the heat which flows through me, the tingling becoming a flood, my vision blurring so all I can see is a green mountain towering over me, until he resolves into the monster, the beautiful monster who is playing my body like a precious instrument. He drives his finger deeper, curling it up so instead of a blur, I'm seeing stars as I convulse, clamping down on him as he groans over me, that incredible tongue lapping at my breasts, his hand spanning my waist.

I'm pinned by him, consumed by him. I belong to him.

"That's one," Draxx growls.

"I want you!" I gasp, my voice hoarse.

"Come for me again, little mate. Come for me and call my name, then you can have my cock like the good female you are."

He slams his lips onto my clit, and my arms are flailing, grabbing hold of the bedclothes as he strums my clit, both tips of his tongue working in unison before he wrings yet another climax from me, and my mind is filled with all the wonders of the universe as I writhe and pulse under him.

"So good," Draxx repeats, his voice a rasp of desire as he slips in another finger, then a third. "And so ready."

I'm already panting, already soaking with everything he's pulled from me, but the thought of his cock sends a fresh rush of moisture, flooding my thighs as he raises up and pulls me to him, hands hooked under my legs.

"I want to watch our joining, see you stretched around me," he murmurs, his eyes glazed as he looks down.

Huge wings unfold as he parts my thighs farther and notches his cock at my entrance. It feels absolutely huge, as the strangely shaped tip pushes into me. It's slick and warm with his pre-cum, and he rocks slowly, every muscle in his neck straining as he eases me open.

With every movement, he slips in just a little more, and I can feel his cum working its way into my body, my channel opening farther and farther for him until finally, in one slick movement, he drives his huge cock inside and impales me.

I gasp at the feeling of being stretched so damn wide and being filled to the brim by him.

"Good mate," he groans. "Look at you taking all of my cock."

He reaches behind me, sliding a hand under my back and lifting me into a curl until I can see where he enters me. I can't believe it, but he is buried deep, and I shudder with the erotic thrill of seeing my pussy wrapped tight around him.

Draxx supports me so I'm straddling him as he withdraws and slips back, causing both of us to exhale with pleasure. I can feel every ridge, every bump on his big green cock as he lifts me easily up his shaft and allows me to descend slowly, dangerously slowly, because I'm about to come again.

"Do you want to let go, little mate?" Draxx murmurs. "Do you want to cover my cock in your nectar?"

"Draxx!" I can't help myself as yet another orgasm crashes through my body. I hear myself scream out his name, and I'm flipped onto my back as the massive male cradles me in his arms.

"You undo me, my Jem. You make me feral for your sweetness, for your slick cunt, so nevving tight I don't think

I ever want to be free." He groans, circling his hips and driving even deeper into me.

Not only does Draxx have wings, but his tail is curling up my leg, the soft heat of his scales increasing as it nudges up against my bottom, teasing my little pucker with something warm and hard. I feel it pulse, even though I'm an ass virgin, my body wants more. It wants to consume every inch of my big green dragon.

Draxx is setting a demanding pace, and I can't believe he might be able to wring yet another climax from me, but as the ridges touch my g-spot over and over again, I can't stop myself. The edge comes, and I fall over it, my pussy clamping down hard over Draxx, and he bellows like a bull.

"Jem," he groans.

I feel his release, his hot cum firing into me, a slight nip and then a low, delicious heat which sweeps through me, pooling in my lower abdomen as my huge alien slams his fists down on either side of me, his head drooped, his muscles shaking, his cock buried in me as I'm wracked by my climax.

"Mine," Draxx growls, his chest heaving. "This cunt is mine. You are mine."

DRAXX

My head is full of her. Of my *szikra*, my mate, my heartsfire. Her scent, the feel of her skin against mine, the delicious tightness of her gorgeous pussy. My cock is still firing seed into her, my hook buried deep, my barbs gripping her tightly, ensuring her ultimate pleasure.

I don't know how long I will be like this, but I want to see her belly swell with my spend.

"Draxx," Jem says, her hand fluttering on my arm.

"My mate," I croon at her.

"That was..." She drops her head back. "I don't know what that was but...I've never experienced anything like it."

She smiles up at me, her eyes bright and two lovely little red spots on her cheeks.

"I would kill for you." I trace my knuckle down her face.

"That's comforting." Her smile deepens, and she wriggles under me, then she stops suddenly, her face clouding. "We're...locked?"

"I have hooked you, my sweet mate. My seed is filling

your womb." I breathe out in pleasure, smoke escaping from my lungs in the most delicious way possible.

"Oh." She bites her bottom lip in a way which makes me want to bite it too. "What does that mean?"

Some of the mating fog is clearing from my brain, even as my cock pumps more seed into her because she is just so nevving glorious. Of course she doesn't know how Sarkarnii mate. I don't know how humans mate. All I know is being sheathed in her is perfection, as if she was made for me.

"I have hooked you, Jem. My cock is buried in you, and until my rut decides you are filled enough, it will not release you. I have not had a *szikra* before. You are my first and so I cannot tell you when this will happen." I circle my hips, and she sighs with delight. "But I can tell you it will be most pleasurable before we finally part."

I can feel Jem's heart fluttering against me as I enclose her in my arms and my wings. Some parts of me are staying stubbornly shifted, probably because my rut demanded I take her in a shifted form, and I did not.

Nev! My cock still pulses within her. It is not finished, and with each new rush of seed, I'm hardening like I need to plough her all over again.

Jem pulls in a long breath and her smile is back. She trails a hand down my arm, gazing at my scales. "I...I like it, I think." She yawns.

"Rest, my heartsfire." I press a kiss to her forehead and then one to her lips.

Her eyes are wide open as I lean back.

"What if I don't want to rest?"

The groan I release is one straight from the very depths of my being. I did not believe I could ever feel like this again. I feel whole and I feel hungry. For her.

"What if all I want is you?"

I bury my head in the crook of her neck, breathing in all her scent and the mingling of her, me, and our mating. My cock pulses again. She is filled, but she wants more.

Nev it to the bones of my ancestors! I want more of her.

"What if I was promised *consequences* and I didn't get them?"

"Then I shall ensure you reap the harvest of those consequences, as thoroughly as you demand, my heartsfire," I growl against her skin and revel in the ripple through her body, the clench in her pussy. "Starting right now."

JEM

I'm staring at the ceiling. My body aches, in a good way. Next to me, Draxx rumbles, his chest rising and dropping slowly and evenly. The sound of him sleeping is comforting in a way I haven't felt before.

I let him in.

I enjoyed every second of it. And, what's more, as we rested before the second bout, spending time in his arms was even better. Snuggled against his warm green scales, a huge clawed hand curled around my body, his nose buried in my neck.

I felt wanted. I felt cared for.

I felt protected.

And I loved teasing him, being the brat, making him growl. Draxx makes me ten years younger, brighter...happier?

Happier.

I've been divorced and abducted by aliens and I'm actually happy?

Well, maybe I could be even better if we find the other

human women. Then my conscience would be clear. My decision I don't want to go back to Earth would be settled.

Did I make the decision with Draxx in mind? I'm not sure. I'm not sure of anything anymore, other than there's a mountain of green muscle lying next to me and I don't want to leave his side. He shifts in his sleep and releases a huff of two large smoke rings.

He is the male who gave me the best night of my life and my protesting muscles are proof of it.

Along with the ache in my belly. The one he pumped, and I mean pumped, full of cum. Several times. My stomach actually swelling with everything he put inside me. Until we fell asleep.

Whatever is in his cum, it makes the impossible possible. My head spins when I think about it.

None of this should be possible. My life was a disaster zone. But Draxx accepted me anyway.

"Hey," I say as he shifts his enormous hand to cup my chin and his thumb strokes my cheek.

His eyes are so clear, it's as if I could lose myself in the spinning flames, his pupils mere slits as he gazes at me.

"You are so real, so perfect, *szikra*." His voice is gravel pulled over sand, and despite all our activities, he smells of woodsmoke and musk which I can't stop inhaling. "I don't deserve you."

My heart stutters in my chest. This warrior, this *general* thinks he doesn't deserve me.

"I think it's probably the other way around." I smile wanly. "I'm just a little human. I'm nothing really."

"You are my everything, Jem. Sarkarnii do not choose their heartsfire. Fate chooses them, and when you find your mate, you hold on to them with everything, everything you have."

"But you lost yours." My heart turns to drumming in my chest, stamping out a beat which I don't want.

I don't want to be wrong. Again.

"No, I found her, Jem. My heartsfire, my fate, my mate. It's you. It was always you. I thought my time in the Kirakos was a genuine punishment for not being on Kaeh-Leks, for following Draco into the galaxy, for not staying with my troops and my family. But fate tells me otherwise. If I hadn't come, I would never have found you. And finding you sets my soul to rest."

My hand is on his.

"No one...no one in my entire pathetic existence has ever said anything like that to me or about me." Tears prick my eyes. "I can't say I understand fate, but..." I blink hard, wishing the water gone.

Draxx shifts his hand and captures one of my tears on his finger. He brings it to his mouth, and with his forked tongue, he licks at it with a concentrated expression, his eyes widening when he tastes the salt.

"But?"

"But maybe it's why I don't want to go back to Earth. Maybe my life there is done."

"I wouldn't want you to give up anything you didn't want to," Draxx says, his eyes studying mine. "I've lost much in my lifetime, too much. I wouldn't wish it on anyone, least of all you."

The beating against my ribs has become a fluttering, like wings which want to be free.

"Let me dance for you, my *szikra*, let me show the Kirakos, my brothers, my den warriors what you are to me. Let me claim you before them all."

I'm not sure I can trust my voice, even if I can trust Draxx with my heart. Instead, I nod at him, and he drops his head to brush his lips over mine. A kiss which becomes demanding and dominant as his hand curls around the back of my head.

Our bodies mold together as he takes control. I would have never expected to like it in a million years, but I do. I want to vest myself to him. I want him to take it all.

Including my heart.

DRAXX

I never want to leave this bed, this dwelling in the sky, this part of the Kirakos. I never want to close my eyes and not see Jem.

But someone is rattling something far below us, and it's most likely to be Litur. Our time here, and together, was irritatingly brief.

"Stay here," I say as I throw myself out of the opening, shifting into my Sarkarnii form and unfurling my wings.

I swing out over the Ragad village, and below me there is a cohort of the creatures, Litur being one of them. Far from bringing down our dwelling, it appears the movement is some sort of alarm or calling. I dip a wing and swing up into the sky, filling my lungs and taking a moment to stretch out with pleasure.

I am going to dance for my female. My mating gland pulses hard, but this time, instead of the fog from the mix, it makes me feel bigger, stronger, faster.

Draco said his rut was complicated. I'm finding it absolutely glorious. I release a ball of flame into the sky before I spiral back down to where Jem is waiting at the opening of our den, her glorious body wrapped in some of the coverings from the bed. I shift as I land, putting out an arm to sweep her back in.

"You can breathe fire!" she gasps.

"I can do many things, but most of all, I am yours." I bury my head into her neck, breathing in the scent of her which makes my heart slow and my mind clear. "I'm afraid the Ragad are waiting for us, and I need to talk with them." I pick up my weapons and the single bag which survived my shift.

Jem traces a hand over my chest. "Will you be wearing pants today?"

I splay my hands out. "I would, if I had any." I grin insolently.

She gives me a gorgeous smile in return, her eyes narrow. "That's how you're going to play this? Okay then, big guy. I'm going to get dressed." She pats my left pectoral with a smile.

"Wait." I pull her to me. "How is your injury?"

Jem puts her hand to her mouth. "I'd almost forgotten!" She looks down at her leg, still covered in the healing balm and cloths provided by the Ragad. "I can't feel a thing. That stuff is amazing."

I drop to my knees to inspect it, peeling away the dried bandage. Where her skin was a mottled blue and purple, it has returned to pink. There is a little swelling, but nothing worrisome.

Jem gently tries her weight on it again as I look up at her. She is so nevving beautiful, I want to bury myself in her sweet cunt over and over. A growl of desire rises within me.

She cups my jaw with her hand. "I like you like this." She smiles and then pulls away like the bad little female she is, her gorgeous ass swinging as she makes her way to the sanitary area at the rear of our den.

The last thing I want to do is lose sight of her, but I'm pretty sure I won't be able to get into the tiny room with or without her present, more's the pity. Instead I look forward to the day I can enjoy her in the bath within my quarters. Or maybe even take her to the natural aquium.

Is it really this easy? To one day be in the depths of the pit, wasting your time fighting ghosts, and then the next flying so nevving high it's as if there is a new wind under your wings?

Jem returns to my side, sadly fully dressed, which means I can only kiss the bare skin on her neck. She leans into me, and all I want to do is devour her.

But the Ragad are waiting, and I release the catch on the raising/lowering mechanism which allows our den to slowly descend to where Litur stands.

He gives my mate a little bow.

"I trust you are fully healed, mate of Draxx," he says.

Jem gives her ankle a slow circle. "I am." She smiles at him, and I simultaneously want to kill him and kiss her. "Thank you."

Litur bows again. "It is our honor to assist and to have both you and your mate in our small part of this world."

I pull Jem into my side. Litur extends a pair of long pincers in the direction of a large opening in the cliff face where a number of other Ragad are waiting. With no ceremony, I lift Jem into my arms and stride off in the direction indicated.

"Draxx!" she hisses at me. "What are you doing?"

"I don't care if you feel better. Until I'm sure you are healed, I will carry you."

Jem makes a sweet growling noise under her breath. Then she relaxes into me.

"Okay, onwards, Jeeves." She giggles at me.

"Who is this Jeeves? If he wishes to carry you, I will remove his arms," I snarl.

Jem only laughs harder. "It's you, Draxx! It's a name humans sometimes give those who serve them."

I huff out a stream of smoke, utterly confused and yet, the way she settles into me, her tiny hands clutching at my forearm, I see she is teasing me.

"I will aways serve you, my treasure, but there will also always be consequences later," I murmur into her hair.

The flood of her delicious arousal hits me and sends my head spinning. If I thought the rut made things clearer, I was wrong. I want to set her down, rend her clothing, and mate her in my shifted form in the middle of the Ragad village.

But I don't think Jem will appreciate it as much as I might, so instead we continue towards the cave entrance, where I find there has been food laid out.

Having settled her on a comfortable bench and selected the choicest items for her platter, I realize there is no meat available.

"We have what you require, Sarkarnii warrior," Litur says with a gentle laugh as a smaller Ragad hands me a carrying pouch made out of vegetation, the waxy leaves which grow all around this place.

Inside is a slab of red, raw meat. If I was hungry before I saw the food, with the rut, my shift, and all the mating, I am ravenous.

The food lasts for two bites. Jem coughs, her hand over her mouth and her eyes dancing with delight.

"Mating is a seriously energy heavy business." Litur

motions for another basket. "And an important one for a Sarkarnii."

Jem is handed a platter of cooked items as another hunk of meat is offered up to me. It too disappears quickly, and I note my mate is also making swift work of her food. My body warms with the knowledge.

"Why are you in this prison, Litur? Your species are hardly the criminal kind," I say, leaning back and chewing on yet another chunk of meat.

"I could say the same of the Sarkarnii," he replies.

"Hardly. Have you met my brother, Drega? He's stolen from over half of the galaxy. The arrival of our ship in any spaceport had most jewel traders quaking." I huff out a laugh of my own accompanied by smoke and a couple of embers.

Jem makes a choking noise. "I thought you were *entirely* innocent, Draxx." She laughs.

"Not entirely." I hitch my top lip for a flash of fang and revel in the expression of surprise on her face.

"The Kirakos is the home planet of the Ragad," Litur says, oblivious to the sweet perfume coming from my mate. "And we need Sarkarnii help to set it free."

JEM

Draxx slaps the enormous hunk of meat down on the table beside him.

"We came here for one purpose only—to find the star map which will lead us to any of our other brethren left out in the universe." He cocks his head to one side as if listening to an internal voice. "But it has been a long time since I went into battle."

He grins as he picks his food back up and takes an enormous bite with a mouth suddenly full of teeth. Draxx is a predator. I guess all of the Sarkarnii are, given they turn into *dragons*, but right now, I'm more amazed he wants me than anything else.

But also, my soul warms at his words. He and his brothers are here for one thing and yet he is prepared to do what it takes to help others.

Like helping find the other humans.

"Can you help us too?" I butt in. "There are other humans like me in this maze. We were looking for them when we ended up here. Do you know where they are?"

"You have certainly ended up a long way from your

quadrant." Litur's leg twitches, and he looks very insect-y. I do my best not to shudder. "There are no humans here."

A smaller version of Litur scuttles up to him, and I really wish I didn't have particular views on insects, given the galaxy I'm living in could be full of insect based life-forms. It strums its legs over Litur's and then scampers away.

"Humans are being kept in the undercroft," Litur says, as if he's received a text.

Not weird at all.

"I knew that," Draxx says with a mouth full of meat he clearly can't resist. "We were heading to the warden-controlled areas in order to rescue them when the Belek released a vesso."

"The Wardens are not sure what to do with their new human pets," Litur says with a tone I'm not entirely sure I like. "They understand humans have a way of controlling the Kirakos with their DNA, but they do not understand why or how."

My arm gives me a residual throb. My memory of the time before Draxx rescued me is hazy, but what exactly was the slug warden doing to me?

"I don't understand. You said I was from the *old* galaxy. Compared to what I've seen just in this prison, humans are inferior in so many ways, I can't even count. How can we possibly control the Kirakos?" I fold my arms with a furrowed brow.

"Precisely because you are from the old galaxy. This planet was part of your galaxy once too."

"Okay, that's not possible. Humans have been tracking planets for thousands of years. We'd notice if one went missing."

"From your solar system, yes." Litur's tone is light,

amused, as his weird green-black eyes glitter with a thousand prisms. "But not from your *galaxy*."

I pinch at the bridge of my nose. This is getting far too like science for my less than scientific brain. "So, somehow human DNA is here? How did it get to the Kirakos from Earth?"

Litur does the head movement thing, and suddenly I realize why it's so familiar. Why the Ragad are so familiar.

"You've been to Earth?" I exclaim.

It's as if something deep inside me, some sort of long lost ancestral knowledge, is buried and rises to the surface. A remembrance from long ago.

"When the human race was young, the Ragad visited. Our species is very ancient. We liked Earth. We liked humans."

"You abducted them?" I feel my hands balling into fists. Beside me, Draxx picks up on my distress, and he releases a low, blood curdling growl.

Litur takes a step back. They might resemble the predatory insects on Earth, but they know when they're outclassed by Sarkarnii.

"No, not at all. Our species studied humans. So unique in this universe, so wild, so free."

Draxx lets rip with another deep growl which may well be overkill, but I'm going with it. There is a rattling around us, and out of the corner of my eye, even though Litur might have moved back, I can see some of the other Ragad are moving forward with long, sharp poles.

If they think those are going to, in any way, hurt Draxx, they are sorely mistaken.

"My ancestors believed human DNA was pure enough and hidden enough it could be used for many things," Litur says hastily, head swiveling back to where his comrades are approaching. "But without the need for actual human involvement."

"You took DNA and not humans?"

"Your DNA does get everywhere," Litur says with what has to be a chuckle.

I shrug. From the limited amount of exposure I've had to crime TV shows, I know we shed DNA easily. "That's true."

As I relax, I feel Draxx do so too beside me.

"With human DNA, we were able not only to build better technology but to design programs like the one you seek, Draxx," Litur says.

"You designed the star map?" Draxx sits forward, interest piqued.

"Not me, but others like me. It's the reason it is housed here."

"Wait. Housed in a prison?"

"The Kirakos was not always a prison. The Belek chose it because it can be propelled, moved, changed, as we designed it to be."

"So, you allow them to use it?" Draxx's growl is back, his eyes dark as his pupils widen, claws extend, including the one he bit off last night, shorter than the rest but still sharp. "You allow all the poor creatures of the galaxy to be incarcerated here at the whim of others?"

"And what sort of protection do you think we gain from living in the heart of it?" Litur queries, his tone harsh.

"And if the Wardens get hold of your technology? What then for the rest of the galaxy?" Draxx spits out fire, smoke filling the air above him. "You think the Belek care about anything other than themselves? Why else do you think the place is filled with all different species, including humans? They're trying to gain access to your nevving tech!"

He's on his feet and pacing now.

Litur shifts from leg to leg to leg, his head swiveling to follow Draxx's progress with some concern. The Ragad know how dangerous the Sarkarnii are, and I'm fucking glad they do.

"We put in safeguards."

"What safeguards could you possibly have put in in order to stop the Belek? They'll do anything to gain control and make some credits." Draxx snarls, flames licking from his mouth and nose. "And we were called pirates!" He releases a harsh laugh and glares at Litur.

"The map, along with other elements coded into the Kirakos, can only be unlocked when a human mates with one other species within the Kirakos."

Draxx's growl reverberates around the low cave.

"Which species?" I can hardly get the words out.

"The Sarkarnii," Litur replies. "And only the Sarkarnii."

DRAXX

"You did this deliberately?" Jem is staring at Litur. I can't fathom the look on her face, but her body has gone all stiff and again, and my anger, my need to protect her, rises within me and is released as a flame which has all the Ragad standing back.

Jem does not move. She doesn't even look at me.

"We knew the Sarkarnii from our time on Kaeh-Leks. An honorable race who should have never ended up in the Kirakos," Litur says quickly. "Humans should not either. We never expected their planet in the old galaxy to be found."

"But you bloody found Earth though, didn't you?" Jem snarls at Litur.

Her anger matches mine, and for once, I'm embracing the anger. It's pure, not born of my feelings of failure.

"And as for the Sarkarnii, what did you know of Kaeh-Leks and the threats to my planet?"

"We attempted to warn you of the Liderc, but our species was not well known. Our pleas were ignored by those in charge."

My anger stutters. Jem looks at me, then she gets to her feet and walks away.

"This is not over, Ragad," I snarl at Litur.

"We took two species, from opposite ends of the known universe, Draxx," Litur says, extending his mandibles in an action of peace. "You were never intended to come together."

"But fate is fate," I say. "You might think to manipulate it, but there is no denying it."

"You are the product of your ancestors, the original High Bask." Litur fixes me with his swirling eyes. "Fate does not drive this universe."

"I think you've just proved it does."

I turn, my tail and wings shifting because all I want to do is get to my mate who is rapidly walking across the clearing in front of the meeting cave and back toward the river. Regardless of who knows about the Igered, she cannot be alone.

My Jem must always be protected. With a couple of simple wing beats, I am by her side. She doesn't look at me. She keeps on walking, her entire body radiating anger.

I know anger.

"My Jem." I put out a hand to touch her, but she jerks her arm away.

"I've been broken too often for this not to be real," she snarls under her breath. "For it all to be an engineered illusion of...I don't know what."

She stomps ahead of me, but we've reached the river, and she has to stop. I stand next to her, following her to gaze into the clear water which flows swiftly through the valley, its clean scent mingling with hers.

My beautiful heartsfire, my soul. My everything.

"*Szikra*, if we were never meant to be together, then our

match was written in the stars." This time, I take her hand, resisting her attempt to pull back as I turn her to me. "And if fate decrees we are to be together, then I will kill anything, anything at all which tries to pull us apart, on my honor as a Sarkarnii warrior and as General of the One Hundred Armies."

Her eyes are filled with water again, the water which is salty and which indicates she is unhappy. I do not want my mate unhappy.

"Do not be sad, my mate. I don't ever want you to be sad. I want you filled, claimed, rounded with my Sarkarn-ling, but most of all, I want you smiling and laughing. I want you to be content, with me."

Jem sniffles, wipes at her nose with the back of her hand, and bright, bright eyes stare up at me.

"All my life, I've wanted to belong. I've wanted not to have to fight for everything, whether it was love, or affection, or just the simple right not to be passed over for promotion in my damn job." She drops her chin to her chest, removing her beautiful gaze from mine.

I slide my finger underneath and lift her back up so I can see her, my thumb caressing her cheek.

"You don't have to fight for me, heartsfire. I am already yours. I was yours from the first moment I saw you, and I will be yours until the end of time. That is what it means to be mated to a Sarkarnii. Our hearts cannot be traded, bought, or joined in any other way. I love you. I will always love you."

I grip at her chin.

"I have you, my Jem. Because that is what fate is. Two species from either end of the Universe who were never meant to meet. But we did, and here we are."

More water runs from her eyes, down her cheeks, warm

on my skin. She is still unhappy. I cradle her face in my hands, swiping over her cheeks, desperate to stop the water.

"Please, please, my Jem, do not be sad. I want to burn the galaxy to ash when you're sad." I lean into her, taking her lips, tasting the salt and the moisture.

She leans into me, no longer pushing me away, her sweet mouth receiving mine because my *szikra* is perfection indeed.

"I'm not sad," she says when I let her up for air, her voice rough. "Sometimes humans cry because we're happy too. I am happy you want me. I'm happy about everything you said."

"You make water from your eyes because you are happy too?" I huff out some smoke as I study her face. "How do I know which is which?"

Jem puts her hands over mine. They look tiny and pink next to my scales which flow and spark under her touch. She leans into me, and her lips touch mine again before she whispers in my ear.

"You'll know, Draxx. I promise. You'll know."

JEM

So, I'm a human abducted from Earth. I have no agency. I have nothing but a massive Sarkarnii warrior who wants to burn the place down because I'm sad.

This is not how I expected things to turn out, but I am absolutely going to go with it. Because the main thing is Draxx wants me!

Me.

The second I thought our meeting was engineered by the Ragad, or that there was something which made Draxx find me attractive, I genuinely thought my heart was going to implode.

And if I lost my heart to him, I knew it was the end. I've guarded it for so damn long, I've done my level best not to let anyone hurt me, even if it meant I ended up in a loveless marriage, because the little child in me, the one staring up at my adoptive parents hoping for love and care and who didn't get it—that child has been carried with me all this time.

But I just watched her walk away, down the valley,

never to be seen again.

Because I have Draxx.

Because he loves me.

My big green mountain of fire and muscle folds me into him, and he's so warm I could happily spend the rest of my life permanently attached to him. Although the way he likes to carry me around, that might be a possibility.

And I'm not going to say no.

In fact. I think saying 'yes' to everything is my new mantra.

"We need to get back to Draco and Drega, tell them about the Ragad and the whole human/Sarkarnii mating situation. Then we need to try again to reach the humans you saw," Draxx says, his words reverberating through his chest and into my ear.

"Yes," I say.

"It was important before, but now we must make sure we free them from the Wardens, more than ever. No creature, especially the humans, should be at their mercy."

"Yes," I agree.

Draxx narrows his eyes at me, his hands still on my face.

"I agree," I add. "But then finding the other humans was always my thing so..." I shrug.

A smile creeps over Draxx's face, as if he's never smiled in his entire life. It's not fangs, it's not a grin, but absolute joy.

"My mate." He drops his head to gently bump his forehead on mine.

I'm enveloped by the smoke and musk smell of him, and it is so, so good. His forked tongue brushes over my lips, and I get a hint of what might be to come, provided we survive the trip back to where his brothers live. The taste of him sets me on fire.

"You need to be careful, little mate," Draxx rasps. "If you make my cock emerge from my pouch, I will make you sit on it, whether we are in the center of the Ragad village or not."

A shiver runs through me. I've never been one for public sex, but somehow the way Draxx puts it makes me want to.

"What if that's what I desire?" I lick over my lips, and his hips buck towards me in a way I know is involuntary.

If I can make my dragon warrior come undone...

A toothy smile replaces his other one, far too much fang and far too dangerous a glitter in his eyes.

"You will always get what you ask for from me, little mate," he rumbles. "Just ask for it."

"I -er." We're too exposed, and Draxx is absolutely calling my bluff.

"Oh, sweet *szikra*, you know what the consequences are for setting my fire alight." He leans into me, so his mouth is right next to my ear. "They are when I will bend you over and take you in my Sarkarnii form."

My knees go weak, and a huge hand slides under my back to hold me up as my brain struggles to catch up with what he has just told me, as lust overtakes everything else.

"We'll head back to my quadrant now," Draxx says out loud. It's then I see the gathering of Ragad around us. They look benign enough. "We have some humans to locate and some Wardens to dispose of."

A tail curls around my feet.

This is going to be interesting.

"My hive-brother will take you to the entrance," Litur says, handing Draxx a small clear square. "This will guide you the rest of the way."

Draxx takes it from him and tucks it into the bag he has slung across his body, along with the rest of his weapons.

"When this is over, we will return," he says to Litur. "We need answers."

"And you will get them," Litur says, his long front legs waving in the air animatedly. "I need to speak with my kin, but seeing you with Jem," he taps one leg back on the ground, "it has changed what we intended. I hope we can provide assistance when needed too. But regardless, we will meet again."

Draxx huffs out some smoke and then slides his arm around my waist. "Time to go, mate," he says as one of the Ragad peels away from the rest and starts to walk down the side of the river.

"Here." Litur takes a green woven sack made out of reeds from the mandibles of another Ragad and hands it to Draxx. "Sustenance for your journey."

Draxx gives him a little bow, eyes not leaving the assembled Ragad for a second. He's not on edge but watchful, ready, like any predator. Then we turn and follow the swinging rear end of the Ragad who heads back towards the cliffs we climbed down the other day.

It seems like a lifetime ago. Draxx's arm is warm around me and I feel...safe. I trust him and he trusts me. The enjoyment of being quiet in each other's company as we slowly wind our way back to the huge slab wall and begin to ascend spreads like hot chocolate through me.

Draxx is many things—slightly unhinged, lover of all things violent, but he is also my hot chocolate. Sweet, satisfying, and endlessly pleasing. I snuggle into his side, breathing in his scent of smoke and musk. It doesn't matter what comes next.

Because I have him.

DRAXX

The rut roars through my veins. The last thing I want is to be reliant on the Ragad to get my mate back to the relative safety of the Sarkarnii quarter. I need Jem all to myself. I need to fill her again, I need my cock to stop pushing its way out of my pouch, I need...

To take a breath. Jem is by my side. She isn't going anywhere. I was a nevving Sarkarnii general once. Where the nev has my composure gone?

It's gone with the mating mix and my refusal to engage with my den-warriors once we arrived here and were collared. Not being able to shift nearly broke me.

I am not the same Sarkarnii I was before we ended up incarcerated in the Kirakos, nor am I the same as the general who led armies across the vast plains of Kaeh-Leks.

With all the mix the rut has put into my system, I don't ever want to be the same again. I want to devour my treasure, protect her, and keep her.

"Everything okay, Draxx?" Jem is looking up at me. "You're growling."

I want to lift her into my arms, but something tells me

it's probably not a good idea, given we are some way up the cliff face.

"I'm fine, my *szikra*. I am considering our next move, once we are rid of this Ragad." I smile down at her.

Probably with too much fang as her beautiful brow furrows at me. "We're going after the humans, aren't we?"

I contemplate the position for a moment or two. "As much as I know I can take on whatever the Wardens wish to throw at me, I cannot, in all honesty as a warrior, say I want to do so without assistance."

"Oh," Jem says, and I want to pop my thumb in her mouth, have her suck it like she sucked the tip of my cock.

"I don't need an army, but I do need my den-warriors. It's not just about finding and releasing the humans, my mate. It's about taking control."

Jem huffs at me. "It should be about finding creatures who are at the mercy of others wanting to do them harm, nothing else." She absently rubs at her arm.

The one injured before I was able to pull her from the Belek's clutches.

"I agree, Jem. But what was a foray into enemy territory has become so much more. Draco and Drega need this information. We need to plan our next move carefully."

Jem doesn't look at me. Instead, she watches her feet as we continue to climb. I dislike her silence.

"I just feel responsible for them, you know," she says to the ground. "They weren't even awake. I could have done something, but I didn't. I couldn't."

I don't hold back any more. I take my mate into my arms and hold her, ignoring the Ragad staring impassively at us.

"But you will help them, soon. You have my word as a Sarkarnii warrior, as the General of the One Hundred

Armies." I dip my head to touch her lips with mine. "As your mate, my heartsfire."

Jem raises herself up, arching into my kiss, my tongue sweeping her, owning her, except she owns me.

I am no longer Draco's brother, a member of the High Bask, or the general.

I am hers.

"Well then, General Draxx, I will hold you to your word," Jem says when I release her.

There are two gorgeous red spots on her cheeks, her eyes are half-lidded, and although she smells strongly of our mating from last night, there is a new aroma of her arousal which has my cock aching to be free of my pouch.

"I should think so, heartsfire," I rumble into the soft skin at the nape of her neck.

The nevving Ragad chirps his hind legs annoyingly, causing me to snarl and smoke. He takes a step back.

"You can re-enter the undercroft here." He indicates a large boulder.

I release Jem in order to inspect it. The stone is large, but if I shift, I should be able to move it easily. The Ragad disappears down the side of the cliff in the instant my body changes. I grip at the now much smaller boulder.

"Draxx?" Jem is inside the cliff, and only her head is visible. "What are you doing? You'll never fit in here if you're that size." Her head disappears.

I hesitate for a seccari. I want to remain Sarkarnii to protect her, but if she's inside the cliff, I cannot do so. With a final flourish of my wings, I shift back and step to one side of the boulder.

Hidden from view, in a way which plays tricks on the eye, is the entrance. I should have known. Even in the center of the maze, nothing is simple. Everything is a puzzle. With some difficulty because my tail is having absolutely none of the whole shifting back situation, I squeeze my way inside.

Surrounded by a green glowing light, my Jem stands waiting for me. Her smile is enough light for me in my life. She holds a light stick from a pile next to the entrance.

"The Ragad must occasionally leave the Igered." I pick up a light stick and inspect it. "It is strange we have not seen them."

"Everyone has secrets," Jem says. "Maybe they only came out at night."

I'm beside her in a heartbeat, a little flame flickering from my nostrils. "I am as deadly in the night as in the day, little mate," I rasp in her ear.

"I should hope so." She laughs at me. "You're big and bad enough."

It doesn't matter the passage is narrow, too narrow for what I want to do to my mate. I still clutch her to me, my tongue licking at her skin, tasting her.

"And you are a delicious snack I don't deserve, but I'm going to devour you anyway."

The second Draxx says he doesn't deserve me, my heart flip-flops in my chest.

"You do." I stroke my forefinger over Draxx's scaled cheek. "But bear in mind, you're not exactly getting the best end of the deal if all you deserve is me."

"By the bones of my ancestors," Draxx croons in my ear. "They gave me the best when they sent you to me."

I want to laugh, and I want to cry. I've never thought of myself as "the best." A nuisance, yes. Unworthy, yes.

Not the best of anything. Not the best for this huge warrior who can change into a dragon at will. And whose tail is presently curling around my leg, the tip tickling my thigh.

"I want you so very much," Draxx murmurs, his breath soft on my cheek, his chest heaving.

The tail slides higher. He is unable to contain himself. My big, brave warrior is losing control.

Not that Draxx has much control, and I love that about him. I love he does what he wants, when he wants. I love his chaos, his desire for control, and his complete lack of it.

Suddenly, he stills, his tail clutching me. "Hold up the light stick a little more, sweet mate," he says.

I lift the glow stick which is far brighter than any glow stick I've ever had before. Draxx swaps me from arm to arm, and he studies the wall to our right. There are symbols on it, ones I find I vaguely recognize, despite them being in a language I cannot read.

"What is it?"

"These are directions throughout the Kirakos. The Ragad must have mapped every nevving part of it," he says, voice deep and dark as he studies the markings.

"Is it going to help us get back to your quarter?"

"Most certainly," Draxx says. "But more than that." He places a claw on one of the symbols. "This is going to help us find both the humans and deal with the Wardens. I've seen it in the control room."

"Control room?" I query as, with an all too short snuggle, Draxx releases me.

"Draco's mate led us to a control room, one which had the necessary technology to assist us in locating the star map and gaining power over our own quarter. It also has various assets which have helped us keep one step ahead of the wardens, but this marking has been puzzling all of us."

I stare at it. To me, it looks like a hieroglyph from ancient Egypt, a dagger stabbed through an eye, a tree growing strong.

"The soldier of fortune." The words trip out of my mouth, and I gasp, covering it with my hand. "I don't know why I said that. I can't read any of this."

Draxx traces his claw down the list of symbols. "Soldier of fortune or warrior. You are correct, my mate. It was the fortune part we could not decipher. But now we have our treasure." His eyes glitter at me in the glowing green light. Sparks fly around his scales. "It's you, my mate."

He breaks another glow stick and hands it to me before taking my free hand and ushering me ahead of him. Occasionally, we stop for Draxx to consult the map given to him by Litur, the clear square lighting up as he traces the pad of a finger over it, huge claw hovering like a dagger above.

Each time, he turns to me, smiles, and my heart seemingly turns to liquid. I don't profess to understand any of this or what my place is in this new world, but I do know that being here, with Draxx, is the place I want to be.

We reach a dead end.

"Where now?" I ask.

Draxx's smile widens, and he points a vicious claw upwards. I follow his gesture, and high above us is a pinprick of light.

"You can't fly up there," I say. "It's not wide enough."

But when I look back, he's already changing, scales flipping, a whirl of energy, of beauty, and of change, until I have dragon Draxx filling the space.

He drops his huge head until his massive eye is level with my face. He is a dragon, eye slitted and filled with fire, skin scaled, hard, beautiful. A great muzzle out of which flicks a long, dark, forked tongue.

"I don't need to fly to protect my mate."

I'm scooped up in a set of claws the size of elephant's rib bones and deposited on a scaly back, in between his wings, folded hard against his body.

"Hold on, heartsfire," Draxx rumbles, and his bulk moves under me.

I lurch to one side with a yelp, grabbing at the spikes at the rear of his huge scaled neck for balance. Draxx makes a deep growling sound, a shiver running through his body, then he goes vertical, those great claws slamming into the stone as he climbs. The noise is incredible as he moves with ease up and up. The bones of his back create a natural seat for me. So as long as I hold tight, I'm in no danger of falling.

In fact, the movement of him under me as he climbs is having all of the wrong effects. Or right ones. Is it okay to get aroused when your big warrior, who's just turned into a dragon, has you on his back and is demonstrating his strength and size in a very sexy way?

"*Szikra*, you are a little distracting." Draxx turns his head on his long neck disconcertingly to look at me, even while he continues climbing.

"Sorry," I say and shift my position, but I think that makes it worse.

Draxx resumes his climb. "You like my shifted form, little treasure?"

I gently squeeze the bony spurs on his wings. "Yes." It's easy to say because this huge beast I'm riding is one I've already had.

"Good," he rasps. "Because I fully intend on taking you and hooking you, just as soon as we are back in my quarters."

Oh. Dear. God.

DRAXX

I f I could climb faster, I would, but the last thing I want to do is dislodge the female who perches on my back because I have much greater plans for her. The mere thought of caging her under me, flipping her over and sliding my cock into her willing cunt has the thing pushing out of my pouch.

Nev the fact we have to get back to the Sarkarnii quarter, and I need to report my findings to Draco. I have a female, I am in rut, and nothing else matters. The light above us is growing larger as I spike my claws into the rock. I know where I'm going to come out, and if I'm right, I will need all my wits about me when I do.

I absolutely do not need them concentrated in my pouch and cock. Jem isn't just distracting, the scent of her arousal means I will do something I don't mean to. Both desire and violence rise within me, warring and entwining. Jem is the creature who grounds me, who makes me whole.

She is my heartsfire.

The top of the shaft is nearing, and I slow my climb.

"We are not in the Sarkarnii quarter yet, my mate," I tell her. "This is the pit."

"The pit?"

"The place all those who have been in the Kirakos a long time end up. The lost, the wild, the feral, and the dangerous are here."

I clamber over the top, finding we are in one of the main chambers, as I had hoped.

And it is filled with Mosum. They bare their teeth, knives glinting in the light from above. The light I followed to get my Jem out of danger and the light I will see again soon.

"Hold tight." I release a sheet of flame which has them all running. Spears and blades clatter off my scales as I open my wings wide.

I feel Jem scrabbling at my back to get a further hold on the bony spurs I raise on the back of my neck.

"Go, Draxx, go!" she cries out, voice strong and filled with confidence.

I let rip with another stream of flame and roar of anger, and it frees me. She frees me from this place, this hole I hid myself in. I will emerge a Sarkarnii reborn.

With a couple of beats, we're in the air and in a few more, we are out of the pit and in the air above the Kirakos. I do a lazy turn as I orient myself, and I hear Jem on my back. She's whooping with joy.

Forget nevving Draco. This little mate has to be claimed, right now.

I spin around as quickly as I can in my descent, shifting as soon as I can once we're on the ground, swirling Jem from my back to my arms, pressing my lips to hers and eating up her delicious squeak of alarm.

"Don't we…" she gasps as I swing her through the doors of my quarters and head for my bedroom.

"If I don't mate you within the next seccari, *szikra,* I will not be responsible for my actions."

"I should think so." Jem pouts up at me and my rut roars in my veins, my mating gland filling every inch of me with mix.

"Oh, you do, do you? Are you ready to deal with a Sarkarnii general in rut?" I growl as I toss her onto the bed.

"And what's different this time, Draxx?" she says, her eyes bright with badness.

"Everything." My voice is a mere rasp as she places a trembling hand on my breast, and the heat which infuses within me has my mating gland thrumming beneath my skin.

"I am different, my treasure. I am different because of you." I trace a claw through her hair, down onto her clothing. "I am whole because of you." She shudders as the claw hooks into the material. "Do you trust me, little mate?"

Her eyes are closed, and she surrenders herself to me with a breathy, "Yes."

I slice through the flimsy stuff as if it is nothing, stripping her bare with an ease I wasn't expecting but most definitely enjoy. My cock has fully emerged from its pouch, and a stream of pre-cum is already hitting the floor with a sound like a waterfall.

"Taste me," I order, and Jem's eyelids flutter open.

My cum splatters her naked form as I lift myself over her, one clawed hand cradling her body as she parts her lips and I drool into her mouth. She swallows, and her pupils dilate as my seed settles into her system.

"Are you ready to take your Sarkarnii mate, my heartsfire? Take all he has, be filled and stretched?"

She moans in response as I flip her over, exposing her delicious cunt to me. She's already slick with moisture which glistens around her thighs as I prop her on her front, supporting her in my claws, I part her, exposing her more to me as I slip my cock between her folds, coating her with my seed, slipping the head in and out until she moans and arches her back.

I feel the flood on me as I push deeper inside her, inching my way in as she opens to me.

"Oh, you feel so good, little mate, my sweet one, wrapped around my Sarkarnii cock, such a good, good mate."

JEM

Draxx feels even bigger than before. I'm entirely supported by him, huge claws sheathed as he traces another hand down my back, making me shiver, his cock pressing at my entrance which is dripping wet. The sweet, tingling, fizzy feeling from his amazing pre-cum buzzes through my body.

I want him, all of him, including his dragon.

"Take me, all of me," I whisper. "I'm yours, now and forever."

Draxx rumbles, and I feel him slide inside me just a little more, but it's not enough. I wriggle on his hand, pushing myself back, impaling myself on him, every single last one of those ridges scraping over my channel and making me feel incredible.

I feel the press of his huge stomach against me as finally he seats himself. Something teases up my leg, and as I drop my head, chest heaving as I adjust to the huge member only just contained within me, I spot the tip of a scaly green tail. It teases at my folds, tripping ever so lightly over my clit and making me see stars like I've never seen before.

"Nev! You look so beautiful stretched over my cock, treasure," Draxx rasps as my pussy flutters over him, pulsing and grasping as the orgasm takes me to new heights.

The tail tip dances farther up, over a buttock until its teasing at my tight pucker.

"Draxx..."

"Just breathe, little one. Let me take you, fill your every hole with Sarkarnii."

My bottom tingles in the same way my pussy does as Draxx withdraws his cock achingly slowly and the very tip of his tail slides through the ring of muscle, creating a burn which causes me to hold my breath, and he makes a gorgeous snickering sound which sends my stomach into spasms, and my channel is soaked once again. I breathe out, and the tail slips in deeper, just as Draxx slides back inside me.

"So...full..." I stumble over the words as pure pleasure courses through my veins.

I'm stretched to my very limit by this gorgeous male and all I want is...

"More."

"More, little morsel? You think you can take more of me? When you're stretched so tight and filled so well?"

"More."

I feel Draxx contracting against me, his huge ridged belly stroking over my buttocks.

"Little mate, you will be the death of me." His words are hissed in my ear, then a forked tongue laps up my naked back as Draxx drives his cock and his tail in.

I am stretched to the breaking point. I can't take any more of this beast, and yet I want more. As if to answer my desires, Draxx pumps at me, taking no prisoners as I am sandwiched in his hands, held fast as he fucks me long and hard, my body consumed by him, my mind a whirl of lust and pleasure, my orgasms coming thick and fast. Each time I pulse over him, my channels clamping down hard on his tail and cock, he roars with desire, until I feel a pinch and a hot wave in my stomach.

I'm tipped over the edge again, shocked I'm climaxing when there have been so many, but the more I buck, the more he comes, and I can feel my belly filling with everything my delicious Draxx can give me.

"My sweet mate," he croons in my ear as he withdraws his tail, his cock remaining buried deep within.

I feel his shift, the reduction of the bulk behind me, but as I always anticipated, his cock remains the same whatever form he takes. Draxx might have shifted, but he's still coming as he rolls us onto the bed, making me comfortable, one massive hand splayed over my inflated belly, which both aches and feels incredible, wracking my body with continuous aftershocks.

He nibbles his way up my shoulder and neck, staring down at the swelling he's created with only his cum. A swelling which is continuing as his chest heaves and his hips flip involuntarily against my bottom.

"Nev, little one, you take me so well. Look at my seed filling you." He strokes a huge thumb around the edge of my swollen stomach, making me shiver and flutter over his cock.

Lips kiss at my skin, and that talented tongue swipes over my skin as Draxx encloses me in his unshifted bulk, hips still circling, chest still rumbling with pleasure. I am enclosed, I am full to bursting, and most of all, I am his.

My eyes close, and I drift off with a contentment surrounding me I've never felt before. I never thought I would want any of this, a dominant, possessive, and frankly, half feral partner. But Draxx is the dream made real.

"Heartsfire." I hear his velvet voice as if down a long corridor. "You are claimed, and I will dance for you in the morning."

———

A long, low hiss filters into my sleepy mind.

"Don't mind me, little mate. You don't need to wake," Draxx murmurs in my ear, his massive bulk rising over me, his cock already inside, stretching my soaking pussy wide, all the cum he filled me with before making his entry oh-so-easy.

He rolls his hips, achingly slowly, as my core pulses and my hips lift, allowing him easier access so he can sink in deep. Real deep.

I've lost count of how many times we've done this, but him waking me like this is a first and I love it.

I think I might love him.

Wait. What?

"Jem." Draxx moans my name as he withdraws and pounds back into me, his body getting larger as he shifts. "I'm sorry. I needed to be in you. I hope you don't mind. I am in rut."

He lifts my legs, and I open wider for him, allowing my big, green muscle mountain to get farther, to grind himself against my clit, the rough scales just above his cock sending spikes of pleasure. I lift my hips. He's so big I can't wrap my legs around him, so I'm here for the ride.

And to try to ignore the strange feeling I've told him how I feel, I've revealed myself to him as he curls my body into his, plundering every single part of me, ensuring I know how he feels, every single inch of his cock, his skin, his scales. Every lick of his tongue sets my skin on fire. I never want to forget a single thing about him, about now, about the way he tried not to wake me, but he needed me.

He needed me.

And I love him.

DRAXX

My rut is unabashedly not slaked in any way. Each time consciousness reasserts itself, I want to be in her, making sure her belly is rounded with my seed, enjoying every seccari I am within her or by her side, inhaling her perfect scent.

This is my new pit, the best pit, the one where I do not fear and have no need for any excuses. Being mated is the best experience I've ever had. Being mated to my Jem is everything I ever wanted.

What I don't want is the pounding on the door to my quarters when I was just contemplating slipping inside my sweet mate again.

"What the hell is that?" Jem grumbles, shoving herself back into me.

"A nevving Sarkarnii who doesn't know when to leave a rutting male alone." I heave myself upright.

My tail has decided it never wants to shift back again, but I'm just going to have to deal with the reluctant appendage later. For now, I give my Jem a kiss, cupping her chin and making sure she knows exactly what I want to do with her.

"I'd better go deal with my brothers," I murmur over her lips. "Or we'll not get peace."

Jem doesn't open her eyes. She hums happily as I peel myself away from her. Nev my brothers! I stomp out of my bedroom, through my ante-room, and pause in front of the door.

Once it's opened, the reality of the Kirakos will enter my life once again. I am so nevving in love with my mate, I don't want anything to spoil it, to wrench me away from the one creature who made things okay again, after all the loss, all the fight, the collaring, and the pit.

"Draxx, you nevver! Open this nevving door!" Draco roars. "Or we will break it down."

I pull in a breath, filling my accelerant sacs before I slam open the door and let rip with a sheet of flame I'm actually quite proud of.

Draco glares at me, and Drega rubs his hand down his face.

"Have you quite finished?" Draco asks.

"No, I nevving have not. Nev off unless you want some more."

The pair of them growl, Draco's tail thrashes from side to side.

"I have a mate. I'm in rut," I add, not wanting to give an explanation but wanting to bring this meeting to a close.

"We know." Draco beckons to the side of him, and Drasus appears, a very irritating grin on his face. He holds a platter piled high with roast tralu.

My stomach whines. Draco and Drega grin. I want to kill them all.

"What's going on?" A glorious sleepy voice has me turning rapidly.

Jem is wrapped in swathes of cloth—from where, I have no idea—her hair is rumpled, and she is rubbing at her eyes. I take her in my arms.

"Nothing, my heartsfire. They were just leaving."

"Ooooh, is that food?" Jem slides out from under me and approaches Drasus.

He rapidly puts the platter down on the floor and retreats, his eyes wary on me as I display my fangs and extend my wings. Jem drops down next to it and starts to eat.

I risk a look at my brothers as Drasus departs swiftly.

"He was always trouble, that one," I snarl.

"Who out of all our den warriors on the *Golden Orion* wasn't trouble, Draxx?" Draga sniffs. "Because I recall who the greatest problem always was."

I look down at Jem who is happily chewing on the tralu. Although my skin crawls at my brothers being this close to my mate, she is happy and unconcerned about their presence.

"We found Igered," I state.

"What?" Drega's eyes widen.

Draco huffs out a smoke ring and folds his arms, leaning against the doorframe. "About time you did something useful outside the pit."

"Even the control room couldn't locate it." Drega looks between us.

Our younger brother was always a firebrand in more ways than one. He might have trained to be a healer, but he loved the fight as much as Draco and I did. His ability to manipulate tech has been useful over time too, even though

Draco and I will never tell him. Don't want it to go to his head, which is big enough as it is.

"My mate and I did," I say proudly. "The Ragad are there."

"Ragad?" Draco rubs at his chin.

"You don't seem surprised." I incline my head at him. "What do you know, brother?"

I'm suppressing yet another urge to do some damage to him. Instead I feel the cogs turning in the dusty corners of my brain. It's been a long time since I thought strategically, like a general.

"The Kirakos is not only a prison. I knew that. You knew it too," he says. "It contains the star map we want, but it has to be something else, something which would be conducive to the storage of such a powerful item."

"I had dealings with the Ragad on Kaeh-Leks." Drega leans back against the wall and contemplates the destruction surrounding us. "They are a very old race. Some useful ideas around healing too."

"This place is ancient, far older than what has been built upon it," Draco says, "I'm beginning to suspect the Ragad wanted the prison built here. After all, what better protection can there be than this?" He waves a hand vaguely at our surroundings.

"The Ragad have used human DNA to make this place a fortress." Jem is on her feet, slowly licking at her fingers in a way which makes my pouch uncomfortably tight. "We have to find the humans."

"You always said your mate was a key," I say to Draco, as I pull Jem to my side, enjoying her scent, part Jem, part roasted meat. "But it is the humans who can set this place free, by mating with the Sarkarnii, and only by mating."

Drega draws in a hissing breath as Draco throws his head back and roars with laughter.

"Then you'll need to dance for your mate today, my brother." He claps a hand on my shoulder. "For tomorrow, we will be storming the Kirakos for the final time, and I need my general."

He releases a stream of satisfied smoke as he turns on his heel, exiting my quarters with a flourish of his tail.

"Did he just declare war on the Kirakos?" Drega asks me as he watches our older brother leave.

"I believe he did." I grin widely.

Drega huffs out some smoke, but it's not in the same satisfied way Draco just did.

"This is the nevving space worms all over again." He shakes his head.

"And we know how that ended." I laugh. "Join me in the control bunker when you can, brother." It's my turn to put my hand on his shoulder. "We'll make plans."

Drega gives me a side eye. "You don't plan, Draxx. You just do." He looks around my ante-room. "And this place could really do with some furniture, for your mate if not for you."

He's out of the door before my first growl reaches him.

"Why *is* there no furniture in here? Draco has some." Jem holds up a perfect sliver of roast tralu to my mouth, and I take it from her, making sure I capture her fingers with my lips.

I want to devour her, pleasure her, dance for her.

"There was an incident." I swallow the meat, reveling in the feeling of food in my stomach and heading over to the platter on the floor for more. "I destroyed everything."

Jem tips her head to one side. "Why?"

I pull her down into my lap as I pick out a choice morsel

for her. "I was angry."

"But you're not now?"

"I am." I offer the food to her, and without hesitation, she takes it between her lips, the pillowy softness enclosing the tip of my claws, items which shouldn't feel. But they do. "I don't want to be who I was anymore, Jem. You've changed all that for me."

She gazes at me as she chews the food. "That scares me, Draxx," she finally says.

"You are never to be scared, my *szikra*. Not by anything, not as long as I am here."

She smiles, and my heart wants to burst. "I've never been loved, not really. I know I've never loved anyone in return. My heart has been encased in ice forever. If I didn't love, I couldn't be hurt. Only I could, over and over." She shakes her head, looking down at her hands in her lap. "I got used to not being much to anyone. That's why I'm scared. I don't know what to do."

I take her chin in my hand, lifting her beautiful face up until I can take it all in, every sparkle in her eyes, every strange little brown fleck on her skin.

"You are perfection. You are my mate. You do not need to do anything, other than be mine. You quiet my soul, heartsfire. You make this lapsed general want to fight again."

Her laugh comes easily, and the brightness fills my heart with something so great, I feel like it might pound out of my chest.

"And you make me feel alive, Draxx. More alive than I've ever felt in my entire life." She takes my face in both hands and kisses me for a long, long time.

Long enough to have my cock pressing at my pouch. Long enough I don't want it to end.

I just want to be here, with her, until the end of time.

DRAXX

Drega leans back in his chair, one leg slung over the arm as he contemplates the smoke ring he's just made and which is slowly lifting to the ceiling.

I check over the weapons he's laid out. My brother was a healer once, now he's a warrior like the rest of us.

He's also very irritating and has taken me away from my mate. To say I am not amused is an understatement.

"We just go in and get the humans. It's simple," I say as I snap the plasma pulsar back together.

"It's not simple," Drega snarls. "The wardens are expecting us to try something like this. It's why they released the vesso last time we were getting close. Our weapons are a pile of tor, and in the tunnels, our shift means nothing."

He picks up a pulsar and slams it back down again with another snort of smoke.

I shake my head. "Drega, how many times have we been in this situation?"

"Too many nevving times," Drega grumbles. "And how many times have I suggested we take a different route?"

"Every nevving time." I grin at him. He furrows his brow at me, his piercings glinting in the light of the consoles behind him.

Drega has always taken a different path. A healer with a penchant for destruction and a temper to match. Draco thought I was the loose cannon? He had no idea what Drega was doing most of the time. The pit was a safe place when he was around.

And for some reason, I can see all of this clearly. I can see my next move. I can strategize what will happen if we storm the warden-controlled areas, how we can counter their defenses, what we need to do in order to be victorious.

It all involves bloodshed, but then that's what Sarkarnii are bred for.

No one ever said this was going to be straightforward. And I will do anything to protect my mate and my den warriors. Even Drega, who is punching at a console and muttering to himself.

"Brother." I slide the pulsar into a holster on my pants (yes, I am wearing pants). "This attack will be fine. Once we have the humans, we can move into the main Warden quarters, and our shift will be an advantage."

"But because we are no longer collared, they will throw everything at us." Drega rubs at his chin.

"Then we need more weapons." I give him wry smile. "Now we know what their energy signatures are like." I nod at the flashing console. "Which, I believe, is your department."

He grunts at me, but I see the smile on his face. "I'm going to speak with Draco."

I turn to leave.

"You must dance for your mate today, Draxx. She cannot go with you."

I pause. "Why would you think I want to take my mate into danger?"

"Because she's a key, like Draco's mate." Drega raises a pierced eyebrow at me. "The Wardens will not hesitate to use her against you, if they get even half the chance."

"My Jem will be protected, always. And we don't need a key, not if what I'm planning works out."

"Why does that not fill me with confidence and makes me fear for my wings?" Drega asks.

"Just do what you do best, brother. Leave the planning to me." I grin.

"That's what I'm afraid of." He heaves out another huge smoke ring.

"Drega, if there's one thing I know I can rely on you for, it's organizing destruction in extremes." I shove my face into his, my fangs elongating. "So, don't disappoint me."

"Yes, General," he says, with a look of shock on his face as the words come out with a smart snap.

This time, I don't correct him.

This time, when I think of Jem and my mating gland pulses, it makes my head clear. The rut has come at the very best time for me. Jem has come at the very best time for me.

It's time to deal with the Wardens and get the nev out of the Kirakos.

It's time for this Sarkarnii general to prove he's worthy of his title.

JEM

The Sarkarnii part of the Kirakos couldn't be any different from the center, the Igered. On the one hand, I can understand why the Ragad would remain there, but on the other, if they are not being held here, and I don't for one minute believe they are, I can't see why they would stay.

But then, sometimes, when you don't have options, you do stay in your lane. Sometimes for years, sometimes for your entire life.

I've been given a second chance with Draxx. One I couldn't have possibly imagined on Earth or the second I found I was at the mercy of aliens whose existence I hardly believed in. I can actually have a whole new life with him, wherever it may be. In the Kirakos or out among the stars.

"You made it back," Amber says from behind me.

"We made it back." I smile at her.

"And?"

"Were you always a matchmaker, or is it only something you do with aliens and humans?"

Amber throws her head back and laughs. Now I look at

her, it's easy to spot the signs of pregnancy. I find myself wondering if it's only her and Draco, if there's something special about them, or whether Draxx and I...

"Hey, are you okay? You went a bit white." Amber has her arm around me.

"Oh, it's nothing. But in answer to your leading "and," yes, Draxx and I are an item."

"His mate."

"Maybe he's my mate. Did you consider that?"

This causes another peal of laughter from Amber, and I love it. I've had so little laughter in my life, I'm not sure I've laughed so much, ever, than when I've been with Draxx and here in the Kirakos. He makes me happy in a way I didn't think possible.

"Believe me, it is one hundred percent the other way around. It doesn't matter how much you love them, Sarkarnii don't just love, they consume you. You become part of them, souls entwined as it were."

"What does that mean?"

"A Sarkarnii who loses his fated mate is broken. I don't know how it works exactly, but they can't function properly," Amber says somberly.

A dark shadow passes over us and a thump shakes the ground behind me. I don't have to look to know who it is.

"Hi, Draxx." Amber smiles as a pair of arms wraps around me.

Draxx buries his head in my hair and inhales deeply. His smoky scent curls through us both.

"*Szikra*," he murmurs in my ear, just before he raises his head and gives Amber a nod. "Little female."

"Less of the female. Her name is Amber."

Draxx looks me straight in the eye. "She is Draco's mate," he says, as if that explains everything.

"Told you," Amber says, as if being right explains everything.

"I literally don't understand any of this." I drop my head back, and Draxx takes full advantage, lips on mine in a delicious, long kiss which leaves me gasping.

"I want to dance for you, mate, today. Then I want to mate you." He nibbles up behind my ear and sends shivers down my spine. "I want every Sarkarnii to know you are mine. I want the entire universe to know you are claimed by me."

I am, for a moment, speechless. I hadn't exactly contemplated what a dance was, but I didn't expect what Draxx has just described.

"Told you," Amber says again with a laugh.

And I guess, perhaps I do, especially as Draxx is moving down my neck, hands in places I shouldn't be contemplating publicly.

"You're going to dance for your mate?" Amber claps her hands together. "Wait until I tell Draco."

Before either of us can do anything, she rushes off.

"You've done it now." Draxx pushes his head into the crook of my neck. "Once my brother gets wind of this, he will insist..."

He stills against me, his body tensing. I turn to see what has changed. His eyes are on the sky, or what passes for the sky in the Kirakos.

"Stay here." He releases me suddenly, and in a whirl of change, he is in his dragon form and in the air.

Fire escapes his huge muzzle with a roar. He's joined in the air by several multi-colored dragons, blue, which has to be Drega, a red one, and a purple one. I run farther out into the main square in an attempt to see what has riled them all up.

It's then I see it. Dangling below what has to be an alien drone is something which looks like it's been dragged up from hell. Part slug, part leech, and all teeth, it writhes in the bonds holding it, slime falling in great curtains. Whatever it is, it's coming this way, and it is big.

Another weird screeching sound has me spinning on the spot. There's another one, and another, and another, all of which are converging on the Sarkarnii area. Following along behind are flying platforms. I don't need any guesses as to what is crammed into them.

This is a full on attack. It seems like the Wardens want their prison back, and they're willing to risk everything to do it.

One of the drones reaches the main square, and before any of the dragons can react, the bonds release, and the vile thing drops with a horrible squelch. But if the fall causes it any injury, there's no sign of it. The thing rears up and releases a whine like the sound of a chainsaw starting up only a thousand times larger.

Something grabs at my hand. I attempt to pull away as I look down into the small pale blue face and three discordantly blinking eyes of a creature I don't recognize.

"Vesso!" it says, pointing at the monster which is sat in a puddle of its own goo.

The word is familiar. It's what we were fleeing from in the tunnels, I think. Although surely nothing as huge as this thing could have even got inside the passageways?

The blue three-eyed alien pulls at my hand. "We have to go."

I look around wildly for Draxx, but he and the other Sarkarnii are attempting to incinerate the vesso and the platforms containing the warthog aliens all while dodging what look like laser bolts.

"Where?" I say, my throat dry and my voice croaking. "Where can we go where that thing cannot follow?"

"Here." The small alien drags me over to a blank wall where a group of its species are huddled, eyes all blinking wildly with fear at the vesso which is, it appears, looking around for a new meal. "Open it," they beg.

I'm absolutely sure this is the wrong idea, but I put my hand on the wall and feel it depress under my touch. A door swings open, and before I can even look back for Draxx, I'm dragged into the underworld, the door slamming closed behind me.

DRAXX

"Circle around!" I snarl over at Drasus. "Get behind them and take that platform out."

He responds immediately, dipping a wing and following my order. Drasus is an excellent warrior, and in one firy emission, he's dealt with the Xicop threat...or at least one of them.

Draco flies past me. "What the nev is going on?" he calls over, sucking in a breath before releasing an enormous fireball which easily incinerates one of the smaller vessos, the remains tumbling harmlessly into the Kirakos.

I spread my wings wide and lash my tail. "We're under nevving attack, brother, in case you hadn't noticed."

Draco returns, his eyes dark with anger. "This is not a battle they will win though, is it, General?"

"Not a nevving chance," I reply.

Firing up farther above the fighting, I can see it looks like all the Wardens have decided to throw at us are in play, contained within the Sarkarnii quadrant. There are three large vessos still in the air and one on the ground.

"Daeos!" I call over to the flame red warrior. His eyes

are filled with a death wish, and in each hand is a primed plasma grenade. "Take out all the remaining vesso. Drop them in the pit if you have to."

"Yes, General," He returns smartly, flicking his wings and heading towards the largest vesso.

He's never minded getting his claws dirty, and with a vesso that size, and the explosives he has, he is going to be one filthy warrior.

"Drasus, Drega! With me."

There are two remaining platforms, the occupants firing wildly with little regard for what they're trying to hit, including each other. None of this seems like a properly coordinated attack at all.

"Drasus, disable the propulsion system. Drega, you know what to do," I order as I peel away. "Draco! Where are the females?"

"Nev!" He's diving down, and I'm following him.

We both hit the ground at the same time. He takes off at a sprint to his quarters as the vesso in the square squeals.

"Jem!" I bellow out, flames licking from my mouth.

A few Jiaka scuttle past me, backs against the wall, their dark eyes fixed on the vesso.

"Jem!" I roar again before taking a few strides towards the Jiaka, grabbing one by the arm. "Have you seen a human female?"

One of them looks fearfully at me, the vesso, and then nods, pointing across the square at an exit into the maze.

"Don't leave us, Sarkarnii." A female Jiaka holds a small bundle, a pudgy blue hand curled over the material. "Please."

I need to get to Jem. Every atom of my being needs to be with her, have her close to me, making my mind clear and my heart beat.

This is not the rut.

This is real. Jem is my fate, my heartsfire. She is why the universe continues, the stars shine, and the planets turn.

And if anyone, anything has hurt her, I will burn it all, past and future. I will not care.

"Fine." I glance at the exit I was told she took and then shift.

The vesso rises up as I release a flame ball. It whines, teeth spinning as the thing which is basically a stomach prepares for its next meal.

Vicious, unpredictable, and always hungry, the vesso are a formidable weapon in the hands of the Wardens, only not so much a threat for a fully grown, fully shifted Sarkarnii general.

I fire a selection of fireballs at the thing in order to disorient it before rising up above and looking for the weak point, the breathing hole. If I can scorch it, the vesso will disintegrate.

And although it will cover my quadrant in guts and goo, I need rid of it before I can go find my mate. After all, as well as stopping a whole cohort of Jiaka from being digested, I can't exactly bring Jem back while the thing is still here.

"Draxx!" Drega is above me, along with Daeos and Drasus.

"Any of those plasma grenades left?" I call out.

Daeos gives me an unhinged grin but shakes his head. "All out, General." He splays his claws and releases a strip of flame in triumph.

"I guess we're going to have to do this the old-fashioned way, then." I winnow out my wings and take in a deep breath, filling my accelerant sacs and priming my fire. "With me, warriors."

As one, we dive at the vesso, each Sarkarnii releasing

balls of neat accelerant which stick to the vesso's otherwise slimy skin. Daeos manages to hit the breathing hole too. As the rest of them get clear of the jaws, I fire a single stream of fire, and the entire creature lights up with the most tremendous shriek.

"Get clear!" I warn my fellow warriors, although, given Daeos's state already, I doubt he'd care what else he gets on his skin.

The vesso trembles, then it explodes in a shower of foulness. Having successfully dodged most of the vile innards, I land, along with my fellow warriors, and shift back.

It's at the moment of shift I feel something pierce my neck. Beside me, one by one, Drega, Daeos, and Drasus drop to the ground and lie still. My vision illuminates wildly, then it begins to close in as I see Xicops heading towards us. Not many, but enough. I snarl, or at least I try to.

"Hit this one again," one of them says, and my neck spasms as something sharp slams into it. "Their hides are tougher than an old Laxian whore's cunt."

I drop to my knees. Nothing making sense at all. I reach out one hand to Drega while I swipe out with the other at the Xicops. Something hard connects with my arm, and I hear a crack, but by then, my body has given out completely, and my mind follows.

Darkness envelopes me, and my last thought is for my Jem. If they have her, I will destroy the Kirakos and all who reside in it.

I will kill them all.

JEM

"Where are we going?" I say as I hold onto the shoulder of one of the little aliens.

It's pitch black, I'm stumbling around, and I really, really hate it.

"In the Kirakos," someone says, possibly the one I'm hanging onto, but I can't be sure.

"I need to get back to the Sarkarnii. Draxx is my..." I hesitate because, despite everything, the word remains alien to me. "Mate."

There's an echo of choking sounds.

"We are aware." Another voice, slightly softer. "When the Sarkarnii mate, they are not quiet about it."

"What?" I spin around, letting go of the creature. "You could hear us?"

Why am I in any way embarrassed by the thought I might have been overheard having riotous, incredible, and literally the best sex of my life with a seven foot plus beast and his talented tail? I mean, I did decide not to give a fuck.

Only then I did. I gave multiple fucks to Draxx, both literally and figuratively, and I let him steal my heart.

My chest contracts. I crouch down, clutching at it, whining with the pain. It can't physically hurt to be in love with Draxx, can it?

Next to me, a light flicks on, bright enough to be blinding after all this time in the dark.

"The human is here." Arms grab at me, not little and blue, not gentle.

These ones are hairy and grabby. It's then, finally, my brain wakes up.

This was a trap. It was always a trap. Whether for the Sarkarnii or me, it was engineered to split us all up.

How else would they know where I was?

I fight. Of course I fight because Draxx would want me to fight and because I am not ending up at their mercy again. But despite everything, all my swearing, all my kicking and punching, it doesn't matter because something is plunged into my neck, and my world swims. I'm still fighting as I go under.

They are not going to win. And they are not going to take me away from Draxx.

―――――

The lights flicker on. I cover my eyes with my arm and groan. Aliens are doing a tap-dance in my head. Bloody aliens.

"Fuck!" I lever myself upright despite the wave of nausea which threatens to overwhelm me.

I'm not in a cell this time. I'm not in the horrible pod either. Instead, I'm in a room which looks quite...normal. I'm on a bed. There's a chair in the corner, admittedly it doesn't look like it's made out of wood or any material I recognize.

"Awake at last." A voice penetrates the fog, and I narrow my eyes to make the place stop spinning.

Then I immediately shrink back against the wall behind me. One of the purple slug-like Beleks is squatting in the corner of the room. A large gold collar studded with jewels glints around his neck.

"Warden Gondnok at your service, human." He dips his head as I stare at him. "It seems my task force did its job well." He shakes like an unpleasant blancmange and waves an unnaturally small hand in the air.

Part of the wall dissolves, and unable to help myself, I squeak with alarm.

"Do not be afraid, human. You are not to be harmed. I need you."

"I won't do anything for you," I spit out. "I don't have to. You don't own me, whatever you think."

"My masters went to some considerable expense to find and bring humans here." It slithers towards me, skin scraping over the floor like sandpaper. "And we had to deal with creatures outside our usual remit."

It's not like he has a face to speak of, merely glinting piggy eyes in rolls of purple fat, two slits for a nose, and a wide mouth which streams with spittle, but it is possible I might have glimpsed a hint of disgust at the mention of 'creatures'.

"We made it so you could converse, even though your primitive bodies could have rejected the expensive translation nanos. We even kept you well cared for and fed."

A horrible, creeping thought dawns on my still shaken brain. This alien *knows*. It knows what Litur told us. It knows the Kirakos is hard wired to accept human DNA as instruction. It has to be the only reason we were brought here.

"If you're expecting me to say thank you, I have another phrase which also ends in 'you.'" I spit at him, sliding off the bed onto Bambi legs and skittering away from his foul bulk.

I forget the open side to the strange and familiar room, but when I bump up against it, turns out it's not open but a clear window, looking out on a vast open area, which stretches away into gloom. Bright lights illuminate one patch down below me. Inside the lit area are three brightly colored dragons, chained to the floor and muzzled.

As I watch, the green one lifts his head, as if he senses me.

"Draxx!" I whisper, splaying my hands on the window.

A guard steps forward and slams a long stick into his flank. Light crackles over his scales, and I hear the long moan of pain from him. He slashes out a claw, but the stick lights brighter, and eventually, he slumps to the ground.

"Draxx!" I hear myself scream in a voice I don't think I've ever heard before.

Because I've never despaired, until now. Seeing Draxx, my proud warrior, my dragon mate, being hurt and not being able to reach him...

That is despair.

That rips my heart out through my throat.

"Fear not, female. We don't want to damage the Sarkarnii too much."

I risk a glance at him before I look back at the dragons. Drega is lying very still. The red dragon, Daeos, nudges gently at Draxx before he too is shocked into oblivion.

Tears spring to my eyes, and I blink furiously, not wanting the Warden to see I'm upset.

"Although, if they don't comply, there will be punishment." Gondnok intones next to me. "We thought collaring them in their biped forms was the answer, but it seems that keeping them as Sarkarnii is much easier. After all, we know what we have to deal with."

"Monster," I grind out. "Let them go. You've already got them in the prison. What is the point of all this?"

"The point is, if you behave and do what we ask, your mate will remain *relatively unharmed*."

"If I *behave*..." I gasp, unable to take my eyes off all three Sarkarnii below but especially Draxx.

His huge flank rises and falls. He is alive, at least.

I do not want to acquiesce to the Warden. I don't want to do anything for any of these horrible creatures who think ripping another species from their home and trading them like cattle is appropriate. I don't want to help them because having met the Ragad, I know the Kirakos holds more than just the map the Sarkarnii seek.

I've been around deviousness enough with my ex and his cronies to know ambition when I see it. I've spent time among other lawyers for god's sake. I've stared into the pit of vipers.

"Very well, but don't hurt them anymore, please," I say, my voice dull.

"Oh little human, absolutely, absolutely." The Warden rubs his tiny hands together. "We have no intention of hurting them. In fact, quite the opposite. They are going to get to have the time of their lives."

He presses on one of the jewels on his collar, and the wall goes blank.

"And now, your journey begins."

DRAXX

I open one eye carefully. The last thing I want is for the Xicop to see me apparently awake. The nevving shock staffs they use hardly have an effect on Sarkarnii hide, but I'm getting bored of pretending while we wait to find out what the Wardens want from us.

It seems like they're taking forever, and all I want to do is get back to our quadrant and find my Jem.

My head cleared quickly of the paraxio given to us, although it seems to have had a worse effect on Drega who remains stubbornly unconscious. Daeos is following my lead however, and other than the occasional muscle twitch, he stays still. There's no sign of Drasus, and that concerns me.

We are all collared again. I believe they're trying to keep us in our Sarkarnii form, presumably because they think us a bigger target, but I can feel the ability to shift within me. Having checked the Xicops are not looking, I shift out one of my hands. The collar doesn't shock or whine and it is as I thought. The Belek put too much faith in their tech.

The Wardens think they are clever, but there is so much

unknown about Sarkarnii. Our physiology is something we've guarded for eons. The collars worked, to a degree, but keeping us from shifting back—that is impossible.

Although the use of paraxio is something we're going to have to be wary of. I give Drega a surreptitious poke, and he doesn't move.

"Get them up." The voice of a Belek Warden reaches me. I'm tickled by the shock staff again and roll my eyes open.

"Gondnok."

"General Draxx." He wobbles, his segments undulating. "You see, I do know about you before you came to the Kirakos."

I glare at him before I remember I'm supposed to be meek and drugged, so I roll my eye in its socket.

"A feared warrior, known for his strategy and bravery. You've spent a lot of time in the pit while you've been here, haven't you?" He sneers.

I know Draco didn't trust him. It's not possible to trust a Belek, given the only reason these blobs ever made it to positions of power was via the most devious ways imaginable. Thing is, I left deviousness to my brother.

And I did spend too much nevving time in the pit, instead of taking note of what was going on around me. While I could never anticipate finding my heartsfire, I should have taken heed of everything I learned and everything I was taught. I should have been ready for anything.

I used the collar as an excuse to wallow in pity, something I had refused to do while we were free on the *Golden Orion*. Our time among the stars as space pirates and brigands, I believed, was a distraction.

But I was still a general, I still fought with my warriors

alongside my brothers, until we came to the Kirakos, and I allowed all my woes to take me under.

"What the nev do you want, Gondnok?" I stretch out my neck and shake my head. "I'm as high as nev on the paraxio your minions gave me, and I'd like to enjoy it before it wears off."

Gondnok makes a bubbling sound, which is the Belek equivalent of a growl. The least frightening thing his species can do.

"You have another function this time, Draxx. You have mated, and you will unlock the Kirakos for me."

I roll languidly onto my back and put my legs in the air.

"Maybe later, Gondnok."

The noise he makes this time is one of pure frustration, and I chuckle happily to myself, given I'm supposed to be in the grip of paraxio.

"How much of the drug did you give him?" Gondnok fires out at one of the Xicop guards.

From my upside down position, I see them all shift uncomfortably. "He had two doses, Warden, because he wouldn't submit."

Gondnok whines with frustration. "And the others?"

"The usual dose."

"Take those two to the factory, but leave the general chained here until he's ready for the Mecha." The Warden turns back and regards me with glittering, nasty eyes. "If General Draxx decides he's bored, let him know I have his mate, and her safety depends on his co-operation."

My internal organs freeze. He has Jem?

The last thing I can do is give away the fact I'm not affected by the paraxio. I need time and space to shift out of these bonds, and now I need it more than ever because I have to find my mate, and then I have to kill every last Belek and Xicop in this place because they threatened her.

I close my eyes and listen instead to the sounds of Drega and Daeos being dragged away. They can look after themselves, but even so, it tears me apart inside to have to stand by without saving them.

If my heart wasn't filled with my mate, it would hollow me out all over again.

I have to get to her.

I have to save her.

I have to save everyone.

JEM

I don't get to stay in the nice room. Of course I don't. Instead, I'm grabbed by two guards (overkill much?) and shoved down a few corridors until a door opens and I'm pushed into a narrow space. The walls, ceilings, and floor are all metal with a dull silver sheen. By the smell of things, there has been another occupant in here relatively recently, which means I don't want to look closer at the stains on the wall and floor.

"How long am I going to be here?" I turn on the two guards. "How do I know Draxx is okay?"

My voice breaks when I say his name, and I hate myself for showing weakness when he wouldn't. I want to be strong. I want to find a way out of this, back to him, back to a new life which had so much promise.

It didn't matter I was in an alien prison. What mattered, for the first time in my life, was I'd found someone I cared for.

My proud, dominant, and pantless dragon alien, Draxx. What with all his possessiveness, the fact he makes me feel like a fucking queen and the baddest girl ever all rolled into one...

The floor below me slides open with a rush, and I'm plunged down a long chute, my involuntary scream following me down until I finally tumble out in a tangle of limbs.

"Ah, the human female," a grating metallic voice says.

I'm yanked upright, but not by anything organic. This entire place is metal and filled with robotic, or what I presume are robotic, arms dangling from a brightly lit ceiling.

"Get off!" I twist against the pincers holding me, but all it serves to do is make them grasp me tighter. I wince with the pain.

"You are not supposed to be damaged, human. And you agreed to our terms."

I'm wondering if the voice I can hear is a robot or one of the Wardens. It's hard to tell, given it's coming from all around me like a speaker.

"Then don't treat me like a fucking specimen," I grind out.

Something horrible extends from the ceiling, swaying down to me. It looks part organic, part metal, and it looks like it's been butchered from a very large creature indeed. The eye stops just in front of my face, the oblong pupil darting around like the puck in a video game.

"But you are a specimen," the voice says with just a touch of sarcasm. "And you agreed, in order to save your mate further injury, to acquiesce to our requests."

The eye shoves closer, so the orb is almost touching my face.

"So acquiesce," the voice adds with menace.

"Fine." I go limp and let the arms drag me over to a

selection of weird arms poking up from the floor.

One by one, they grab me, and I'm spun onto my back, staring up into the light in the ceiling. I'm suddenly reminded of all those alien abduction movies. I close my eyes and brace myself for the inevitable *probing*.

Only nothing happens, not instantly. Instead, I feel like I'm floating, and then my bum hits the floor with a thump.

"Shit!" A human voice has me opening one screwed up eye. "This isn't Ruby."

A blonde-haired woman is crouching next to me with concern on her face. "I'm Jem," I say, opening the other eye.

"I'm Opal. This is Jade." She gestures behind herself to a woman who is propped up against a wall behind us, knees pulled up, tattooed arms resting on them, her long black hair hanging around her face.

She grunts at me and lifts a single finger in acknowledgement.

"Who's Ruby?" I ask.

"She was here with us until a while ago." Opal bites at her bottom lip. She's very pretty. Shoulder length dark blonde hair, with bright blue eyes and a smattering of freckles over her nose and cheeks. "Then some of those pig guards came in and took her."

"Fuckers," Jade swears.

"We thought when the trap opened up, it might have been her coming back."

"Wait..." I press the heels of my hands into my eye sockets. "Did she have red hair?"

Now I get a good look at Opal, I see the very, very tips of her hair are pink.

"Yes." Opal nods.

"I think...I think I saw you both before I was rescued by the Sarkarnii, on gurneys in the lab."

Opal shrinks back from me and wraps her arms around herself.

"Fuck it, what did you have to go and say that for?" Jade becomes animated. "We've all been in the fucking lab. No one forgets it."

I know we don't have time for anyone to get all arsey about this situation.

"I've been looking for you since I was rescued. I have friends who can help me get you out of here."

Strange way to describe Draxx, but I'm guessing these ladies are not yet quite ready for actual dragons or for trusting any other aliens.

"Oh, great, you're our knight in shining armor?" Jade huffs.

I look down at my filthy clothing. "How about slightly singed leather?"

They both stare at me for several seconds, and it goes on for far too long, until Jade cracks a smile, a bark of laughter coming from her as Opal grins too.

"Do you know what, Jem? That'll do me fine. Just as long as we can get out of here, I genuinely don't care what you wear."

Her accent is broad Yorkshire, and the way she speaks makes me smile too. I don't miss Earth for a second, but hearing her speak makes this place better, even though it's a prison cell.

"So," Opal says excitedly. "What's the plan?"

"Ah..." I give her a wry smile. "I'd love to say there is one, but basically, if we can get out of here, we may need to do some saving of ourselves before we can get away."

Opal cocks her head to one side like a bright little bird. "Okay, I'm up for some saving. How about you, Jade?"

"Anything's better than waiting around for something

appalling to happen again." Jade blows her hair out of her eyes and gets unsteadily to her feet.

Opal is immediately on hers, arm around Jade's waist. "Are you sure about this, hun? They banged you up quite a bit when they took you before."

"I'll be fine." Jade waves her away before her gaze falls back on me. "Seems like their drugs don't work on me. Not that it bothers them." She closes her eyes briefly. "They do what they want anyway, regardless."

"Okay." I put my hands on my hips. "I'm going to give you the short version of what we can do to help ourselves, but in this place, human DNA has unique properties. It gives us the edge, if we know what we can do."

"About bloody time we had an edge," Opal says with a ferocity which delights me.

"Time to kick some alien butt," I say with a smile at them both.

"Ooooh, look at us, going all American," Jade says, dripping with sarcasm. "Or should I say, 'going all American on their asses.'"

Both Opal and I snort.

"Is it 'asses'?" I ask, waggling my eyebrows. "Or should we stick to arses?"

Jade shrugs and winces a little. "I want to channel my inner American. I'm going to use 'elevator,' 'garbage,' and 'zucchini' today, but not necessarily in that order or all in the same sentence."

"Go you." Opal grins at her. "So, what do we do now?" she asks me.

"You're not going to believe this, but we need to check for hidden passages…"

"You're absolutely right." Jade shakes her head. "We're not going to believe it."

DRAXX

After what seems like a nevving eternity, the Xicop guards slope away to a far corner to play picdize, argue, and drink from small flasks. I wait long enough so they are suitably engrossed, then I shift.

It's harder than normal to return to my non-Sarkarnii form, as the collar is attempting to stop me, but I can shift, and I catch the large metal ring as I shrink down to biped form and place it gently on the floor with what I hope is complete silence.

Turns out, it is not. As I look over at the guards, one lifts his head and spots me, but before he can rally the others, I've shifted again.

In close quarters, their weapons are no match for a fully shifted Sarkarnii, and I make swift work of them before returning to my biped form.

Gondnok has everything on his side—good weapons in the hands of bad warriors, terrible creatures like the vesso, and an ability to control the Kirakos. But I have something else.

I have a reason to live. I have a mate, and there is no way

anything is ever taking her from me. Gondnok has put his faith in technology, which means I have the element of surprise on my side. I will find her, find my brother and my den warriors, then, by the bones of my ancestors, I will burn this place to ash.

Just as long as I have the nevving map for Draco, or he'll never forgive me.

There's only one door out of the enormous hangar, and having grabbed a pass key from one of the ruined Xicops, I exit.

Hanging outside the door are a pair of pants in my size. I look down at myself. Can pants remain optional? I might need to shift again...

But here, inside the passageways of the warden-controlled quadrant, any such shift will be minimal and in some cases, impossible.

Maybe it's time to embrace pants, at least for a while. I drag them on, unimpressed with how they feel on my body or why, in fact, they were there at all. Still, I have a mate, I have a purpose. Perhaps pants are required.

I grab a couple of plasma pulsars from the guards and find there is a very useful set of holsters on these pants. It's as if they're made for me. Perhaps pants aren't so bad after all.

Next thing I need to do is find my Jem. Once I have her safe in my arms, anything else will be as easy as producing a flame.

I lift my head and scent the air, not searching for her, as much as I would love to be able to detect Jem this way, but I want to find a Belek. If I can get hold of a lesser Warden, I will be able to find my way around this place.

"Draxx?"

I have both pulsars in my hand as I spin on the spot,

only to be confronted by Litur and two other Ragad, both holding spears.

"What the nev? Why are you here? If the Wardens find you, they will make you show them the Igered," I hiss out.

"We have been a foolish species. Your mate showed us the error of our ways. By hiding away in the Kirakos, we have made things worse. It's time to make sure it is in safe hands," Litur says, inclining his head at me.

"And what makes you think the Sarkarnii are safe hands?" I query.

"It is the humans we wish to give the Kirakos to, not the Sarkarnii." Litur chuckles. "But we know you'll help us to oust the Belek and you will keep the humans safe, no matter what." Litur's many faceted eyes glitter.

I shrug. "Fair enough. As long as we can have the nevving star map my brother wants so much in return for our assistance, I am at your service. Your battle is my battle."

"And you need to find your mate first, while we do what we do best." Litur hands me a map-cube.

"What is it you do?" I eye him and his fellows.

"We cause havoc."

"That's good because I cause chaos." I grin at them with far more fang than is necessary, but it's just how I feel.

However, because I have pants on, I control my shift, and it's only my tail which extends unbidden, which does cause some damage, given the ripping sound, but I feel a nev of a lot better, and I release a long stream of smoke in delight.

"The cube will show you the locations of both humans and Sarkarnii," Litur says.

I stare into the thing. There is a group of dots colored blue near a group colored green. One of the green ones glows at me, and my heart quickens, as the mating gland fills me with mix.

"Your mate"—Litur chatters his long legs with amusement—"of course."

"Save some havoc for me, Ragad." I flick my tail and blow out a smoke ring.

Plunging back into the passageways, taking out any Xicop who attempts to stop me as I fix my gaze on the green dots and how I'm getting ever closer to them.

"General!" This time, I don't need to point my pulsars at the voice.

"Drasus, how goes it, warrior?"

The massive purple Sarkarnii has several nasty slashes on his torso. They are already knitting together, but they look like vesso injuries.

"We were collared in a shifted state but were able to shift back and escape our bonds."

"We?"

Daeos and Drelix step out from behind him. Daeos looks particularly unhinged. He's dripping in blood which is clearly not his own, breathing heavily. Drelix looks as calm as always. He is an incredible warrior, with a stealth beyond anything I've ever known and an ability to use any weapon the second he picks it up.

He has also not uttered a single word since we learned of the fate of Kaeh-Leks and our people.

Drelix cocks his head to one side and raises a pierced eyebrow. He and Drega are close given they both prefer the old Sarkarnii way of decorating their bodies.

"Warriors!" I grin. "Drega?"

"He and I were taken in different directions when the guards moved us. I was placed with these reprobates," Drasus says. "But we do not know where Drega is."

"I have a map." I juggle the cube between my claws. "It's a long story, but it should allow us to find Drega, any other Sarkarnii, and the human females, including my mate."

"We are with you, General," Drasus says smartly. "Whatever you need, we are your warriors to command."

Even Daeos stands a little taller, his claws reducing, even though his breathing doesn't change. Drelix snaps easily into warrior mode.

"It's time for the Kirakos to really understand what happens when you attempt to cage a Sarkarnii and threaten his mate," I snarl. "It's time for this place to burn."

JEM

"**A**re you absolutely sure about this?" Opal asks me as we continue to feel over the walls. "I'm not doubting you. I have been abducted by aliens, so all my disbelief is duly suspended, but..."

She hesitates as something under her hand clicks.

"Push down," I exhort as she gives me a terrified look but does as I ask.

Cracks appear in the wall, and she springs back, nearly knocking into me. A door swings open. Opal gapes.

"Fuck me, if I'd known it did that all along, you wouldn't have seen me for dust," Jade says as she saunters through.

"Same," I reply.

Opal is staring at her hands.

"Yeah, we can do magic here. You're a wizard, Opal," I say as I follow Jade into the darkness.

"It's bloody dark in here," she calls back to me.

For a second, I hesitate. I don't really want a repeat of bumping into one of those shadow monsters like the first time I ended up in these passageways, nor do I want Jade and Opal to have the dubious pleasure either. Suddenly it comes to me, and I delve into my pocket, my hand closing around the two light sticks I picked up just after we left the Igered.

"Here." I hold one out to Jade. "Snap it like a glow stick."

She does as I suggest, and I do the same with mine. The passageway illuminates, and I slide past Opal to pull the door shut.

"Won't they know how to follow us?" she whispers.

"What's she saying?" Jade bellows as she walks off ahead.

"From what I understand, this place is ancient, far older than the guards and the Belek who use it as a prison."

"A prison!" Opal stops whispering.

"What?" Jade is striding back to us.

"Yes, this is a prison...for aliens, but don't get too hung up on it. We're not here because they think humans have done something awful, we're here because we can do what Opal just did. We can control this place."

In the weird yellow light cast by the glow sticks, Jade narrows her eyes at me. "I don't want to sound ungrateful, but my experience so far of being abducted is pretty shit. Why in hell would these aliens allow us to be able to control a prison?"

I take in a deep breath, feeling like we're probably wasting time but remembering how much I wanted answers when I first escaped.

"It wasn't always a prison. The aliens who inhabited it used to come to Earth, and they took our DNA because the genetic coding was complex and ancient. They somehow, I don't know how, coded it into their planet, this place, and it means we can find hidden passageways."

"Seems excessively complicated for hide and seek," Opal says, staring straight at me.

"Yeah, it all makes my head hurt because I'm no scientist." Jade snorts. "So, you got us out of one box. What's next?" she asks, folding her arms.

"We follow this tunnel until we come out somewhere, then we need to find the Sarkarnii."

"And how exactly do we do that?" Opal asks.

"I don't know," I say quietly. "I'm hoping Draxx is looking for me."

"Draxx?"

"Um..." I twist my hand in my clothing. "There's no real easy way to say this, but I'm...I..."

"Spit it out," Jade says.

"Are you with one of the aliens?" Opal clasps her hands together and is smiling widely. "Is it even possible? Does he have tentacles? Have you, you know, slept with him? Do you love him?"

"Jesus, Opal, let Jem get a word in edgeways!" Jade snaps.

Only I can't breathe. I almost can't even see.

I do love Draxx. I absolutely love Draxx. I trust he isn't going to abandon me, that he isn't going to leave me behind. And he will do it for no other reason than he cares for me.

"He is looking for me. He will come for all of us," I say quietly.

But most of all, he will come for me.

DRAXX

nnoyingly, as we close in on the human signatures, they move farther away. I growl in frustration.

"General?" Drasus is beside me, releasing a stream of smoke and sparks. I stab a claw into the moving green dots.

"The nevving guards must be taking them somewhere."

Drasus leans a little closer to the cube and shakes his head.

"They're not going fast enough. You know what the Xicops are like."

He's right. I rub at my chin. We still haven't located Drega. There's one faint blue marking, which I presume is him, buried much lower down than our current level. I'm concerned at both the distance and the strange mixture of color surrounding him. The humans are closer, and I have to get to Jem first.

"We need explosives, a tame Xicop, and a route to the Wardens' quarters," I announce. "Daeos, you get the explosives. There's an armory down one level. Drelix, I need you to find me a guard who will be co-operative or one which will help with a little coercion. Drasus, I need you to go find my brother." I hand him the map-cube and tap at the light blue dot.

"General." As one, they bow to me, claws thumping over their accelerant sacs.

"I'm going to get my mate and any other humans I can find. Meet me back here as soon as you can." I turn and release a lick of flame. It dances onto my finger, and I dab it onto the wall as a marker. "And Drelix." I stop the mauve warrior before he slips into the shadows. "I want the Xicop alive," I warn.

He gives me the evilest of grins. I take one last look at the map-cube, and we part ways. I need to get to my mate. The pull I have to her is overwhelming, incredible, and fires through me like the first time I made flame as a Sarkarnling.

Jem is what keeps me going. My mate is everything, and I will not have her used against me. I stride down a number of passageways until I'm sure I've reached the area where the green dots were congregated.

But there's nothing. No cells, no guards. The whole place is deserted. It does not fill me with a good feeling at all.

I want my mate. I want my heartsfire. I want Jem. Releasing a stream of smoke does nothing to assuage my rising concerns, so I roar out some flame.

"Draxx?" The voice I hear is like nectar sliding into my ear.

Standing a short distance away in a small doorway which wasn't there a few seccari ago, is my Jem.

I cover the distance between us in no time at all, and I have her in my arms, covering her in kisses.

"You came for me," Jem whispers.

"I will always come for you, heartsfire. You are the

reason my heart beats, my body shifts, my fire burns. Without you, I am nothing. With you, I can do anything. I will always come for you, my Jem. I love you."

As my lips hit hers, any time passing stands still, saluting us, making our joining absolute.

Then there is the cough.

And the sigh.

Jem pulls back from me a little. "Draxx, I want you to meet my friends, Jade and Opal."

Hovering in the doorway are two faces, and they creep forward. I see they are humans who are a little like Jem. One has hair lighter than Jem, and the other has darker hair. The lighter haired one has her hands clasped together and looks like she has been given a dose of paraxio. The other looks displeased.

It makes me happy Jem has found the humans and that I can read them because I have spent time with her.

"Hello," I say.

"Is this your alien?" the dark-haired one, Jade, asks, stepping out. "You didn't say he was built like a brick shit-house and *green*."

Jem winds an arm around mine, and I revel in the feel of her against me, her tiny frame delicate but so much easier to protect, now she is with me. My mating gland gives a pulse.

"This is Draxx. He is a Sarkarnii."

"And Jem is my mate," I rumble, looking down at her, unable to help myself. "Any friend of my mate is a friend of mine."

The other two humans stare at me, mouths slightly open.

"He's very...big." The light-haired one, Opal, stumbles over her words.

I give them both a bow.

"General Draxx, of the One Hundred Armies, descendant of the High Bask, at your service, little humans," I tell them. "And I can get bigger."

My arm is pinched, and I look down at Jem. She shakes her head at me.

"Not just now, Draxx. I think seeing you as you are is enough for my friends. But I did promise them you would rescue us, so..."

Her eyes are wide and pleading. While she scents of arousal, there is also another tinge to her scent, one of fear.

My mate will not be frightened. And she needs to know the truth.

"Warden Gondnok has Drega. I have sent Drasus to retrieve him and my other warriors to obtain what we need in order to get out of here before the Ragad unleash whatever it is they are planning. Are these all the humans you have found?"

"There's another one, called Ruby, but she was taken away before I got to Jade and Opal," Jem explains. She looks over at the other humans, who nod.

"It's just us," Opal says.

"Come then, little humans." I give them a smile which I hope is reassuring, but just seems to make them both take a step back. "It's time to be saved?" I suggest.

"Honestly, Draxx and the Sarkarnii are friendly, I promise," Jem says.

"But the...fangs?" Opal stutters.

"All the better to bite you with." Jade snorts a slightly manic laugh.

"I don't bite." I look between Jem and the others. "Not much anyway, and never humans," I add seriously.

It's Jem's turn to laugh, but hers lights up my heart, my entire body.

"Shame," Jade says, walking past us and giving me a long searching look. "I'd have thought being eaten by you would be an interesting experience." She raises her eyebrows at Jem.

My mate's cheeks turn a beautiful shade of red as Opal saunters past us, also smiling widely.

"I'm pleased you're wearing pants," Jem whispers as she squeezes my arm.

"I'm not." I shift left and right, my misbehaving cock pushing from its pouch because I have my heartsfire again and my rut is nowhere near over. "But I am wearing them."

"I look forward to no pants again." Jem looks up at me, her eyes bright, a naughty smile playing on her lips.

I know I never want to lose her. And if I want to keep her, I will be ensuring Gondnok burns for attempting to take her from me.

JEM

I wanted Draxx back—of course I did, after everything we've shared—but I didn't expect my body and brain to react to him the way they did.

Hot, cold, bright, and bliss. Waves and waves of it. Is this love? Is it really?

I hope it is.

I don't want to leave his side. Not now, not ever. I always, always want to be with my big green warrior who has a love/hate relationship with trousers.

This has to be love, doesn't it?

Draxx, with me in tow, moves past Jade and Opal. He rasps at them to stay behind us so they can be protected. They stare at him, spellbound, until he releases a stream of smoke, and then they shrink back.

I have absolutely no idea how to tell them he changes into a dragon. Even if I did, I'm not sure they'd believe me. Perhaps the way I found out wasn't such a bad way after all. You can't disbelieve what you see with your own eyes.

Only I'm pretty sure before all of this is over, there will be dragons.

We move relatively swiftly down various passageways. Some are lined with metal, some with a sort of white translucent plastic. None of them are like the ones we were using, and I wonder how deep we are within the Kirakos.

"Did you say the Ragad are here?"

"Litur and some of his warriors. He says they have decided to take action for once."

"They started this, or at least their species did. It's about time they took some responsibility for it." I grunt. "What are they doing?"

"I'm not sure." Draxx grins down at me. "But apparently it's going to be destructive."

"That'll suit you."

"I am only destructive if there is a strategy," Draxx says, lifting up his head and attempting to look regal.

"Is there a strategy, General?" I ask him, filled with mischief.

I'm rewarded with a slight break in his stride and a hitch in his movements as my words take effect. He leans into me, lips close to my ear. "You will call me General later, little mate, when you are impaled on my cock."

Heat floods my body, proper heat, as if Draxx has lit me up. He inhales deeply, and his eyes glitter with badness. He knows what he does to me, as I him.

"Down here," he announces, and I see a couple of warriors waiting for us. Along with one of the guards.

Behind me, I hear someone take in a breath.

"Do not fear, little humans." Draxx grins over his shoulder. "This time the captor is the captive."

He strides ahead, hailing the other Sarkarnii, a dark red one and one with neon fuchsia scales.

"Daeos, Drelix! You were successful?"

"He's not dead if that's what you mean," the red one, Daeos says. "A first for Drelix, surely."

"And the explosives?"

"The Belek and the Xicops weren't using these." Daeos holds up a selection of clear balls filled with glowing lights. He smiles widely, and I'm pretty sure I hear more of a gasp behind me as he shifts a little and is, briefly, a dragon.

At the sound, both warriors crane their necks to see. Jade and Opal have eyes so wide I'm not entirely sure they're not going to pop.

"There are more of them," Jade whispers.

Daeos makes a deep rumble in his chest, not taking his eyes off Opal. Drelix is otherwise occupied with the squirming Xicop in his grip.

"Why do we have him?" I take hold of Draxx and pull him down to my level. "Not only do I not like them, but Jade and Opal have, up until now, been at their mercy."

"Then maybe they'll want to watch how I extract information from a Xicop?" Draxx suggests, eyes filled with innocent assistance.

I look over at Jade and Opal, seeing Daeos edging closer to them, the explosives still in his hands, and I feel like all of this is spiraling out of control.

"My sweet mate." Draxx takes hold of my hand, and his warmth seeps into me, until it is just him and me and no one else. "I promise you, there is a plan. We will get out of here, all intact, and not only will we be free, but the Belek will regret the day they hatched. I just need you to trust me."

"Okay." I press myself closer to him. "But if you can keep the bloodshed to a minimum?"

Draxx looks over at Daeos who has his eyes fixed on Opal, and the woman is staring at him while attempting to hide behind Jade.

"Daeos! Warrior! To me," he snaps out.

As if in a dream, Daeos turns his head, sees Draxx, and immediately comes to attention. "General."

"The Xicops. Find out from him where the Wardens' quarters are, but *keep the bloodshed to a minimum.*" He grins.

Daeos furrows his brow as if this not a concept he is used to.

This is going to be messy, whatever happens and as much as Jade and Opal are grown women who want to be strong, I know I'd have preferred a more gentle introduction to the Sarkarnii. It's perhaps the only thing I can give back to my new human friends, who are going to be my only human friends.

I've never been very good at making friends, so I don't want to lose these ones.

"How about we have a look around for some more passageways? You know, the hidden ones?" I suggest to Draxx. "Opal found the last door."

"You are all keys?" Draxx breathes out a stream of smoke at the revelation.

"I guess so. It sort of fits with what the Ragad said." I shrug.

Draxx smiles, and it makes him look so handsome my knees go all melty. Green sparks flow under his scales, and he is like a firework I really want to climb. And do dirty things to.

Somewhere in the distance, there is a low *whump* and the floor under my feet trembles slightly.

Daeos shakes and whines, his eyes closed.

"The Ragad promised havoc, and it sounds like it has started. Take your humans and see what you can find, but don't leave sight of me." Draxx nuzzles into my hair, sucking in a breath, and I'm surrounded by the most delicious smoky scent of him, warm, musky, and delicious. He drops his voice so only I can hear. "Together, my heartsfire, we can do anything."

DRAXX

If the Ragad have started their attack, then we need to work quickly. My entire being is buzzing with having Jem back with me, although I have a nagging concern about the lack of Drega and Drasus, especially with the next steps being so critical.

Because if we're here, if Gondnok thinks he can control Sarkarnii and humans alike, he needs to be disabused of that notion with some extreme prejudice.

The Belek never controlled us. Our intention in coming here was to find the map, something which is proving more complex than even Draco imagined. But it's time for the Sarkarnii to rise.

It's time for the Kirakos to become ours.

"Where are the Wardens' quarters?" I ask Daeos.

True to my instructions, the Xicop is not covered in blood. Daeos's chest heaves, and his eyes are bright red.

Under the Xicop is a rapidly spreading pool of black. I roll my eyes but ignore it.

"Two floors up. Apparently, we cannot miss them," Daeos growls. "I'd like not to miss them."

"I need you to hold off the rest of the guards and look after the human females while I pay Gondnok a visit," I reply. "There will be plenty of battles ahead for you to slake your bloodlust, Daeos," I add as I see the look of disappointment flicker over his face.

"General!" Drasus pants, appearing from down one of the passageways.

The big warrior is covered in pulsar scorching, adding to the damage to his hide. He's missing the claws on one hand.

"My brother?"

"The area he was in, I don't know what it was, but it was heavily guarded by mecha-bots. I tried to reach him, General, but I could not." He hangs his head in failure.

I put my hand on his shoulder, avoiding the worst of his injuries. "You did what you could, Drasus, that's all I ever ask. We have human females to protect and get to safety. We will come back for Drega."

My heart beats twice. I do not want to leave my brother in this place. The Kirakos is bad enough, but my brothers and my den warriors made it bearable, even when I didn't want anything to do with them.

And because of my kin, I'm still here to claim my hearts-fire. Without Jem, I would have never discovered I am still a Sarkarnii general. I simply lost sight of who I was until I had her.

"Draxx!" Jem's voice has me running in her direction.

She's stood next to a wall with the other two humans, and rather than a door, they seem to have activated a viewer.

And there's another human, laid out on a slab, surrounded by mecha-bots.

"We have to save her," Jem says, her eyes brimming with tears. "Draxx, we have to."

"Is this the other human who was with you?" I ask the one called Jade.

"No, this isn't Ruby. We haven't seen her before," she says.

I growl under my breath. I cannot deny my mate's wishes. I also know we cannot leave any humans in the Wardens's clutches, not now we know how important they are to the Kirakos.

This is getting more complex by the minz.

"Drasus, Daeos!" My warriors are next to me in a seccari. "You are to escort the females back to the Sarkarnii quadrant. You must keep them safe at all times." They both nod, although I see Drasus's eyes wandering to the vid-viewer. "Daeos, give Drelix the explosives."

Telling my warriors to look after the females is one thing, asking Daeos to give up things which go bang? Something else entirely. I watch his internal war.

"Yes, General," he eventually says, teeth gritted.

"Drelix, I am going to find the other human. You are to get to the Warden-controlled area and unleash everything there, cause as much disruption as I know you're capable of and more."

Drelix grins from ear to ear, a tail appearing and swishing wildly. My warriors are simple beasts. Food and destruction are all they require. He nods enthusiastically, grabs the explosives from Daeos who holds tight to them for a few seccari, before finally releasing the things. In one of his characteristic moves, Drelix melts away into the labyrinth of passageways, his scales changing color to match the surroundings.

"I'm coming with you," Jem says.

"You are not."

"I am." Her eyes blaze. "I know exactly how hard it is to

suddenly find yourself being stared at by a huge, green Sarkarnii, and believe me, she's going to want to see a human face."

"I cannot put you in danger, my heartsfire."

"I won't be in danger, Draxx. I'll be with you."

I want to argue with her logic. I'd like to have Drasus throw her over his shoulder and carry her away...

Actually no, I would not like that, not at all, and Drasus might find himself without a shoulder for just touching my mate.

Jem has her arms folded. She taps one foot, and the other humans giggle.

They are giggling at a Sarkarnii general.

Daeos blows out a ring of smoke but manages to keep his features neutral.

"Fine," I grumble. "But the other humans go with Drasus and Daeos."

"Oh, mister, if it means getting out of here, you do not have to force me to go anywhere," Jade says, grabbing Opal's hand and strolling past me towards my warriors. "I'm all for escape."

"It's settled then," Jem says, unfolding her arms.

"It's settled," I reply. Who am I to deny my mate anything, after all? "Let me have the map-cube."

Drasus throws it to me, and I inspect it, working out where the human is being kept.

"Over here," Jem calls out.

She's found another passageway, the door hanging open. I check the cube. It will lead us into the heart of the Warden area, but it is the closest to the human. Once again, I allow myself to marvel at the way the Kirakos works with the humans and wonder if this is the intention of the Ragad.

Another explosion, closer this time, has me tossing the map-cube back to Drasus.

"Take the humans. I will see you back in our quadrant."

He gives me a curt nod, then ushers the humans in front of him, shoving Daeos behind him, and they hurry away.

"Time to go into the belly of the beast," Jem says with just the tiniest of trembles in her voice.

I wrap an arm around her and slide a finger under her chin, tilting her face up to mine.

"I promised to protect you, and a general never lies. While you are with me, you will come to no harm, heartsfire. My heart is joined with yours, and once we get out of this, I promise I will dance for you and cement my claim."

"Good," Jem says. "Because I am never going anywhere without you again, Draxx. You are my soulmate. I see it and I understand it, for the first time in my life. I will never leave you either."

She raises herself up and presses her lips to mine before she slips out of my arms and into the hidden passageway.

JEM

This passageway has its own lighting, coming from above, high above. It's like we're walking through a crack in the surface of the Kirakos, only I'm sure the light is not natural.

"The map-cube suggests we will come out somewhere near where the human is being held," Draxx says from behind me.

"Once we have her, we need to go look for Drega," I say because I feel terrible we're chasing after a human neither of us know when his brother is still missing.

"Once you and the other humans are safe, we will return for Drega. He's a Sarkarnii and a tough one at that. We've faced down many foes in our time," Draxx says quietly. "He knows we will come for him because I know he would do the same for me."

Ahead of us, there is a scraping sound, and Draxx places a hand on my shoulder. The passageway is too narrow for us to pass easily, so he lifts me up as if I weigh nothing and puts me on his shoulders. A set of wings extends in order to make my seat comfortable.

"If I cannot go in front of you, I will still keep you protected," Draxx says, and my heart swells.

Of course I feel quite absurd perched up here, but he thinks it's right, and my stomach turns to jelly because I am so damn in love with him.

We move easily through the passage as the scraping sound ceases. There is an archway ahead, and the area around us opens up. With some reluctance, Draxx helps me down and gently pushes me behind him, shielding me with his wings.

"Finally."

I do not like the disembodied voice which greets us, and neither does Draxx, given his entire body tenses.

"The Sarkarnii general and his mate. We've been waiting for you."

Draxx curls a hand around my wrist, and we step out into a large room, lined with metal. In the center is the bed with the woman tied to it. She is gagged by what looks like a metal band. Her face is red and wet with tears. When she sees me, her eyes widen, and she shakes at her bonds.

Between her and us is another of the slugs. Only this one is a particularly violent shade of purple, vast and oozing.

"Warden Gondnok," Draxx grinds out through sharp teeth.

"It's good you remember your place, *General*," the massive slug replies. "All the Sarkarnii should remember why they are here and who is in charge."

Draxx makes sure I'm tucked behind him and snorts out a stream of smoke and embers.

"Perhaps you should be collared again, to enforce that reminder?"

I'm not quick enough, and something plucks at my

clothing, spinning me up and away from Draxx who roars out in anger. I'm being held from the ceiling in some sort of metal pincers which are gripping ever harder. Draxx goes for me.

"No! Don't!" I call out. "I'm fine. Don't give him any reason to hurt you."

The pincers make it through my clothing, and I feel them digging into my flesh. Below me, the other human is still squirming and groaning against her gag, her eyes darting around as I grit my teeth, trying not to cry out at the pain.

I don't want Draxx to do anything which might get him in any worse position.

"Listen to your mate, Draxx," the Warden croons nastily. "I need the both of you, mostly intact, but it's not entirely necessary, so why not accept the collar and be done."

A metal arm zips forward, dangling a silver-colored hoop. Draxx stares at it, then at the Warden, as if his look alone could melt the creature.

"Let my mate go, give me your word she will remain unharmed, and I will do as you say," he growls.

"How about you ask me without the growl?" the Warden says, as the arm with the collar moves closer to Draxx.

He closes his eyes, I see his fists ball, and then he extends his fingers, huge claws sprouting from them. The pincers dig deeper, and I can feel the blood running down my back, one of them grating on bone, but I can't move, I can't do anything because I don't want the Warden to hurt Draxx.

He's lost enough. I know he has to have a plan.

"Just do it, my love," I say quietly, my chest heaving as I

try to hold back the tears and the pain. "I trust you. I will always trust you."

"You heard your mate."

"Let Jem go. Give me your word she will remain unharmed. I will do as you say," Draxx says, his voice dull, the claws reducing.

"Good. I knew you could do it. Put the collar on, there's a good Sarkarnii, and your mate will be released."

Draxx reaches for the collar. I can feel my vision dimming as one of the sharp pincers pushes past the bone. I hear a muffled squeaking sound, and I look down. The woman below me is rolling her eyes wildly as well as squirming hard against her bonds.

Only she's not having a fit. And she's actually attempting to get me to look to her left. I stifle a groan as my body slips farther onto the pincers.

Just within reach of my foot, there is a glowing translucent orb. It flickers with a rainbow of colors. I look at the woman just as I drop down farther with a pained grunt. Consciousness wants to desert me so much, but until I know Draxx is safe, I can't possibly let him know how much this hurts.

I see a drop of blood hanging off one boot. The other is close enough to the orb I could touch it. The bound woman groans and blinks hard at me, almost as if she's trying morse code. She wants me to do something with the orb, but I don't know what. From this position, all I can do is stamp on it.

I hear a click. Draxx has the collar around his neck. It bites into his scales, and his eyes are dull. I know I can't hang on much longer, so I do it.

I slam my foot on the orb, and everything goes black.

DRAXX

J em groans, and my attention snaps to her. There is blood curling around the fabric of her pants, black and terrible She gives me one last look, her eyes fever bright, before her foot presses on the orb directly below, and the mecha-bot arms release her.

The collar falls away, and the lights fail.

Everything goes into free-fall.

Gondnok levitates, his small arms flailing, I shift out my wings and stab the claws at the tips into the walls to hold myself steady as my tail wraps around the spinning body of my mate. She is soaked in her own blood, and I roar out as I clutch her close to me.

The other female remains bound to the slab, her long brown hair floating above her and around her face.

"Sarkarnii!" Gondnok screams. "Help me or your mate will die."

"I'm not entirely sure if you've realized it, Warden, but it seems to me like the only creature dying today is you," I growl.

He's almost completely flat against the ceiling. The

control orb my mate touched must have flipped the gravity in the room, although why it would be necessary or even useful, I'm not sure.

Regardless, I'm not going to question it, not when I have a mate who urgently needs medical attention and a female human who also needs to be freed.

I slam my wing claws into the floor and crawl towards the human and make quick work of her bonds, pressing my hand to her chest to keep her in place.

"Thank you!" she gasps as the gag is removed.

"We need to get out of here, and I'm going to have to carry you," I say, "My mate is injured. Can you get on my back?"

She looks at Jem with some concern.

"There are medical supplies, or at least what I think are medical supplies, in a cabinet over there." She points to a metal storage hub. "I'm a doctor. I can treat her."

The relief which flows through me is tempered by another high-pitched shriek from Gondnok.

"You will comply, or I will order all Sarkarnii to be terminated."

I look up at him as I extend a wing, stabbing the claw into the wall near the storage hub. "Go get the supplies," I say to the human. "Gondnok, you don't have the ability to terminate anything, least of all the Sarkarnii."

As I speak, the entire room shakes.

"Hear that? It's the sound of you losing power on the Kirakos." I grin up at him. His dark gimlet eyes are darting around, looking for an escape, but there is none. "And today is your last day here."

The human clambers back to me, her clothing stuffed with supplies.

"Get on my back. This might be a little rough," I warn her.

With one final look down at my Jem, I see her face is pale and her eyes stubbornly closed. Her usual scent is masked by that of her blood, and it simply makes me hate the Belek even more.

The orb stops flashing. Inside fills with a black smoke.

"Oh, no!" Gondnok cries out. "Now you've done it. This room is going to purge."

I spike a set of claws into the door mechanism, and it slides open.

"Purge?"

"I'll be expelled. Everything will be expelled." Gondnok screeches.

"Where?"

"Into the core."

"That doesn't sound good," the human female says over my shoulder.

"No, it does not. Time to leave." I scramble out of the door, and immediately, gravity reasserts itself.

The human slips from my shoulders, and she sits down heavily, panting. I cradle my mate.

"Jem? My heartsfire? Please don't leave me. You promised, just as I promised you too."

I hate the pallor on her face, the fact her eyes remain stubbornly closed, the chill to her skin compared to the heat of her blood on my arms and hands.

"I cannot live without you, *szikra*." My voice is a whisper now as I hold her close. "I love you with my entire being, with everything I am." A tear rolls down my nose, and it drops into her hair. "Without you, I am nothing. My heart will be no more. I need you to fight, to come back to me. I need you to live forever."

"Please." The other human has her hand on my arm. "Let me tend to her."

"Draxx!" Gondnok shrieks.

I don't want to let Jem go. I never want to let her go.

"You saved me," I murmur into her ear. "Please stay with me."

The human tugs gently at Jem, and my arms release her, even though my heart wants to join with hers, to beat and to give her my life force. A wind whips at us. The room where Gondnok is stuck to the ceiling is starting to disintegrate.

"Can you close the door?" the human calls over the noise as the wind snatches away a piece of medi-sheeting. "I can't work like this, and I have to stop the bleeding." Her voice is calm, but I catch the concern held underneath.

"Yes." I reach for the mechanism, but my touch doesn't close it. The wind increases, along with Gondnok's shouts.

I see the closure button is inside the room. I look back at my mate. The other human is doing what she can, but the pool of blood under her is growing.

Jem has to survive, no matter what.

"I love you, my Jem. I will always love you."

I dive into the storm. For her.

DRAXX

Alarms are screaming, but Gondnok has gone strangely silent, staring at me with his tiny dark eyes. The room will purge, and he's going to go with it. Perhaps he's ready to meet his ancestors after all.

"If you save me, I will reward you well, Sarkarnii," he says, his voice penetrating the wind and alarms.

I'm clawing my way across to the closure mechanism, hoping I can get the nevving thing operating and get back to my mate. I need Jem like I need air.

"I have my treasure, Belek. I have no need of you," I growl. "Not when you threaten her and my den warriors in one breath and promise to save them in another."

They are without honor, these creatures, but as a Sarkarnii general, I know I have honor.

I know the best death is one in battle.

And I hate that Gondnok is not going to end by my claws.

I reach the door mechanism. It snaps at me, part of the covering torn away by some debris which spins around the room. This is Drega's territory, but I've learned enough from him over the years to sometimes choose intricacy over violence. I make short work of the damage, enough to allow me to operate the door from the outside.

The wind and the screaming alarms ramp up a level, indicating the purge is imminent. All I want is to get back to my heartsfire, my gorgeous Jem, take her in my arms, and never let her go.

I'm not sure I want to be anything other than her mate. Not even the general. I don't think that's too much to ask from the universe, is it?

Except, I need to shake off the pit, shed the past like I shed my skin, with ease and grace. Now I have her, I have a future, I have a life, and we will be together.

So, letting things die isn't honorable. It never was, and it isn't now.

A large piece of debris flies past me, and I hook it with my wing claw, sending it on a different trajectory towards Gondnok as I activate the alternative exit. It slams into him, scraping his bulbous form from the ceiling, and with a rush, he's half pushed, half sucked out, the door snapping shut behind him.

Even in a partially shifted state, I'm struggling to cling on as the wind and suction are reaching their peak, and below me, the floor drops away. I slice my way back around the walls, heading to the door where my precious jewel remains unmoving and the other human tends to her. A heat fires at my tail as I reach the opening.

"Get back!" I call, and the human drags Jem farther from the door, words coming from her which don't translate.

I'm holding on with all my might, attempting to heave myself through the doorway. With one final push, I make it. Slapping the palm of my hand on the closure mechanism, the aperture spirals closed, and all I can hear is the sound of my own breathing as the sudden silence grips us.

Jem opens her eyes, beautiful and pain filled. She whimpers, and in that seccari, she is in my arms.

"I thought I lost you," she whispers.

"Never. Never. Never," I reply, chanting into her fragrant hair, ignoring the tang of her blood. "I will follow you into the heart of a dying star if only to be by your side, my heartsfire."

Jem goes limp.

"Help us," I say to the human female, my voice a rasp of nothingness.

"She's fainted. It's lack of blood." She tugs at my arms. "I've managed to stop the bleeding, but she lost a lot. If I was on Earth, I'd say she needs a transfusion."

"Jem needs blood? She can take mine," I growl. "Anything she wants, she can have, human."

"Coral." She stares up at me. "And I doubt very much lizard aliens are compatible with humans." She turns away, pulling at various items in the medi-kit. "But I might be. If there's anything in here which I can use."

I put out my hand and still hers, closing it around the multi-functional medi-device. "Give her my blood," I say firmly, fitting in the two transfer devices.

"No," Coral says. "If you're not compatible, it will kill her."

"She is my mate. I'm not going to argue with you. Do it now."

As much as I want to help Jem, I do appreciate this humans concern. I'd much rather she felt this way than wanted to gamble with my mate's life.

There is a low rumbling thump, causing the floor to shake and cracks to appear in the walls around us. I jab the collector into my arm, allow it to fill with what it needs and toss the device to her.

"No time to administer my blood. We need to get out of here." I gather Jem into my arms as gently as I can. I press her to me. "Hold on, my love," I murmur.

Coral scrambles the medi-kit together, and we set off at a run down one passageway after another. I can smell the Kirakos. It's strong and pungent as always. Not so long ago, I couldn't imagine running back to my prison, but it is currently the safest place for us, for my Jem.

The Wardens are already undone. With the help of the Ragad, we have taken the first step in gaining control.

And with the humans, maybe finding the nevving star map.

We reach a cross-passageway.

"Which way?" Coral says, her voice trembling as yet more explosions rock the Warden area.

I scent the air. It's filled with the smell of the detonators used by the Ragad and possibly my den warriors. I strain every sense I have until a noise, way off in the distance, reaches me. It's Drasus, and he's calling out for me.

"This way." I grin and set off at a run, trusting the human to keep up.

The small corridor comes out in a much larger one. We are exposed, but I don't care. I hear Drasus's voice louder up ahead.

There's a volley of pulsar fire from behind us.

"Get in front of me," I yell at Coral, shifting out my wings to provide a larger target as I run, and she is pushed ahead of me, legs scrambling.

"Draxx?" Jem murmurs, her eyes opening briefly.

"Don't worry, my little jewel," I croon. "We'll be out of here in no time."

A pulsar bolt strikes my wing claw, pinging away to the roof and sending a spike of pain through me. Jem's eyes widen and then close.

Fear for her hurts far more than any pulsar bolt. I spot an abandoned weapon on the floor to the other side of the open passageway. I have no option. I have to return fire or we will be destroyed.

Another explosion, this time significantly louder and closer, rocks the entire place, and with timing I couldn't have hoped for, a large section of the ceiling slams down behind us.

"Over there." I shove Coral behind it, my tail scooping up the weapon as we pass.

I place Jem down on the floor, stroking her hair, making sure I can remember the feel of the silky strands between my fingers, that her beautiful face is burned into my brain. Smoke fogs out of me, and I draw in a breath, allowing time to stop. For it to just be us.

It will always be us.

"Time to finish this."

I roar as I rise and shift out my wings. Fire streams from me down the passage as I release a stream of pulsar bolts.

For a second, I have a hope my shock and awe has worked, then a bolt hits me in the shoulder and another in my chest. I fill my accelerant sacs once again and breathe flame to scorch ever part of this ancestor-forsaken place. But the bolts keep coming, and unless I can take out the nevvers, I cannot create a safe passage for my injured mate and the other human.

I'm struck in the thigh and in the wing, causing me to stumble. Only I will not give in. I will not. My body doesn't matter. I will heal.

More fire, more pulsars. I have to keep going. Even as I dodge another volley, mostly.

Then the air is filled with weapons discharge. But not towards me, firing the other way. By the sounds of things, they're hitting their marks.

"General." Drasus greets me, firing two pulsars at the same time as he advances.

"Warrior." I nod at him.

"The others are waiting at the new entrance." He nods over his shoulder, continuing his stream of bolts. "You've held this lot off long enough, so you might want to get your mate to safety, especially as Daeos has found more explosives. I'll be right behind you."

It's then I spot them, Litur and his warriors, the bolts passing around them as if deflected somehow.

"Go, warriors. We will deal with the Belek today," he says with a slow nod, his words crisp in my ear.

I fire a few more shots and scramble to my feet, Jem in my arms.

"Let's go, Drasus. Help the other human. It's time we left the Belek to face the original owners of the Kirakos."

JEM

This is a very bumpy car ride. I groan and grab for the door handle.

I touch scales.

"Be still, my treasure. We are nearly home," Draxx murmurs.

I'm held close to his chest. I think he's running, but it's all lopsided, and where my hand touches him, it's wet.

"You're hurt," I say, my voice cracking.

Bolts of light zip overhead, and when they slam into the walls, huge chunks explode outwards.

I feel like I've been trampled into the ground. All I can remember is touching the orb and then...nothing. Yet here we are, in the middle of a firefight, and my Draxx is injured.

"I'm fine, Jem. Just hold on."

His body shudders suddenly, and his pace slows. Ahead of us, I see light, even as destruction reigns. Drasus, the dark purple warrior, appears by Draxx's side.

"General?" he queries.

"It's nothing, Drasus," my big green warrior intones.

"Get to the exit. Make sure the others know the Ragad are going to blow this place."

Drasus races ahead, and for a second, I think I see another human with him, but then they are in silhouette, and Draxx stumbles.

I slip out of his arms, onto legs which don't want to hold my weight. Everything swims violently. A bright laser fires past us, only just missing Draxx, who has his hand on his side, blood flowing from it.

"No, no, no!" We're using each other to stay upright, and I'm reaching for his injury. "This isn't happening!"

"I have to get you to safety, my *szikra*," Draxx says, his eyes glassy.

"Not at any price. And I'm not going without you." I snatch at one of the pulsar weapons hanging from his chest. I can see two, although my hand only closes around one. "Together or not at all."

Draxx straightens, his eyes clearing. My chin is enclosed in a huge finger and thumb as he brushes his lips over mine.

"Always, my perfection."

Something slams into his back, and he topples. I fire out widely, not caring what I hit. Just as long as I keep them away from my Draxx, I don't care.

"Jem," he says, and a huge clawed hand encloses mine, ceasing my firing.

"You're hurt. They hurt you," I growl, pain over-whelming me.

"I have a tough hide." I can see his smile, and it's like the world is lit up. "I'll survive as long as you do, little warrior."

The weapon is plucked from me as Draxx gets to his feet.

"Together or not at all." He smiles down at me, strong arms scooping me up.

With a low, deep rumble, the entire place ripples alarmingly. And then there is the explosion to end all explosions.

But it doesn't matter. Because we are together.

Or not at all.

My shoulders are burning at me. My eyelids feel gummed together. I groan.

"Fuck! She's awake!"

"'Fuck, she's awake?" I rasp. "Thanks for the vote of confidence." I attempt to lift my arm to clear my eyes, but it feels like lead.

"Let me, my mate." A gorgeously familiar voice, all velvet and sin, rumbles through me.

A cloth is removed from my face, and I blink a few times to clear my vision. An impossibly handsome face is hovering above, subtle green scales flickering over his sharp cut cheekbones, eyes a whirl of colors. His lips are drawn tight as he inspects me.

"Draxx." I smile, attempting to lift my arm again. This time it's easier because he assists me, and I'm able to place my hand on his jaw.

"Heartsfire." He holds my hand and nuzzles into it.

"What happened?" There's a dull ache in my back, a thumping in time with the blood pumping through me.

"Stuff I don't understand, but whatever it was, he saved your life," a female voice on my left says. "I'm guessing it had something to do with the machine he had."

I turn my head, probably a bit too quickly as it makes things hurt more. There's a dark-haired woman, familiar, I think, sat next to me. She has my wrist pinched between two fingers, and she's looking at a watch on her wrist.

It's the most incongruous thing I've seen since being abducted by aliens.

"I'm Coral Haines," she says, not looking up. "Doctor Coral Haines, if you were wondering what I'm doing."

She is the dark haired woman in the room. The one we went to save. The one we both nearly died for.

"I was more wondering how you still have a watch." I say, dryly.

She looks up. Her face is pretty with kind, dark eyes which crinkle at the corners, I would guess she's in her late thirties. She looks down at the watch again and shrugs.

"I don't know. I also never expected to be treating any human patients again, so today has been full of surprises."

"Thank you." I take her hand.

"Thank Draxx. If it hadn't been for him, none of us would have survived. And without his blood, again something I cannot fathom, you wouldn't be here either."

I look back at my mate. He is still staring at me with an intensity which is almost burning into my soul.

"Everyone means everyone, my *szikra*. Drasus and Daeos got the other humans out."

"Drega?"

He drops his head to nuzzle against me. I feel his breath and the intake of it as he inhales over me, sucking in whatever it is he likes, and I close my eyes again, dragging in his warmth, the feel of his skin against mine, the utter joy of waking and seeing his face.

"We have not yet found him, but my brother survives, and it is only a matter of time until we do locate him," he murmurs in his sinful, smoky voice, one which sends shivers through me. "Then the Wardens will pay for what they have done."

I struggle to sit up.

"Hey." Coral puts her hand on my chest. "Take it easy, okay? I'm going to leave you in Draxx's capable"—her eyes wander to his claws—"hands. But I'll be nearby if either of you need anything."

She gets up, and Draxx tears his eyes away from me.

"You have my eternal thanks, human," he says with a nod.

"Not a problem," Coral replies, and she is gone.

"How are the other humans?" I ask as Draxx helps me sit.

"I have not seen much of them, other than the healer. She refused to leave you," he growls. "But because she helped, I let her stay."

"Thank you." I lean into him.

"You have nothing to thank me for."

"Your blood, apparently, and for saving the humans."

Draxx's eyes are fixed on mine. "I did it for you, Jem. You are mine. Whatever happens here in the Kirakos, or out in the stars, I will always be here for you."

He streams out a long breath of smoke.

"Come on." I pat the bed. "I can't move much, and frankly, you look like you can't either."

Draxx opens his mouth, but I put a finger on it.

"Don't say a word about being some big bad Sarkarnii general. I might not remember everything, but I do remember you were injured."

I study his skin. There are scorch marks, even if there are not actual wounds.

"As long as I can shift, I can heal," Draxx says.

"And I don't care. I want to rest, and I want to rest with you."

With a sigh he could have dredged up from the Igered, Draxx levers himself out of the chair stiffly and slides onto the bed with me. Every muscle in my body screams at me as I huff and wince to accommodate him, but soon he's here, his head pushed into the crook of my neck.

I brush at his hair, trailing my fingers down his neck and marveling at the beauty of his scales.

"If you keep touching me like that, mate, I might not be able to have this rest you speak of," Draxx murmurs.

"Oh, you had other plans, did you?"

"I plan to mate you until you can only see the stars," he replies, words slightly slurred as another long stream of smoke curls from him.

His eyelids droop as I continue to rub my fingers through his hair, gently massaging his scalp.

"And I'm going to hold you to that promise, my love," I whisper as his breathing deepens and my huge Sarkarnii general falls into a deep sleep he justly deserves.

Because he saved me.

And I intend to stay saved.

DRAXX

I don't know how long I slept. I don't care either. Because when I wake, I have my sweet mate in my arms, and there is no better way to open your eyes.

"Hey, sleepy head." Jem is smiling at me, her hair rumpled and some of the pink back in her cheeks.

"I slept like my ancestors were watching over me," I rasp, attempting to stretch out my body in such a way it doesn't pull on the healing areas of my scales.

"Is that a good thing?" Jem furrows her brow.

"The Sarkarnii believe the bones of our dead contain their essence. On Kaeh-Leks, we kept them all in caverns which went deep into the mountains, bones upon bones. All watching, all knowing. Our ancestors were our past and our future." I smile to myself, thinking about the ossuaries. "Before Draco decided we were to all give up our ranks and privileges, instead head into the stars to search for treasure and glory, I liked to go to where we kept the bones and spend a quiet time there among the dead, learning and listening."

Jem is watching me closely. "You were lucky. The best

quiet time I got was a sandwich in the shoebox of an office in my dusty law firm." She smiles, and her eyes are far away for a second before snapping back to mine. "Yours sounds much more grand."

"I am an ancestor of the High Bask, I'll have you know. One of the original ruling families of the Sarkarnii."

"So, basically, yesterday, I saved a prince?" Jem's eyes sparkle with mirth.

I draw her into me, inhaling her scent so deep into my lungs I never want it to escape. "I'm no prince."

"I don't doubt it for a second, *General*," she replies with a snort and then a little cry of pain.

"What is it, my jewel? Do I need to fetch the human healer?"

"I'll be fine." She shifts uncomfortably on the bed. "I think. It feels like parts of me are on fire."

"Sarkarnii blood." I grin at her.

"You really did give me your blood?"

I nod.

"And Drega really is still missing?"

"He did not make it out with the rest of us. Daeos and the Ragad did some significant damage to the warden-controlled area, something it will take them time to fix." I draw in a breath. "There will need to be a rescue."

"Of course there will. I would expect nothing less," Jem says, leaning her head on my chest. "And I expect you'll be going."

I'm not sure my heart has ever felt this calm. My mating gland is still pumping away, but rather than filling my veins with fire, it provides a balm to my soul.

"I want to dance for you, my Jem. Will you let me?"

She lifts her head slowly as I hold my breath for her answer.

"I'll do whatever you want me to do, Draxx. I love you."

Unbidden, my hips do a little snap, and I have to hold back a hiss of pain.

"But what exactly does it mean?"

"It means you are mine."

"I thought I was already yours. After all, isn't that the first thing you ever said to me?" Jem laughs softly.

"My dance is only for you. An ancient ritual to tame the wildness which is the female heart. To show her, in all her glory, she is the only mate I will ever take, the only one I will ever claim, and that I belong to her, body and soul."

Jem's laugh dies in her throat. Her hand is back on my chest. Her eyes, wide and beautiful, filled with water, are on mine.

"You would do that for me?" she whispers.

"I already have, but I want to show the universe, my treasure." I hold my finger to her cheek, capturing the water which runs there. "Are these"—I furrow my brow, wanting to get it right—"happy?"

Jem curls her hand around mine.

"I couldn't be happier, Draxx." She kisses me on my jaw. "Now go back to sleep."

And I can't think of a better time to start obeying my female. I close my eyes and sink into her scent and her skin, my heart gladdened by her acceptance of my dance.

JEM

Sleeping with Draxx, my own personal heater, has been a healing session in itself. Which is why, when I wake and he's no longer beside me, I feel completely empty.

But he is a general after all, and I guess he has things to do. I spread myself out in the bed. Draxx's smoky scent covers me like the sheets.

Did he really ask me to sort of marry him?

Did I actually agree?

I stare at the ceiling in Draxx's quarters, attempting to work out if what has happened in the last few days is real or makes any sense.

It doesn't, and I love it, just like I love him.

"Oh, hey." Opal pokes her head around the door. "It was open so..."

I go to push myself into a sitting position, and it's not a pretty sight. Opal runs to my side and helps me up as Jade, Amber, and Coral all troop in behind her.

"Yeah, big, green, and scary is with the others." Jade

does a circuit of the room, her dark eyes missing nothing. "And when were you going to tell us about the dragons?"

"Um…" I can't avoid her gaze. "I've not been well?" I suggest.

Coral laughs out loud as she plonks herself on the bed and grabs my wrist.

"It's okay, I'm down with dragons." Jade cracks a smile.

"There's no easy way of finding out," I say.

"I like them," Opal adds.

"You like anything." Jade snorts. "You told me you liked quiche."

"Who doesn't like quiche?" Opal retorts.

Around the room, a number of hands rise.

"Fine." She huffs, folding her arms. "I didn't like being abducted by aliens though."

"Universally agreed," I reply.

"Although if there's more who look like the Sarkarnii, it can't be all bad," Coral says, dropping my wrist. "You look like you're getting better."

"I'm still pretty sore, but yeah, I think I am."

"I could do with checking your dressings at some point. That you survived a blood transfusion with the big green guy is something else." She shakes her head.

"He's my…mate." I look around the room. The new ladies have blank faces. "You haven't told them?" I query with Amber.

"I thought I'd let everyone get over the dragons first." She gives me a wan smile.

"We're never going to get over the dragons," Coral says. "So, you may as well explain." She folds her arms.

"Humans are compatible with Sarkarnii," I say. "And I mean compatible. At some point in time, our DNA has been manipulated with theirs to make us compatible." Coral opens her mouth and Jade looks like thunder. I hold up my hands to stop the onslaught. "Look, I don't understand any of this, but it means we can control the Kirakos, and it means we can...be in a relationship...with a Sarkarnii."

"By 'in a relationship,' do you mean fucking?" Coral asks.

I look at Amber, and she looks at me.

"Oh yeah, they certainly do," Jade says, with possibly the dirtiest cackle ever heard in this galaxy.

"But I've seen them." Coral furrows her brow. "They don't have any obvious genitalia."

"Spoken like a true doc, Doc." Jade can hardly speak for laughter. "But ask this one how she got a bun in the oven."

She points at Amber who opens and closes her mouth like a fish.

"About the dance," Amber changes the subject in a way my politician ex would have envied. "You'll need a dress."

"I will?" I query. "I mean, the way Draxx put it, it's sort of private."

"If by private you mean it's in the main square with everyone watching, then yes. It's basically their equivalent of a marriage ceremony, although it's not like you're going to be able to get rid of your big green Sarkarnii any time soon."

I wrap my arms around myself.

"Hey." Opal rubs my shoulder. "Are you okay with this?"

"I've been married before. It was not...good," I reply. "But I want what Draxx wants, and if this is it, then I'll do it for him. I was just not expecting anything public, that's all."

I hate the fact tears are threatening again. After all we've been through, doing some simple marriage ceremony is hardly the end of the fucking world.

"My mate is supposed to be resting." A deep velvet voice rumbles into the room.

Draxx is leaning against the doorframe, huge arms crossed and, thankfully, wearing a pair of pants. A stream of smoke leaves his nostrils as he glares around.

"It's fine, Draxx. The humans are my friends, and they were checking on me."

He nods, narrowing his eyes a little as he takes in all the women, until he spots Coral. There's a further huff of smoke.

"Very well," he says.

And he doesn't move.

"Probably time for us to go." Opal gives me a gentle hug and stands, grabbing at Jade and Coral.

"We'll see you later." Amber smiles at me. "Help you get ready for the dance."

"What?" I exclaim.

"You'll see." She chuckles as she follows the others out of the door.

"I thought the dance was just for you and me?" I say to Draxx, who has remained in the doorway.

He leans back, obviously checking to see if everyone has left, before he stalks over to me, sinuous and predatory.

"My dance is for you, my Jem, but a Sarkarnii must show his den warriors his mate is claimed." He sits next to me and takes my hands oh-so-gently in his huge clawed ones. "In all of this, I realize I wished for a salvation, and it is you, *szikra*. I want to show my den there is a salvation for all of us."

"Okay, I guess." Draxx's gaze is so earnest, so solemn, I can feel any reservations I have dropping away.

"But most of all, I want you," Draxx says. "I'll dance for you now if you want me to."

"You will?"

Draxx withdraws from me and walks across the room, turning to face me and then slowly tapping his foot on the floor, creating a lazy, easy beat, which is joined by his tail. His hips swish from side to side, and I'm reminded of the very first day we met.

The movement is almost hypnotic as he stalks in my direction, those eyes fixed on me like he wants to devour me whole.

What pain I had in my body is dissipating as Draxx gets closer and closer. Instead it's replaced by a delicious heat and a feverish anticipation.

DRAXX

I want my mate, so very much. She is injured, but she is alive. Mating has healing properties, everyone knows it. Sarkarnii seed is a great healer. It's the reason it assists females in taking Sarkarnii cock.

Jem's eyes sparkle with mischief, and I can't control myself. I slide my arm under her, cradling her lower back so her injured shoulders are not in contact with anything. As much as I've wanted to mate, I've known her injuries needed time to heal, and, I'm not going to deny it—just being in her presence was enough for me, enough to assuage my rut in the past few days.

But now, the aroma which rises from her sends my mating gland pumping the mix into my bloodstream.

I slide a claw down the sheet, slowly, inexorably ripping it, peeling away the fabric to reveal my delicious snack.

"Now you have seen my dance, do you want to be mated, little morsel?"

Jem pants at me. I dip my head and capture one of her sweet nipples in my mouth. She tastes like nectar. I flick my tongue over and over the tight peak until it is solid, and she moans out loud.

"Draxx."

"That's my name. I always want to hear it on your lips, but more so, I want to hear you scream it for the entire Kirakos to hear...again."

"That's a big ask, big guy. Are you going to make me?"

This female will be the death of me, and not because I managed to stop a purge and allow a foul Belek to go free.

My cock has pushed out of my pouch and is constrained in my pants. It nevving hurts, and I circle my hips to shift position, groaning gently as the fabric rubs over the sensitive head, my hook already forming. I flick open the catch and allow it to spring free, taking myself in hand and giving it a couple of long, slow pumps.

Jem licks her lips.

"I am absolutely going to make you, wicked little mate. Not only will you come at least twice before I fill you, I'm going to lick you to oblivion and back."

Jem bucks under me, wincing and moaning at the same time.

"Hmmm." I look down at her. "How best to enjoy my tasty mate's pretty cunt while she is *injured*?"

"Please, Draxx," she says, breathless.

"Oh, now you beg, do you?" I nuzzle into her neck, nibbling at the skin and enjoying how she squirms. "I love it when you beg, little one. Beg me to pleasure you."

"Draxx, I-"

I flip her over. She has large white patches stuck to her back, but I try not to look at them.

Gondnok paid the price for hurting my mate. The Belek will pay as a whole for any injury done to her or my brother, as is my vow. I trace a claw down her spine, cupping one of her glorious buttocks before sliding a hand under her pussy and feeling how wet she already is for me. I pause only to bite off a claw. Jem is helpless against me as I cradle her in one hand and slowly slip in a digit.

Her sweet cunt clenches on me but floods with more and more of her delicious juices the deeper I go. I tease at the little bundle of nerves I found last time I licked her with the very tip of a claw. She goes rigid, her pussy convulsing, her body shaking as an orgasm wracks her sore little body. I plunder her as her channel goes from achingly tight to deliciously right to take my cock.

Only I promised her another climax, and a Sarkarnii always keeps his promises. With her body still trembling, I gently deposit her back on the bed. Hands curled around her thighs, I feast on her, lapping up her sweet juices while she moans and writhes under my ministrations, continuing to produce her nectar faster than my tongue can suck it up.

"Draxx! I can't...I...Oh! Draxx!"

Jem screams out my name, loudly and with some force, as I shove my tongue in deep, finding the spot within her, which all females have and which is guaranteed to produce a body shaking orgasm. My perfect, beautiful mate obliges me with such a rush of her moisture, I have to partially shift in order to take it all, my snout nudging at her glorious little bottom hole.

She's going to be filled there too, soon enough. I give it a lick as it convulses, before shifting back.

My cock is streaming with pre-cum, and if I don't bury it in her, I'm sure I will explode everywhere. I coat my fingers with my seed and push it inside, making sure it goes deep. Jem sighs with delight, her body limp over my hand.

"I'm going to mate you, my love. I'm going to be as gentle as I can, but I need to be inside you. I need to release and fill your womb with every drop I have." I notch my cock at her entrance, the obscene size of it compared to her causing even more pre-cum to spurt out and coat Jem's skin.

"Fill me," she moans. "I want to be achingly full of you."

I push forward, her gorgeous cunt giving just enough to allow the tip inside. My seed pumps out, flooding her channel and easing my passage as I inch in, slowly, carefully, enjoying every hot seccari as I push deeper and deeper, until I'm seated within her.

It is glorious. My tail shifts, and I know just what it wants to do. With Jem in one hand, fully impaled on me, I use the other to swipe up my spill and her slick to coat the tip, before I trace a finger around her sweet hole.

She groans and pushes back at me, causing my cock to jerk inside her. I slowly work my digit into her.

"Are you ready to take all of me, my mate, like the good female you are?" I rasp. I'm so close to my orgasm, I don't know how much longer I can hold on.

"Take me, Draxx, make me yours." Jem moans.

I plunge my tail into her tight back hole, and she screams my name with absolute perfection.

JEM

Draxx has filled me in every way imaginable. I
didn't even think it was possible to move, but
when he replaces his finger with his tale in my
bottom hole, he rips an orgasm from me I didn't think I had
left.

I was wrong. Draxx can play my body like a musical
instrument. His hands carefully hold my body so nothing
presses on my injured back, his claws pinching around my
nipples with just the right amount of pressure as his cock
withdraws and then thumps back into me, each ridge, each
barb hitting nerve endings I did not know I had and which,
yet again, are hiking me back up to another climax.

I am so full, every channel stuffed with him, his tail
doing things to me which causes stars to spark in my vision.
I feel Draxx growing, and I know he can't contain his shift.
My huge male has needs just as I do. Feeling him move with
grace and ease, finger strumming me, cock plundering me,
tail...doing terrible, wonderful things to me, Draxx is
drenched with pleasure, and it's all mine.

He is all mine.

I am all his.

Draxx presses his hand down on the small of my back, and his other hand cups my belly.

"I am going to fill you, heartsfire, fill your belly with so much seed, enjoy every last part of you until you can't even think, let alone breathe."

"Do it, my love," I cry out because I want Draxx more than anything in the entire universe.

He's generous, considerate, sexy as hell, and he makes my body do things which shouldn't be possible, but they are.

He is my everything, and as all of him withdraws, to plunge back inside me, I'm tipped over the edge of desire into pleasure and then into an orgasm which absolutely should not be legal. My entire being feels like it's being turned inside out as I clamp down on Draxx. He roars and, with three final irregular thrusts, I'm flooded with his warmth, and I feel the pinch as his hook penetrates my cervix and he starts to pump his cum into my womb.

None of this should be possible. Draxx himself should not be possible. But then I never thought I'd find real love, real peace, real life, until I found myself in the Kirakos. So, the fact my belly is swelling as he groans his release is both incredible and pleasurable.

"My sweet mate." Draxx presses kisses up my back as he continues to slowly circle his hips, each time a new wave of heat sweeping through me with every fresh rush of his seed. "You are my flame eternal, and as soon as we are unhooked, I will dance for you, because I want to claim you and make sure every Sarkarnii male knows you are mine."

He encompasses me, gently putting us both on our sides so he can continue to fill me and also hold me, his huge hands spanned over my expanding stomach.

"I want to fill you with a Sarkarnling," he murmurs in my ear. "I'd love for you to grow ripe and plump with my progeny."

"I..." I swallow hard, tears pricking at my eyes. "No one has ever said anything like that to me before. No one ever wanted me."

Draxx kisses at my neck, his touch feather light, sending shivers through me.

"I don't care about anyone else. You are my mate, my heartsfire, and I want you to have my Sarkarnling."

I think of Amber, how she didn't want to scare me off with her pregnancy.

"I'm pretty sure you've already done that." I slide my hands over his, resting on my pot belly. "Because if this hasn't made me pregnant, I don't know what will."

"You want my Sarkarnling?"

"Oh, Draxx, I want whatever you want, just as long as I'm with you. Of course I'll have your baby." I find myself laughing with the pure joy of having this conversation.

He burrows into me, and if my wounds hurt, I can't feel them. "I promise you, my heartsfire. If I have not filled you this time, we will try over and over until you are. And then I will keep you happy and healthy with constant mating as you carry our baby."

I shiver with delight.

"That is one promise I will hold you to, General, above all others."

"And it's the one promise this general will enjoy keeping, above all others."

DRAXX

"I know you'd prefer it if Drega was here for the dance. I would too," I say to Draco as we watch the large hole, high above our quadrant in what was once the sky and we all knew was the wall shielding the wardens.

The hole Daeos and the Ragad blew in the Kirakos in order to get back here with the humans. The reason it was easy to make my escape too.

Our warning to the Wardens. This prison maze is no longer entirely their playground.

"I said nothing of the kind," Draco growls. "I merely pointed out he would enjoy watching you claim your female."

"Enjoy watching me squirm, you mean," I reply, firing out a stream of smoke.

"Exactly."

"In that case, I wish to claim my female tonight. I will dance for her, and we will feast," I state, glaring at my older brother and daring him to contradict me.

Instead he claps a hand on my shoulder and squeezes, his tail lashing as he looks me up and down.

"If you can find a mate you want to wear pants for, I don't care when you claim her or when you dance for her, brother. Just know I will be with you, even if Drega is not. That nevver can hear all about it when he finally shows his face."

"We're going to have to send out a rescue party," I reply. "The last time I saw him, I don't know, there was something wrong. The fact he's still missing means there's definitely something wrong."

"And you will direct the rescue party *after* you have danced for your mate. I assume you have already filled her belly?"

My brother is nothing if he is not direct.

"I would hope so." I stare directly into his eyes. "She has been thoroughly hooked."

"My mate is with sarkarnling," he says, his face suddenly coming over all dreamy.

"The Ragad suggested a mating between a human and a Sarkarnii might be more than just chance."

"I need to speak further with Litur and the others about their meddling, when I'm sure we have the control of the Kirakos I believe we have. Until then, not only do we need to find Drega, but we need to ensure the Wardens know this place will not remain in their clutches for much longer."

I give him a nod. "I am at your service, Draco."

"I should think so, *General*, and it's about time." He grins at me. "We also still have a star-map to unlock, but every blow we strike against the Belek brings us closer to our prize."

"I have my treasure, and she is all I need," I reply. "I'll make the preparations, but I trust you will be my second."

"Always, brother." Draco grins. "After all, dancing for your mate is far easier than dealing with space worms."

"Nev it! Why did you have to bring that up?" My mouth is suddenly dry. I was not nervous. A Sarkarnii general does not get nervous. "I can dance for her. I can," I repeat, mostly to myself while my nevving brother chokes out a smoky laugh.

But I am about to dance for my mate, claim her in front of all my den warriors. And I have to get it right.

First time.

"It gets to you, doesn't it? Warrior, general, or not." Draco's grin is even wider. "But at least you have pants."

"Nev you!" I turn on my heel.

"It's easy, Draxx. You just put one foot in front of the other, just like the space worms," Draco calls after me.

I curse at him under my breath. I need to see my Jem, hold her in my arms, let her ground me once again.

I make my way through to my quarters but pause a while to watch Drasus put a few warriors through a drill for shifting and fighting, one I asked him to refresh with everyone a few days ago.

There is going to be a battle, and we need to be prepared.

My mind wanders, though, to what Draco said. His mate is already with sarkarnling. Jem and I have only been mating a short while, and carefully, since her injuries mean we need to take things slowly, but could it be possible? Could she also be carrying my young?

I give Drasus a sharp nod of approval as he looks over at me. He has always been a strong warrior, and the others look up to him. We're going to need all the leadership we can get as we prepare for the coming storm.

The door to my quarters is open, and I can hear female

voices inside. As I reach the threshold, Draco's mate, Amber, appears.

"Nope," she says, holding up her hand. "You can't come in."

"I need to see to my *szikra*." I attempt to crane my neck past Amber, but she steps to one side to shield the view inside. "She has been injured and she is my mate."

"From what I hear, it hasn't stopped your other *activities*." Amber giggles. "I do hope Draco and I were never that loud."

"You were," I reply. "Now let me past."

"I'm fine." Jem's voice rings out. "I'll see you later."

"See," Amber says firmly. "She's fine, and you have a dance to organize."

"I don't like this," I grumble, but I can't lay a finger on Amber, as much as I want to lift her up and put her to one side.

Draco will most likely remove my head first and ask questions later if he scents me on his mate. I would do no less myself if the situation was reversed.

"You don't get to like it," she replies. "But oh, boy, are you going to like it later. Now get moving and get that dance organized."

I leave, grumbling about females and with my heart in my throat. I might have fought the creatures of the pit, space worms, Belek, and Xicops. I might have commanded armies with thousands of warriors at my beck and call.

But today I have to dance for my fated mate, and I am more terrified than I've ever been in my entire life.

JEM

"Are you sure about this?" I smooth the dress down over my stomach.

I'm pretty sure it's my imagination, but it seems a little rounder in the last few days. But then the amount of times a day Draxx fills me up means I also have a sexy residual ache.

The dress Amber has got for me is beautiful. A shimmering green blue silk, somehow it's even more gorgeous than the one she had me wear for the feast when Draxx captured me the first time. The fabric flows over my curves. Tight in all the right places, it dips low over my cleavage. I sort of feel like I have everything on show.

And I like it.

"I'm sure. If Draxx is anything like his brother, he'll need something to concentrate on while he dances, and you, my dear, are going to send him skywards!"

"You mean I'm going to scare him off?" I mock gape at Amber.

Behind me, Coral snorts with laughter. She's been

keeping an eye on the puncture wounds in my back and today pronounced them 'healing nicely'.

I know Amber is relieved we have a human doctor among our small number, especially as she knows she's going to have a baby.

"I don't begin to understand any of this, but if you're taking on a relationship with one of those big beasts, I'm very impressed," Coral says and raises a golden goblet to me. "And also, what is this stuff? Because it is strong!"

"Ale-wine. And those 'big beasts' drink it, so it has to be strong." Amber laughs as Coral puts down the goblet and pushes it away.

I wonder if Amber has noticed I haven't touched any of the plentiful ale-wine, despite all the butterflies in my stomach. If she has, she's not said anything.

"Draxx is ready," a warrior calls through the door to our quarters.

"Oh, shit." I look at Amber. "What do I do again?"

"Be calm." She puts her hands on my shoulders and stares me in the eye. "And enjoy your big growly mate doing something he's been waiting to do since he came of age, dance the claiming dance for his mate. That's you, by the way."

I draw in a shuddering breath, drop my head between my shoulders, and stare at the floor.

"Jem. Draxx chose you. I know things have been bad in your past." She doesn't let up with the staring, and now she's raking up the things I've shared with her in the past few quiet days, ever since Draxx told me he wanted to do the dance, regardless of whether his brother was present. "I know you think you're not worthy of him, but you are. It's the reason he chose you. Don't you remember what I said when you first got here?"

"I remember," I mutter.

There's silence.

"Sarkarnii mate hard, and they mate for life," I say.

"So, go out there and let him claim you," Amber exhorts me, and before I can do anything, I'm spun on the spot and given a good shove in my rear.

Out in the central square, all the Sarkarnii warriors are arranged on either side, almost like a guard of honor. At one end, closest to me, is an open-sided tent with a chair. I walk over, noting the lack of eyes on me from all the warriors, although there is a cohort of the smaller Jiaka, who rustle with what seems like excitement, so many eyes blinking at me.

Amber, Coral, Jade, and Opal appear, and Amber nods at the chair, so I sit.

A deep drum beat booms out. It thumps through me with a bass note any percussionist would be proud of. Ahead of me, the warriors part, and Draxx stands in the center. His scales are shining brightly, lit by an inner glow. He looks absolutely magnificent.

He sways his hips in time to the beat, hypnotic and sensuous. He shifts and then he doesn't, his tail swishing behind him and curling up around his legs. All around, the warriors move in time to the beat, but not in the way Draxx does.

I heat the more he moves, sliding, snapping in time to the heady beat of the drums. The more he moves, the more I want to run to him, ask him to devour me and devour me again. By the time he's close enough, smoke curling from his nostrils, his skin sheened now with sweat, I'm virtually a puddle myself.

In a swirl of green and black, I am encased in a pair of

strong arms, a single claw under my chin, tilting my head up to him.

"You are wearing my colors, heartsfire," Draxx rasps, his lips brushing mine.

"I am," I reply. "Because I am yours, General."

"Call me general again, little mate," he says, hips closing in on mine. "Because I've only filled you once today."

"So, the claiming is public then, *General*," I growl.

"Oh, no, it is absolutely private. At least until my den warriors can see I have filled your belly."

He spans his hand over my stomach as his mouth claims mine, hard and fast, his tongue dancing and robbing me of any breath I might have had.

When I'm finally released, I have no balance, no composure, nothing.

Except Draxx.

"I want you to be mine, Jem. So I can protect you, always. So I can burn down the universe for you if you ask me, and so I can light a fire to warm our young at night. If you take me as your mate, all my promises forever belong to you."

"I don't need your promises, Draxx." I run a finger along his strong jaw, and when he closes his eyes in pleasure, my heart nearly beats out of my chest. "I just need you."

"Then I am yours. In front of my den mates and under the watch of my ancestors, we are bound until the suns and stars go out." Draxx lifts me into his arms, and a huge roar goes up from the surrounding warriors.

"Do you think they were waiting?" I ask him.

"All they ever want is a feast." Draxx inclines his head at his brother, Draco, who has an arm wrapped around Amber. "And all I ever want is you."

EPILOGUE

JEM

Over the past couple of weeks, there have been several attempts to infiltrate the warden-controlled area to look for Drega, given there is no sign of him getting out on his own.

Both Draxx and Draco are concerned, I can tell. Losing their brother was not in their plan, or Draco's plan. Draxx doesn't plan. Most days, he still doesn't wear pants. But then, most days, he also sports the most enormous grin, and unless he's searching for Drega, he doesn't leave my side.

I've never felt more loved in my entire life.

My stomach is churning in a very unpleasant way as I sit in the main square, attempting to look like I'm interested in what the Jiaka are doing as they scuttle back and forth. I am absolutely not watching the huge hole blasted in what looks like the sky but is actually more of a hidden wall.

The Sarkarnii have control of a large part of what lies beyond, and they are using it for greater incursions into the rest of the Kirakos, looking for the map Draco wants. Some of my fellow humans have even been helping out. Jade is hell bent on finding the woman they call Ruby and constantly petitioning to go with the warriors. Some of them seem keener on her being there than others.

Amber sits down next to me. She has developed a little pot belly recently. Most of the time, she thinks she's hiding it under more flowing clothing, but none of us are actually blind.

"Any sign?" she asks.

This is one trip which Draco has also joined, something about wanting to meet with the Ragad. I'd say he's a politician like my ex-husband, only Draco is considerably less reptilian, even if he can turn into a dragon.

"Nothing yet, but you know they're rarely back in a few hours," I say, in order to reassure her.

Of course, my heart remains in my throat the entire time Draxx is gone. He knows it too, and the chances of me remaining upright once he returns are minimal.

My big green warrior likes to make it up to me by ensuring every single hole is filled, and I am absolutely not complaining. The more he mates me, the better I feel.

But when he's away from me, I feel decidedly ropey.

"You look a bit pale," Amber says. "Have you seen Coral recently?"

"What for? My shoulders are healed, just about. I'm fine."

Amber snorts. "Have you felt light-headed today? Stomach off?"

"Yeah, but then...you know...I'm worried about Draxx. Same as you and Draco."

"If you say so."

"I do say so." I glare at her.

"It's just I bet Coral would know."

I roll my eyes upward. "Know what?" I grind out.

"If you're pregnant or not."

"What!"

"What? Seriously, Jem. You're an intelligent woman who is having a hell of a lot of sex with a very big male. Do you think you're immune or something?"

I shake my head at her. "I was married for ten years. I can tell you, I do not get pregnant at the drop of a hat."

"Not with a human man anyway," Amber says. "And do you remember our conversation when you just arrived? About periods?"

"What about it?" My head is starting to ache. I go back to staring up at the scorched hole.

"It was well over four weeks ago."

I cluck my tongue and ignore her, willing myself to see a flash of green scales, anything which might indicate Draxx has returned safely.

It was over four weeks ago.

I don't look. I just grab her hand and squeeze it. Hard.

"Ow! Oh, now you get it."

I can't look at her. I can only look up, every fibre of my being willing Draxx to be there. "I don't believe it."

"If that's what you want. But numbers don't lie, Jem."

A cloud of smoke puffs out of the opening. Beside me, Amber gasps as two huge dragons sweep through, one gold and one green. They swing around in a lazy arc before dropping down into the main square.

But there are only two. Two who resolve themselves into their usual forms and stride towards us. Amber runs to Draco, but I hang back, waiting on Draxx.

"Any sign?" I ask as he reaches me, holding out his hand until I take hold and he can wind a tail around my feet.

"Nothing," he rumbles. "But Litur believes there is an area masked from the rest of the Kirakos and he is probably being kept there. We will try again."

He nuzzles at my neck, sending sparks of arousal flying through me. My heart leaps into my throat.

"Maybe you should go on fewer missions. You can direct your warriors without needing to go yourself, can't you? Like Draco?"

Draxx looks over his shoulder. Draco is now dressed, or at least wearing pants, and walking back to his quarters with an arm around Amber.

"I am not like my brother," he says.

"No, but I am like his mate."

Draxx huffs out a smoke ring, his brow creased. "His mate has light hair, you do not. Her eyes are different. You are not like her at all."

I can't help but laugh, wrapping my arms around his waist and pressing myself to his warm, hard chest.

"But what I have inside me is like her," I say.

I think Draxx might have stopped breathing. He is very still for what seems like a long time.

"You are with sarkarnling?"

"I think so."

I am tossed into the air as Draxx roars with delight.

"You are with sarkarnling! My sarkarnling!" He grins from ear to ear. "Did you hear that?" he roars at a passing warrior. "My mate is having my sarkarnling!"

He buries his face into my hair. "My Jem, you have made me the happiest male in all the universe."

"And you, Draxx, have made me the happiest female. Ever."

Book 3: DREGA: An Alien Warrior Romance is available as an early bird pre-order from my store. You'll receive an ebook copy along with stunning SFW and NSFW Art before anyone else on the 26th December 2023.

DREGA will be available on Amazon in January 2024.

You can get an alert for all my new releases before anyone else by signing up for my newsletter or you can also sign up on my website www.hattiejacks.com

And you can follow me on Bookbub, Amazon or even join my Facebook group - Hattie's Hotties!

JOIN ME!

Why not join the Hattie Jacks Alien Appreciation Society?
Subscribe to my newsletter for a free sci-fi romance novella:
www.hattiejacks.com/subscribe

You can also join my Patreon
https://patreon.com/HattieJacksAuthor
Where I post chapter serials of my ongoing work in
progress, the occasional poll and little snippets of character
art.

Additionally, if you wish, you can stalk me on Instagram:
www.instagram.com/hattie.jacks
or join my Facebook group:
www.facebook.com/hattieshotties

ACKNOWLEDGMENTS

My thanks to the following Kickstarter backers:
Emilie Kunz
Chance C. Hightower
Hillary E Spencer

ALSO BY HATTIE JACKS

FATED MATES OF THE SARKARNII

DRACO

DRAXX

DREGA

DRASUS

DAEOS

DRELIX

WARRIORS OF THE CITADEL

SAVAGE PRIZE

SAVAGE PET

SAVAGE MINE

ELITE ROGUE ALIEN WARRIORS

STORM

FURY

CHAOS

REBEL

WRATH

JUST WHO IS THIS HATTIE JACKS ANYWAY?

I've been a passionate sci-fi fan since I was a little girl, brought up on a diet of Douglas Adams, Issac Asimov, Star Trek, Star Wars, Doctor Who, Red Dwarf and The Adventure Game.

What? You don't know about The Adventure Game? It's probably a British thing and dates me horribly! Google it. Even better search for it on YouTube. In my defence, there were only three channels back then.

I'm also a sucker for great characters and situations as well as grand romance, because who doesn't like a grand romantic gesture?

So, when I'm not writing steamy stories about smouldering alien males and women with something to prove, you'll find me battling my garden (less English country garden, more The Good Life) or zooming around the countryside on my motorbike.

Check out my website at www.hattiejacks.com!

Printed in Great Britain
by Amazon